Acknowledgments

We are thankful for all of the people who took the time to proofread and correct for us. We also apologize to those who were forced to listen to all of our weird discussions while building this fun reality

Weightless

Peter Anderson & Jordan Nuffer

Table of Contents

Chapter 1 1

Chapter 2 15

Chapter 3 30

Chapter 4 41

Chapter 5 56

Chapter 6 79

Chapter 7 94

Chapter 8 106

Chapter 9 121

Chapter 10 137

Chapter 11 156

Chapter 12 178

Chapter 13 192

Chapter 14 203

Chapter 15 214

Chapter 16 228

Chapter 17 241

Chapter 18 253

Chapter 19 268

Chapter 20 277

Chapter 21 295

Chapter 22 316

Chapter 23 331

Chapter 24 345

Chapter 25 358

Chapter 26 376

Chapter 27 389

Epilogue................400

Chapter 1

"Hello? Somebody help me! Hellooo?!"

John slowly pulled himself along the left side of the wall of the living room of what appeared to be a small two-bedroom apartment. The run-down government apartments, surprisingly enough, always had the best food. The room was decorated with several cat paintings on hideous, peeling, mustard-yellow wallpaper. Many small, dust-covered glass cat statues were floating all around the room. It was a surprise to John that someone could fit so many felines into one room. He slowly made his way into the kitchen and opened the nearest food pantry to find nothing but cobwebs and disappointment.

His eyes swept the area once more, shuttering as he caught sight of a dead cat drifting through the air. It was one of those hairless cats that always made him uneasy just by looking at them. For a moment, he wondered if any portion of the long-dead animal was edible, but thought better of it.

Good thing I wore this rag over my mouth, or I'd be breathing in more than air.

He drifted down the row of cabinets, hoping to finally find something to fill his aching stomach. His luck finally took a turn for the better as he reached the last row. Pulling back the cabinet door, he found a small can with a brightly colored, smiling cartoon character on the front that he didn't recognize. After four hours of going through the ruin of a building, all he had to show for his troubles were a can of oranges, two sandwich-size Ziploc bags full of murky water, and a knife that had been badly decorated with fake jewels. He was pretty sure the knife was just one more piece of junk, but he figured someone would trade for it, thinking it to be of value.

John had one last scan around the room before drifting to the door closest to him. He pushed it open to find a bathroom. Upon first glance, he could tell this room hadn't been disturbed in a long time. Even in the dim light provided by the tiny window above the tub, he could see the heavy layer of dust floating stagnantly in the air. Nonetheless, bathrooms made for good looting. There was almost always a little bit of water in the showerhead to be salvaged. He found the best way to pull the small droplets out was to draw them in like a straw. Very rarely did you ever get more than a mouthful. Also, there was almost always medication, a box of bandages, or a shaving razor. Most of the useful medications were starting to exceed the expiration dates printed on their labels at this point, making them less valuable in bartering.

This bathroom resembled one you would find at a rest stop that required a key from the cashier, one usually attached to a comically large item. Using the bathroom in zero gravity was both difficult and messy, but this bathroom gave a whole new meaning to the term “Poocaso.” John instinctively covered his nose, as the cloth he wore over his face did little to combat the stench. He didn’t even dare try his luck with finding water here, knowing he would end up paying for it later. John did, however, notice that at some point someone had written in the dust on the mirror. It read, "true desperation is eating ur own friends.” John’s stomach sank. He really hoped that whoever left this message was referring to the cats. He pushed away from the bathroom, catching a small piece of debris on the side of his cheek, causing him to jump.

It used to be so easy to drive down to the grocery store and fill your cabinets and refrigerator for a month. You had accessible water everywhere you went. John thought about what he would do for a middle-of-the-park water fountain. He wouldn't even mind the strong metallic taste of the impending flu that would follow. Now, he had to wrench open pipes in the walls and search toilet bowls just to satiate his dried, cracked tongue.

John heard a soft cry from the next room. He pushed himself against the wall and slowly drifted to the opposite side of the living room toward the call.

Stupid... he thought to himself. People left traps and ambushes in places like this all of the time. John briefly remembered last week when he floated through a tripwire made of fishing line tied to some cans, put in place by the presumed owner of the home he had ventured into. He had found the owner shortly after his arrival, who was hardly more than a rancid pile of decay secured to his recliner ironically by fishing line. John rotated his body so his stomach faced the ceiling and pulled himself along, being careful not to make any noise. He had grown accustomed to surveying rooms upside down and at right angles. It had become second nature from traversing rooms along ceilings and walls. He started to smell an overwhelming mixture of sweat, piss, and fecal matter as he drew closer to what he assumed was a bedroom.

The door where the noise was coming from was

closed all but a small crack. John stopped himself on the door trim and peered inside. He immediately noticed the middle-aged woman floating dead center in the room. She was wearing a torn blue shirt with dirty brown pants. Her skin was drawn back and her eyes were sunken like she hadn't had anything to eat or drink for several days. Floating around her were newborn diapers and colorful baby toys. From the looks of it, the room was once used as a nursery. John had never seen a person perfectly suspended. Truthfully, he had never really believed others when they told him their witnessing. He supposed it was possible, in certain instances, to zero out, such as when people go to sleep and forget to tie themselves down.

The woman yelled again, "Please is there anyone out there!" The whole scene gave John a bad vibe. Ever since The Lifting nothing had been the same. Two years ago if you needed a cup of sugar from your neighbor you could simply walk across the street, only needing to concern yourself with looking left and right for potential traffic. Now, most people can't even remember what refined sugar tastes like.

The woman rotated in the air, trying to grasp any nearby object, but was not nearly close enough to reach anything that could help her. John watched her for a moment, weighing his conscience against his gut instinct. She truly seemed to be alone in this place, and John found it hard to believe for a moment that someone would purposefully put this woman in such a predicament just to draw in a random straggler to rob. He decided that this woman, helpless as she may be, wasn't worth risking his mediocre haul that day – or, ultimately, his life. As gently as he could manage, he pushed himself away from the door frame, doing a full 360-degree check before doing so. It always seemed easy to accidentally run into something when meddling with no gravity.

The room was littered with small floating objects like cat hair and dust. As he drifted away from the door, he found himself swatting small pieces of trash and semi-faded old newspaper clippings. Drifting through the center of the room, his shoe clipped a baby's rattle, the beads moved inside just slightly enough to make his presence known.

"Hello?" the woman said. "Please. I won't hurt you, I'm just so thirsty… please..." She started a long drawn-out coughing fit. Each cough made John flinch because he could feel the pain she was feeling. After several days without water, your throat looked like a cracked desert landscape. John's last coughing spasm had him spitting up blood. He knew the real pain of coughing that hard and the relief that came after with a small amount of moisture to relieve your throat was of his own making.

Anxiety and adrenaline started to well up in John's stomach. He knew the right answer was to go and help the woman but he just couldn't.

I can't do it. I shouldn't. Not every person is my responsibility. I'm just trying to live one day at a time. If I keep adding distractions I'll never find my dad.

John propped his legs against a coffee table. He went into a kneeling position. John used the counterweight of the table to push himself back toward the bedroom where the woman sat suspended in her own nightmare. At the door frame, John slowly applied pressure to the door and found some resistance to it. He looked over and saw that the door hinges were rusted. John made a quick mental note that maybe carrying grease around might make his scavenging runs stealthier. He pushed harder and the door gave an audible creak. The hint of the smell he encountered earlier while floating closer was nothing compared to the assault on his nose now. Between John's building anxiety and the horrific smell coming from the room, John couldn't help but vomit what little he had in his stomach. The woman knew he was waiting in the doorway and tried to crane her neck in a way that she could see her intruder.

"Please, help me. I have a newborn baby who needs my help". She motioned to the right side of the room. John observed an off-white crib filled with several blankets. In no way did the woman appear to be recently pregnant. He didn't believe her for a second that she was ever pregnant. It was unheard of that someone would have a child with all that is going on.

"Please, my name is Crystal and my baby, Aaron, needs to be fed, " she said.

In her predicament I would be just as desperate, too.

Crystal's back was facing John and that's how he preferred it — no chance to be surprised. John glanced back toward the front door, still battling with his decision. He considered that the state she was in proved there wasn't a baby in the crib, and if there was it was likely no longer alive. John had no intention of finding out.

John softly breathed out, "I can't trust you. I hope you understand."

Crystal began to sob and screamed, "How can you let this happen to another human being? Do you have no heart? Look at me! Do I look like I'm in any position to take advantage of you?"

John pulled himself from the frame of the doorway

into the room while keeping his distance from the woman. John saw a picture floating near him and he pulled it out of the air. The picture showed one elderly woman surrounded by several cats. The lady in the picture looked annoyed by one that appeared to have walked off. This was probably the best photo she could manage with that many cats.

"This isn't even your apartment," John said.

He gently pushed the photo forward and released it toward Crystal, keeping in mind that he didn't have to push very hard. The frame touched her back and she recoiled as if she were preparing for a violent end. Crystal awkwardly reached back, searching for the object, and grabbed the photo.

"What are you, a detective or something?" she asked in a condescending tone.

John pulled his backpack around underneath his chin and opened it. He looked at his long sought-after food and water that he needed just as much as this woman. His eyes were drawn to the knife.

Could I actually do it? Kill another person? With the way she looked, it wouldn't even be murder. It would be merciful.

He surveyed the room, hoping to find anything of

use.

Crystal caught John looking around and said, “I know what you want. If you’re hungry, I have food hidden.”

“Do you mean the small can of oranges from the cupboard? You can consider them long gone,” he replied.

“No, I didn't even know those were there. I have a stash in another apartment just down the hall. I have been collecting for days from other apartments,” she pleaded.

John considered trusting that this woman was desperate enough to start giving up real goods to save her life. John pulled himself back into the door frame and started to pull his body into the living room. Crystal panicked,

“Stop! Just… Please, just don't let me die here”. “Where is your food?” he asked with a tone of indifference.

Crystal started to cry again, but no tears came, probably due to the dehydration.

“The food is in the stainless-steel mini fridge four apartments down, room 403,” she muttered quietly. John reached into his backpack and pulled out the small bejeweled knife.

Crystal saw this and started frantically screaming, “I don't want to die! Please, please, I told you where the food was! How can you do this to me? I was a good person. I gave to charity. I never hurt anybody!"

"Shut! Up!" John yelled intensely. Crystal immediately fell silent.

"I don't have the heart to hurt you, but I also can't trust you. So I will give you the option to do what I can't, "John said. John brought the knife up to waist height and gently pushed it toward Crystal. John turned and propelled himself toward the front door. Realizing what he expected her to do, Crystal's pleas immediately turned to fury.

"You bastard! You coward! You're no better than a damn murderer!" she cried.

As John made his way through the door he heard a thud hit the wall. The bejeweled knife was lodged in the wall no more than three inches from where his head had been only a second ago. Old dust billowed from around the wall from the impact. John had a thought to grab the knife and leave Crystal in her tomb. His anger at her attempt on his life soon became overwhelming. He wanted this woman to be reminded of her decision every time her body rotated to face the direction of the knife. John wasn't typically in the business of teaching other people a lesson, but two years of scavenging, starving, and wariness had calloused him enough to feel justified in this decision. He propelled his weight off of the wall to the front door and made his way into the hallway, closing off the screams and wails that continued to stream from the woman.

While scaling the walls toward the supposed food, John couldn't help but notice the amount of graffiti covering the walls. In several places, he found many expletives repeated in different fonts, styles, and colors, which seemed to be the norm in a building like this. As he was about to reach his destination he saw a piece of graffiti that made him do a fast double take and make his heart drop. It was a very poorly sprayed bright-yellow symbol of an Atom.

Two or three years ago this type of symbol wouldn't have meant anything to anybody. But, now, it was a symbol that struck fear into most, at least, anyone who had a shred of sanity left. It was the mark of the Cult of Atom. The cult used these marks to claim territory. The only thing John knew for sure about the Cult from a great many rumors he had heard about them was that they were extremely dangerous, doubly so if you were caught on their territory. John wasn't keen to find out if they were as violent as people made them out to be.

With a little less caution and a lot more speed, John made his way down the hall to the apartment Crystal had told him about. He made quick work of finding the mini-fridge that was poorly hidden in one of the bedrooms, covered with a few matted blankets.

Maybe I'll finally have enough to feel full for once, eh?

He opened the fridge to nothing but loose pieces of rotting cat legs and other mystery components. The stench was so overwhelming that he heaved hard enough to create a sharp pain in his chest, but not spewing anything as there wasn't anything left in his stomach to spew.

Looking across the living room of the apartment, he caught a glimpse of himself from a mirror on the wall. He pushed away from the fridge and drew closer. He hadn't seen his own reflection in months. Where his cheekbones once stood resilient, they had turned loose and pale in comparison.

What has happened to you?

He tugged at his dark brown hair, his forehead dominated more and more as the days went by. John was by no means attractive, but by looking at himself in the mirror, it was apparent that this was probably as good as it would ever get.

Those oranges would be the first thing he had eaten in two days, and he doubted they would go far. He decided he had pushed his luck enough for one afternoon. It would be dark soon enough anyway. The only thing harder than navigating in zero gravity was doing so in the black of night. John retraced his steps (an expression that felt odd to use these days) and exited the complex, still trying to tune out the voice of the woman he had sentenced to death.

Chapter 2

John surveyed the tree line along the edge of Fernwood City Park while at the top of a large, twelve-story office building. It was the tallest building on this side of the park and allowed him an overview of his surroundings. John pulled out the tourist map he had happened across when leaving a gas station on the outskirts of the small town. Large, cartoonish buildings stood out on the paper to display popular visitor sites. He had drawn an “X” over each building as he visited them, scouring every corner for anything that could be of use. He also made sure to check some of the more inconspicuous buildings, such as the complex he had just left, in hopes that they might still be untouched. The last building to check out was The Lonely Man Bar. John thought it a little strange that a bar would be considered a tourist destination, but, in such a small town, the criteria to make the list were easily met. John had been moving from town to town heading west. He couldn't remember the last time he saw his dad but he needed to know if he was alive.

The problem he now faced was that he had to cross the park to get to the final spot on his map. By his best estimation, the park appeared to be about a mile lengthwise and about a half mile wide. John sat on the edge of the roof, drumming his fingers on the head of his pick-head fire axe, wondering if he had good enough aim to push himself from atop the building toward the bar.

No sense in throwing caution to the wind at this point, he told himself.

The handle of the axe, worn smooth from years of use, fit perfectly in the hand of the firefighter who wielded it. Its weight felt familiar and comforting, a reassuring presence in the midst of chaos. With each swing, it cut through obstacles with precision and ease, clearing a path for rescue and relief. The head of the axe was cleanly painted red, the blade maintaining its sharp quality. The shaft of the blade was a deep gray with a metallic sheen.

Normally, areas with a substantial amount of trees, such as the park he now studied, were easier to navigate than the outsides of brick and concrete buildings. The soft wood was perfect for sinking his axe and Halligan tool into and the tree branches provided a bit of a safety net were he to slip up and start ascending. That being said, there was something about the eerie silence of this new, empty world that made these forests and parks give John the unnerving, gut-twisting feeling that was fear. *It's not fear,* John reasoned with himself, *its survival instinct.*

John looked back towards him at the apartment building in which he had the encounter that would probably now haunt his dreams for the rest of his life. How much time had he spent scavenging that one location? John carefully shifted his body to face the park again where the sun was crawling towards the horizon. He raised his right hand to the front of his face, arm outstretched, and measured the sun as being three fingers above the horizon. He had read in an old wilderness survival book that by using this method, with each finger being roughly equal to fifteen minutes, you could determine how much time was left before sunset. Forty-five minutes. He had never bothered to test this technique before The Lifting but figured it offered a close enough estimate for his current lifestyle. He had yet to find a watch with any battery power left while scouring through the shops and markets.

No way will I make it through the park before dark.

One of the biggest problems with moving while in the dark is visual distance. If you were to misjudge the distance from one object to the next, or the speed at which you propelled yourself, it would mean the difference between lightly catching yourself on your feet, as if sinking to the bottom of a pool, and shattering your legs and spine. John was already fatigued from slowly scaling buildings, inside and out, all day. The fact that he got so little resources for his troubles made his exhaustion even more vexatious. He looked down at his arms. His muscles had been receding for a while now. The lack of gravity re-prioritized the importance of his body's muscle groups for everyday tasks, and the physical changes that resulted were noticeable in everyone these days. His arms had transformed from fairly toned to a gristle, bony look. His thoughts briefly took him back to the fire station; the long nights when he couldn't sleep, lifting weights for hours just to pass the time.

It's kind of early to turn in, but it might be smart to go through his haul and set up camp for the night.

John pulled his backpack around to the front of his body and unzipped it. He had only found a couple of cans of sardines and tuna throughout the rest of the apartments after his encounter with Jessica. John thought maybe a little protein would stay his hunger long enough to get him through the night. He took a bag of water out of the pack to complete his meal, the dirt had mostly separated from the water in the bag. Growing up, his mom would make him eat all kinds of food he didn't want to eat. Every time he took a bite of a brussel sprout he would have to wash it down with some juice.

The lengths I would go to for some fresh veggies now.

The thought of his mother and her constant lectures brought a small smile to his face. John took a swallow of water, the taste acrid and earthy. Forcing it down, he took a bite of fish to wash down the taste of what he could only think of as dishwasher juice.

After suffering through semi rotten sardines and a well-aged bag of dirty water he decided it was time to turn in. John pulled out a thin nylon rope and tied it to a large A/C unit on the roof. He then unraveled a brown-colored mummy sleeping bag. John grabbed the rope and secured it to the sleeping bag with a blue metallic carabiner clip. He slid his backpack into the sleeping bag and then slid into it himself. John pulled on the straps, tightening the sleeping bag around his head. John thought to himself how silly he would look from a distance.

I bet I look like a corndog.

John lay in the bag, trying to forget at what angle

he rested. He had been traveling for what seemed forever.

It's weird how I stayed away from my father for so long and now all I can think about is finding him. Traveling from town to town, John had gotten better at scavenging for food and water but had never become accustomed to seeing the horror and death each place brought. A twinge of anxiety welled, creating a pit in his stomach. He wondered if all of the time he had spent as a nomad would be in vain. John's father could easily be one of the billions of victims of The Lifting.

He heard a distant scream from the city below. His thoughts were drawn to the woman in the room. John's heart began to race and a small amount of anxiety started to well in his stomach. He began to ask himself the questions he had been pushing from his mind since leaving her behind. John pictured Crystal's pale skin and blackened malnourished eyes.

"Stop it," he mumbled to himself. He had always thought that it would get easier with time. Seeing the death, the bodies, and the overwhelming sense of just needing to survive. John wondered if he was even, in fact, surviving. In EMT school he went through a course on emotional survival. They taught that in the profession sometimes you are thriving and sometimes you are just surviving. John thought that he would like to add another option to that list, something lower than surviving.

Am I surviving? I'm alive, aren't I?

John decided that the third option was to simply exist. He didn't feel as if he was quite surviving, and he surely wasn't thriving. He was just alive, and the thought made him content enough for now to be able to drift out of consciousness.

STATION 62.

John inspected the large, bronze lettering on the front of the building he could now call his second home. Located on the northeast corner of the main city block, the fire station was surprisingly calm for mid-afternoon. He could hear families playing at the park behind the station. Two teenagers on BMX bikes rode past him, one nearly clipping John's shined boot. It was about eighty-eight degrees outside, the heat of the sun warming the back of John's neck. He tilted his head upward in delight as a light breeze hit the sweat on his forehead.

John walked up the clean gray concrete driveway,

wearing a tight-fitting blue shirt, jeans, and freshly polished boots. John hears the blare of a fire engine revving up and doors slamming shut. He watched as two fire engines peeled out of the garage with their bright red lights flashing. They were off to deal with a controlled burn that had gotten out of hand. These were the most common type of callouts they received involving actual fire, and John knew they would have it under control and be back before dinnertime. He hesitated outside the large rolling door leading into the garage, annoyed by the long list of daily duties he had before him.

Maybe the guys will pick up some food on the way back.

The least he could do was get one of the engines clean before they returned. He grabbed the clipboard holding the list of instructions and checkoff boxes and headed inside.

John located the shelves of cleaners and grabbed a large, empty blue bucket. He dragged his arm across the top shelf pushing brushes, washcloths, soaps, and wax, into the bucket. He put in one earbud and got to work. Part of him felt like he could probably get away with just wetting the outside of the engine and drying it off, saving him the time and effort it took just to clean one of these massive vehicles.

I'm pretty sure this engine hasn't even been used since its last cleaning. If you're going to do something you might as well do it right.

John knew the importance of doing things right though, even if nobody else was around. Besides, he was happy to have the chance to continue listening to the podcast he had put on for the drive to work.

Once he was finished washing, waxing, and polishing, John stepped back to admire his work. His biceps swelled from the constant rotating motion while finishing the polish, a bead of sweat rolling down his forehead. Six years of doing this and he still found it difficult to get the metal side plates up to his standards, but it was hard not to appreciate the shine of the cherry red after a waxing. He moved on to checking gauges to ensure fluid levels were good. Checking the compartments around the engine came next, ensuring each piece of gear was in its assigned location. Satisfied that everything was in place, he swung the last compartment door shut. John grabbed the clipboard and drew a quick check mark in the final box. He knew that if just one item was out of place or missing it could be the difference between life and death for him, his coworkers, or a civilian.

It was then that John felt the sensation that his spine was relaxing as if lying down after hours of intense physical labor. He could not tell if his insides were pressing into or away from each other, making him nauseous. The weight of his body seemed to no longer burden his legs. He started to feel dizzy and, even though he knew exactly where he was, had a sense that he was lost. John grabbed onto the nearby exhaust system hose in an attempt to stabilize himself. As he put his weight into his grip on the hose John became aware that his feet were no longer touching the concrete floor of the garage. His body hovered several inches above the ground.

Outside of the garage door, the air had gone silent like the calm before a storm. The sound of one person yelling turned into two people, then three, gradually growing to the volume of a small sports arena. The cries echoed through the garage, sending shivers down John's spine. The roaring of voices was broken up by inconsistent, loud thuds, metallic scrapes, and snaps of what he interpreted to be large pieces of wood splintering.

Looking behind him he saw through the garage door window to the park. A charcoal grill had been knocked over and was held in suspense a foot off the ground, the charcoal drifting close by and still glowing red. A mother and father had anchored themselves to the pole of a pavilion, desperately reaching for the fingers of the young girl who was drifting steadily away from her parents. The family pug that was tied up to the nearest tree yelped frantically as its paws left the ground.

John's breathing became erratic and his chest tightened, a sense of dread washed over him like a slow-moving river.

What's happening here, am I having a heart attack?

Sweat started flushing out of every pore and he struggled to catch just one good breath of air. With all of the panic going on around him John struggled to focus on one thing, his body frozen with shock.

I need to get out of here, I need to be somewhere safer.

Chaos seemed to explode at every corner of John's field of vision, it was hard for him to focus on all of them at once. He remembered his instructor telling him that in a mass casualty event to use triage. "Triage is to conduct a primary assessment of any situation determining the most important to least important problem," he heard from his memory.

John shakily put one hand in front of the other,

forcing himself to climb along the hose toward the garage door. His body was parallel to the ground. Reaching the large garage doors, he transferred his grasp to the guide rail and peered out of the doorway just in time to see a car soaring through the air. The red, four-door Buick soared head-on through the second-story window of the station. John held his breath, bracing for a barrage of debris. What he saw instead only made him feel all the more perplexed. Shards of glass and chunks of brick shot out in every direction from the point of impact and continued flying in a straight line, losing neither altitude nor velocity.

The car, not held in place by the building itself, hovered within the hole it had created in the side of the fire station. John's focus turned to the scene behind the sedan. Vehicles, people, animals, and objects of all types littered the sky, as countless as the stars at night. Horrified, John could only watch as the townsfolk he loved to serve shot into the sky in every direction except down. An approaching car alarm made him whip his head to the left just in time to notice the dark blue pickup with no driver hurtling toward him-

John was startled awake by a scream emanating

from the park. John groggily pulled his pack from the bottom of the sleeping bag. On his travels, he rarely finds anything of use but he had recently found a small, dark-green set of binoculars that looked like they had come from a kid's meal at a fast food restaurant. John raised the binoculars to his eyes and searched for any light or movement, but couldn't find it. It was dark outside other than the pale glow of light from the moon. He lowered the binoculars to see if his peripheral vision would catch anything. A knot formed in his stomach as he watched a heavy patch of trees light up with several small lights. John pulled his binoculars back to his face and focused on one of the lights in the park. The soft sound of a violin whined through the open air. The sound could only be described as a combination of sadness, serenity, and acceptance. The music felt as if it was flowing through him as he understood the emotions the artist was trying to convey. John couldn't remember the last time he heard such a beautiful sound. It was so seductive that he had to fight the allure to get closer.

Am I still dreaming?

The light appeared bigger and brighter than before. He heard a woman screaming.

"You can't make me do this! No! No!" she yelled.

John watched as a large fireball launched into the

air. It reminded him of a shooting star as it continued toward the atmosphere. The light propelled quickly, out of sight within moments.

"Would you j-just listen this is craziness?" a man stammered. "This won't solve anything! Have you all lost your minds? Please, just let me go."

John watched as a flair of light burst from the center of the park. He then heard the unmistakable howl of a man being burned alive. John had heard that sound more than once, which was infinitely more than a person should ever have to. One thing they never trained you on at the fire and rescue academy is how to tune out the screams of people burning alive, followed by a sizzle and a pop. John watched the light launch into the air in his direction like it was meant for him to see. As the man sailed overhead he saw his burning flesh and the frozen expression of fear on his face. The man had a rough burlap rope tightly wrapped around his upper torso. John watched as the man flew straight up into the night sky. John could not help but compare this spectacle to the sights seared into his mind from years of battling fires. No gravity sure did make for some fascinating views, dreadful as they may be at times.

Another flicker of light in his binoculars caught his attention. John couldn't tell if this person was a man or a woman from this distance. It didn't help that they were wearing a strange headdress that further obscured their heads and faces. They were holding a wooden club with a large flame atop it. Yet one more thing that was impossible for John to get used to was the appearance of flames when there was no gravity. Instead of a streaming billow of fire, dancing and licking, the shape of the flame took on a spherical appearance. John was no physics master, so he wasn't sure why it looked like that, but he knew it didn't start until after The Lifting. The lights were snuffed out one by one in the park and the music ceased. John was certain that he had never seen anyone die – or be murdered – that way in this new world. The image of the blazing man was all he could picture in his mind, not allowing his heart rate to come back down to its normal level. John wasn't able to fall back asleep after the ordeal; before he knew it the sun was peeking over the edge of the rooftop at him, bidding him good morning.

Chapter 3

Two years prior. Los Angeles gridlock.

"Ughhh." Mary let out a breath of annoyance.

She had been stuck in traffic for over an hour now. She told herself that this is one of the many tolls you pay for living in Los Angeles.

On the plus side, she thought, *that's why I bought this car in the first place.*

She was sitting in an old-style white Cadillac with a deep red interior. The aftermarket shocks smoothly handled the potholes littering the freeway, and the leather seat was built like a luxury sofa. The only thing Mary hated about the car was the odd smell of 1970 playboy she couldn't get out of the upholstery. Mary reached over and pressed the scan button on the radio. The first station to catch was playing an old, sad-sounding brass instrument. Another push sent the radio to a rap station playing a song that would make any respectable person blush. She finally left it on the NPR talk station so she didn't feel so alone in the car. Mary adjusted the rear view mirror seeing that there were a pair of semi-trucks tailing her close enough that she could have turned around and spat on them.

Annoyed, she mumbled to herself, "Listen, buddy, it's not my fault we aren't moving."

Mary was on her way to the toy store, she had planned on buying a new game system, the most expensive she could find. When she moved to LA from small rural Montana she didn't realize how hectic everything was. She was set to have her scheduled weekend with her seventeen-year-old boy, Jacob, and wanted to buy something nice. Anything that would make her Ex-husband Tyler look like a bad father. She and Aaron were like two peas in a pod and when the divorce went through she felt like a piece was always missing from her. Jacob is big for his age, but he got his appearance from his father. She loved Jacob but she always saw the failure of her marriage in his face.

She and Tyler met at a time when both of their lives had taken a turn for the worse. He was just getting out of an early divorce with a wife that had cheated on him. Tyler had just started at a new law firm so he barely had time to eat and sleep, let alone have a steady marriage. He blames himself for what happened. He was the tight-bodied charmer that any girl would swoon over. They were introduced at a friend's dinner party and I saw stars. She had never had a person say nice things to her or been made to feel special. She felt like everything he talked about was ecstasy, his voice a soft song and his words the most poetic lyrics. It seemed silly to her now, how fast they ran into life, only to let it fall to shambles. Mary didn't consider herself a catch, but her middle-aged body was plenty to contend with. She kept up with the modern fashion, watched what she ate, and occasionally went jogging. After Tyler, she vowed to only devote real attention to her baby boy.

Mary inched along the highway road having a hard time zoning out. Her eyes landed on the long strip of Blue Ocean that could be seen from the highway. Mary thought about how she moved to LA to see the ocean more but found she only saw it from a distance. It was maddening to be so close to such a pretty thing but never actually enjoy it. She made plans to visit the ocean each month with Jacob but they seemed to always fall through. In the distance, Mary could see a handful of lights that were coming from CHP police cars, likely the reason why traffic was so bad. She started to worry a little.

If this traffic doesn't pick up soon I'm going to be

late to pick up Jacob.

She gazed at the oversized pickup truck to her right. A man dressed in a red lumberjack shirt arguing with the woman in the passenger seat. It reminded her of how she and Tyler argued. Seeing an opportunity to make the time go faster she cracked the window to listen to the couple. Mary's white rusted car didn't have a very good air conditioner, she debated if it was even worth the front row real-world entertainment in exchange for what little A/C held in the car.

The man yelled, "What do you mean you're not hungry anymore? The whole reason we got in the car in the first place was to go get a burger."

"I told you I didn't want a burger. When will you actually listen to me for once?" The passenger retorted. "I knew this relationship wouldn't last. I told you I am a vegan and I don't eat meat."

"How could you not eat meat? That is the sole purpose of any animal's existence. They live to feed us. I thought you were joking, I watched you eat a bowl of ice cream."

"Do you not know what being vegan means? It's about how much time an animal spends in the pasture!" she said.

Mary felt like she was losing brain cells listening to those two dummies argue. She rolled up the window. The taste of the strawberry bubblegum she was chewing was starting to go stale. She opened the middle console and fished around for the gum package to refresh her piece and found that it was empty.

Just another thing to put on the list when she went to the store.

Jacob must have taken a few when she wasn't looking. Mary crumpled up the empty gum package and put it in her purse. She finally inched close enough to the accident to see three people on the side of the road. Mary saw a newly waxed purple Corvette that had been hit from behind by a large rusted red van. *Probably on their phones.* Mary could see "wash me" written on the dirty rear windshield. The damage didn't seem all that bad to the van, but the corvette had taken some damage. One light was smashed out and the LA license plate that read "BIGMONEY" had been crushed.

As her car crawled closer, she heard a man yell, "This car cost more than your life. Do you understand what you did?"

Mary drove further past the van to see a couple

wearing tie-dye shirts. They had a blank expression on their face that led Mary to believe they were too stoned to even really know where they were. The woman stoner was sporting blonde dreadlocks.

"Why does anyone do that to themselves?" she mumbled. Mary imagined small little lice skipping around the unwashed bird's nest of the lady's head. After passing the traffic jam the old Cadillac started to pick up speed.

30 MPH….

50 MPH….

65 MPH…..

"Finally," she thought. Mary felt a twinge of annoyance, she was definitely going to be late now. Mary reached into her leather brown purse and pulled out her cell phone. She pressed the side power button to see a nice photo of Jacob playing at the park with a puppy. She kept half an eye on the road while tracking down Tyler's number. She had him labeled under "Fake Man". She clicked the name with her thumb and was immediately met with three dull beeps. She looked at the screen. No signal.

"That's what I get for going for a cheap plan" she grumbled.

Mary's car started climbing up the two-lane highway ramp that split the six-lane freeway into smaller two-lane highways. She looked at the rear view mirror again, to find two very impatient truck drivers still tailing her car. Her hair caught her eye as it started to bunch like she was playing with a static balloon. An odd sensation started to well up in her body making her stomach turn. Mary felt an overwhelming tickle in her throat and coughed, losing her gum by accident.

Mary watched as her old chewed gum, instead of falling into her lap, floated just in front of her face. She stared in disbelief. The gum though slowly moving, was floating mid-air at eye level. Horrified, she rolled down the window and slapped the gum out. She watched as the gum drifted out of view towards the clouds. This is it she thought, working double shifts for months to pay the rent and she had finally cracked. She heard the radio blaring several noises and a monotone voice came on.

"This is an alert, this is a national emergency. Stay indoors. All communications and the internet have stopped working. We don't know why or how stay safe and God bless".

Mary didn't hear the radio emergency. She was too fascinated with her pale-red piece of floating gum. She had heard many stories about people hallucinating when finally developing schizophrenia, seeing monsters, and having inanimate things talk to them. She was surprised that her snapping point could be something as small as drifting gum.

She looked back up at where she was driving, just about to hit the crest of the bridge. Her car started making violent noises like it was running out of gas. Mary looked at the gas gauge and found it was sitting at the three-quarters mark. Mary felt an extreme blunt force as the Semi-truck driver slammed into the back of her car. Mary lurched forward, the seat belt stopping her from ramming forward more than a couple of inches. Mary felt the instantaneous punch of the airbag deploying. The airbag hit with such pressure Mary felt a crunch that created a violent spurt of pain in her face. The airbag broke her nose causing a steady stream of blood to flow out down her lips. Mary watched the scene unfold like everything was moving in slow motion. Not realizing, she was screaming as hard as she could manage into the liner case material that made up the airbag.

Heaving her body forward she pulled down on the airbag just barely peeking over the top she watched as her car topped the crest of the ramp and drifted sideways into the air. She felt her body go weightless as her car launched off of the ramp. Mary held her breath expecting to feel her car hit the ground. The car continued to rotate in a barreling motion, not fast but continuously rotating. Mary scratched and clawed at the airbag until the air let loose and she could get a better look at what was happening.

Mary tried to look out the window but had a strong wave of nausea from vertigo, the spinning was too much for her to focus on. Mary looked behind her out of the back window and saw hundreds of cars behind her drifting toward the sky. The cars from a far-off distance resembled a floating metal coil pulling away from the ground.

She felt panic and fear. Mary looked out the passenger window and saw she was thousands of feet in the air gunning towards the clouds. Her face went flush, and she felt dizzy like she was going to pass out. In a haze, she looked around the car and saw large balls of blood floating in the air. Looking at the blood reminded her of the old videos she saw of astronauts drinking orange juice on the space shuttle. Mary looked down and saw a stream of blood drifting from her nose. The blood streamed out in a series of tree roots stretching for more nutrients.

How is this possible?

While in her panic she noticed she was feeling short of breath. She looked out the side of her window and couldn't recognize objects. Mary started coughing just trying to catch her breath. Her car pushed into a thick cloud.

The moisture from the cloud started saturating both the inside and out.

I can't breathe. Why can't I catch my breath?

Mary turned in her chair and looked behind her. She didn't see the vehicle train that followed behind her.

The car punched through the clouds that made up the troposphere, Mary imagined this was what the creation of the world looked like. The majestic sun reflected off of the clouds. Though she was panicking she found the sight to be the prettiest thing she had seen since the birth of Jacob.

"Jacob," she yelled. Where was her boy? Was he alive? Will she ever see him again? Mary felt her eyes drying out. She just couldn't breathe.

Why is it so hard to breathe?

She resembled a fish out of water, trying, with no hope, to get one more breath.

"Mom, don't be sad, I'm fine."

Mary looked over at the passenger seat and there sat Jacob, without a care in the world. Jacob had his favorite blue shirt on, the one with his favorite band. Mary tried to say something but nothing came out.

"Mom, you don't have to say a word. I will be with you. I love you mom".

Mary felt tears in her eyes. She felt an intense burn

in her chest, then nothing at all. She looked down and all of the blood that covered her face was gone. She watched Jacob rest his head against her shoulder and they fell asleep together.

Chapter 4

Rubbing his eyes with his fists, John's stomach lurched as he felt a strong cramp. He wondered if it was hunger or rotten food. No matter the cause, he knew he needed to eat. John carefully extracted himself from the sleeping bag and tucked it, along with his tie-down rope, back into his pack. He finished off the last of his water and food. He felt his stomach rumble for more, but he had no more to give.

This bar better have something to eat or I'll have to resort to finding spiders again.

John squirmed at the thought. He looked at the trees that spanned in front of him and considered the potential food source. He pulled his body head first over the edge of the building and rotated his body with his head facing the street below. John pushed against a window ledge with his feet, being careful to maintain a grip on the building at all times. John passed a window and looked inside, pausing his descent momentarily. He saw a kitchen layered with dust. The place was empty, save a few pieces of a cheap, all-black dining room set pieces hanging in the air. No one had been there for years.

He reached the street level and rotated 180 degrees to place his feet on the ground. In front of him was a wall of oak trees wrapped in vines and weeds. The vegetation had taken over every square inch of dirt in the park. Using the sturdy building wall, he lightly pushed off with his toes and hovered just a foot off of the ground through the parking lot. Gyrating his body clockwise, he navigated around a rusted-out white sedan. At the edge of the parking lot, he stopped himself by grabbing onto a park sign that read: "Park hours are from sunup to sundown."

I'll bet they don't want anyone in the park because that's when they start launching people into orbit.

John chuckled at his dark joke and looked up. An almost neon yellow Atom symbol had been spray painted on the tree in front of him. As John inspected further ahead, he saw that most of the trees bore roughly sprayed symbols on them as well.

I should probably go around... but, I'm not going to last another day without finding food.

Next to the pole he was stationed on sat a wide map

that had been discolored by the sun. John studied the map, noting key points in the park that would help him navigate its vastness. A large, green star that read “You are here” confirmed that he was in the eastern parking lot. He took out his tourist map and tried his best to copy down water fountain locations and other points of interest. At the center of the map, John saw a blue pond with a cartoon duck painted on it. If memory serves him right, he was sure that the pond was where the commotion occurred last night.

His stomach muttered a rather loud grumble. John buckled over, grabbing his stomach, strong stabbing pains throbbed on his side. John pushed off from the park sign and drifted in between the first two trees into the park. Upon passing, he felt a familiar grip that tickled his face and he tore through a spider web.

No food and no water yet, somehow, there's an abundance of spiders around.

Frustrated, John brushed his hand across his face hoping that that was the last web he flew across.

The irony of spiders living this long…

John caught sight of the first marker, which was a water fountain. He had little faith in the quality of water contained within any park fountain, apocalypse or not. Almost always the penny-pinchers in city hall never bothered to turn them on. He placed his lips around the metallic spout, cupped his hands around his face and sucked in. He drank five deep gulps of water before stopping for a breath, surprised to find so much. John drew three more mouthfuls before the pipe ran empty. He felt every refreshing swallow roll from his mouth to the bottom of his stomach. The water was a bit warm, but he didn't mind.

John pulled his knees in and pushed himself towards the next tree, in the direction of the bar. He caught the side of a tree branch, trying to stop himself. As his speed slowed he realized he had grabbed more leaves than branches and his grip slipped. This sent him into a clockwise spin, albeit manageably slow. Panic filled his chest as the image of the dying woman stuck in the air entered his mind. Frantically, he flailed at the branches. A pinch was all he needed to stabilize himself. On his fourth spin, he caught it with his pointer finger and thumb, focusing all of his energy into the tips of his two fingers. John pulled himself toward the tree with relief. John held that tree, like a newborn baby to his mother, waiting for the fear to pass.

Focused and calm once more, John picked a sturdy-looking oak about twenty yards away to be his jumping point. He methodically pointed himself at the tree. He put his hands out in front of him and lightly pushed off the trunk with just a tap of his feet, although he pushed a little harder than he had intended. The closer he got to the tree, the more he noticed that there was a fair amount of spider webbing that coated the tree bark. *Great. More spiders.* He sailed just inches above the dry, overgrown grass and weeds. John held out his hands, anticipating the impact. His hands hit the tree, stopping him abruptly. He felt a violent spurt of pain in the palm of his right hand. He pulled his it away from the tree, and as he did, he felt a tug of resistance from a cluster of splinters. His hand had landed on a sharp gnarled knot.

Dammit, that is how people die from infections.

His palm welled up with blood, pooling into a near-perfect sphere rather than dripping down his fingers. John tore off a piece of his dirty shirt and tightly wrapped it around his small wound.

I'll get a cleaner strip of cloth from my bag once I get inside. If I don't come across any bandages, that is.

John continued combing the area ahead with his eyes. He noticed, past the next group of trees, a large, dry crater. A wooden bridge, whose white paint was nearly completely peeled off, separated the two ends.

That's got to be the pond.

John propelled himself once again to the next tree with added caution to not make the same mistake twice. He laboriously crawled up the harsh, coarse trunk and out onto a branch that pointed toward the clearing. Surveying around the bridge, he observed several little floating black blobs hovering within the confines of the shade under the bridge. He took one more wary look around before making his way back down the trunk, then slowly walking his hands along the ground to the edge of the bridge. Even this simple maneuver was incredibly painstaking, as he had to make sure not to push upwards with his limbs too hard, or he may not be able to stop himself from launching upward.

At the bridge's edge, he saw an odd contraption built into the center of the bridge. A small trampoline had been tied down to the bridge with twine rope. The rope looked several times knotted and well secured.

This is a dangerous place. I can't be caught here or I'm just as doomed as those two from last night.

Almost as if it were scripted, John heard the voices of two men approaching, coming from the direction of the bar. John scrambled to the underside of the bridge, using it as concealment, and pressed himself up against the bottom of it, hoping that he hadn't already been seen.

"How many do you think it will take?" one said.

"I don't care how many it takes, it's just easier not to

think about it," the other replied.

"What do you mean you don't care? These are people. I understand that what we're doing is going to save the world, but that doesn't make it easier to do. Those people seemed decent enough."

John watched as the two men passed over the bridge, catching small glimpses of them through the cracks of the bridge. Both of them had loose-fitting, dark tan-colored robes on with a bright green sash tied around the waist. The man on the left was only a few inches taller than the other, and much of their physique was hidden by their robes. John could tell, however, by their broad shoulders and strong jawlines that they were likely considerably strong. Both men grabbed onto the handrail of the bridge and stopped near the trampoline.

"Do you think there are any more around here?"

The other looked out toward the city and then down at the bridge. John held his breath.

I'm caught. He's looking right at me, why doesn't he react?

He tried to focus on breathing as quietly as he could, even though he was convinced the man could hear his heart pounding. The robed man had a metallic gold marking the size of his fist on his forehead of an atom. John had never seen one of them so close.

This shortcut isn't worth dealing with these freaks. I need to get out of here.

The two men cut loose and disassembled the trampoline and continued deeper into the park. John let out a shaky breath. Out of the corner of his eye, he noticed a blob of floating black liquid right as it touched his cheek. He wiped at it, but the consistency was not what he was expecting.

This is definitely oil. Is this what they were using last night on those people?

He pictured someone being set on fire and the black oil droplets floating off of them. John crawled along the underside of the bridge to the other side. He pulled himself from under the bridge and shoved his body away, aiming for a large elm tree with leafy branches. He caught the trunk and crawled to the very top, using the large leaves as cover from the men's view. John spent the better of an hour slowly launching from one tree to the next not seeing any signs of robed people. From the tree top, he saw a shiny metallic square below him.

Hopefully, the next fountain will have as much water as the last one. At this rate, I just might be able to store enough to make the next push across the state.

John was hesitant to make his way to the potential new water source, though. He looked in every direction while poised at the top of the tall tree, but was unable to see where the men had wandered off to. John wanted to believe that they had put plenty of distance between themselves and him, but the nagging worry that ate at him refused to let up. After what he perceived to probably be about fifteen minutes, he pointed his head toward the dead grass and weeds below and pulled himself down the branches until he reached ground level. John took a closer look and found that the shiny object he had found was a toy robot's head covered in rust, its body partially buried in the dry, cracked earth. John didn't let himself imagine what had likely happened to the child that left this here. The children's area had been well covered with vines and weeds. John did another check around him. A massive oak with the center rotted out grabbed his attention. Moving to attach himself to the trunk, he found that the hollowed-out portion from the rot was big enough to contain all of him.

John brushed aside the loose pieces of wood, looking for grubs or maggots. He had found during his journey that worms and grubs, like spiders, were able to attach to surfaces well, so they were mostly unaffected by

The Lifting. John grabbed a handful of moist, foam-textured wood and pulled it aside. There, he found the mother lode of slimy, writhing maggots feasting on the rotting wood. He pulled out one of his unused Ziploc bags and started pushing them in one by one. John studied the tiny insects floating around inside the clear plastic bag for a moment.

First water, now some protein. If it weren't for these damn Atom creeps I could spend all day gathering grub here.

John weighed the chances of getting caught if he kept looking around. Once the bag was full enough that he was having trouble keeping all the maggots from floating out he sealed it and let it hang in the pocket of the tree trunk. He wanted to give a quick double-check for any loose ones he might have missed. The bag looked like a pulsating mass just waiting to explode.

"I'm telling you, I swear to I saw movement near the top of the trees over here," the first man's voice surprised John.

John peaked his head out of the tree, gauging the direction where the voices were coming from.

I can't keep this up. I just need to get out of here before I'm caught.

John was mentally kicking himself for not having

left earlier, regardless of the bag of insects he was able to collect. Stuffing his bag of goodies into his pack, John's mind gave him a mental image of what it might be like to be launched into space while burning alive. He was starting to get sick of these intrusive thoughts. He gracefully moved around the tree trunk, opposite the direction of the voices, and thrust his body away hard, deciding he'd deal with the rough landing when he got to it. But, he was desperate to put distance between himself and the robed strangers.

John never even saw the line. He could only feel the thin line of tension from the fishing wire catch his chest. The wire broke with a snap, and just as suddenly as he felt the wire it was gone. Two cowbells started rolling in circles, their tones deafening in the quietness of the trees. As John's body continued forward, a second line caught the side of his neck and up along his cheek. Another set of bells sounded off.

"I knew I heard someone! Get over here!"

John became petrified.

Shit. I'll be surrounded soon.

John looked behind him and saw six similarly robed people skillfully moving from one tree to the next in pursuit, using all fours to do so. John couldn't help but compare their movements to monkeys as they darted towards him, clearly confident in their maneuvers. The sight of them was enough to snap John out of his shocked state and start dashing through the trees himself. As the pursuers propelled themselves, they were making a series of monotone noises toward each other that didn't quite seem to be real words. One holding too much speed collided into a thick limb of the rotted oak he had been at. There was a loud snap that John knew was likely the man's arm. He let out a terrible scream and held his arm, all while going into an uncontrollable twirl that sent him head-first into another tree, effectively knocking him out of consciousness. This didn't deter John from picking up speed, grappling from branch to limb, and even making use of the scattered park benches as he rushed toward the edge of the park. A line tugged and broke across his shoulder and he heard the more bells violently resonate, confirming to his pursuers his whereabouts in case any of them happened to lose sight of him. John audibly cursed himself for not paying more attention on his way in. It was obvious now that he should have assumed this place would be booby-trapped.

"I've almost got him," a new voice rang out.

John turned his head to the right and found himself parallel with a surprisingly overweight man with a double chin that melted down into his robe. "Stop. Let us save your soul," he giggled.

John moved his stare back to the front of him and noticed that he was approaching a shoddy little building, red-bricked and sun-bleached, with an old neon "Open" sign in the red and green stained glass window. It was The Lonely Man Bar, and he was approaching it at a dangerous speed.

If I don't slow down I'm going to break my neck.

Dead grass had grown up the edges of the front wall along with some green vines. The sign for the bar had the image of a sad cartoon clown holding a mug of beer. John quickly determined two forms of entrance: he was either going through the front door or smashing through the window. Since there was no guarantee the door would give way once he made an impact, John reached behind him and pulled his axe off of his pack. He used the short brick wall that bordered this section of the park to aim himself at the window and dragged the axe along the ground to slow his speed, clanging loudly against the asphalt.

John took one more look behind him and saw that several more robes had joined the chase. The fat man, whom he had gained some distance from, kicked off a tree at dangerous speeds, aiming to meet John under the clown sign. The man, without intervention, was on a course to ram him from the side. He reached out with this hand at the same time John planted his axe into the dirt of the park strip on the other side of the sidewalk from the park, abruptly stopping him. The robed man sailed over him, helpless to stop himself from slamming into a bike rack bolted into the concrete. The momentary pause gave the others chasing time to close the gap between them. As swiftly as he could manage, John pulled his legs in and jumped at the glass window. He glided across the street, gripped his axe tightly, and swung it into the glass right before his body would have hit it. The glass splintered in all directions. Several shards of glass came to meet him as he soared through the window into the bar, cutting his face and hands as he did. John felt an itch on his forehead. He put his left hand up to it and found a small shard of glass had lodged itself in his head.

Hastily taking in his surroundings, John did a backswing with the axe, sticking the pick end into a beam. John felt a stinging pain in his left shoulder as his momentum immediately halted. Frantically looking around the room, he saw the only other door that could have offered a way out had a locked padlock. There was no escaping this room except for the way he came in. He turned back toward the window, ready to leap out of it, only to be met by four figures between him and freedom. John didn't have time to notice as a fifth individual approached him from the side, knocking him over the back of the head with the thick end of a pool cue. John's vision blacked, but he stayed conscious. Two of the four people near the window approached him. One grabbed the axe from John's hand as he raised it to defend himself, and the other threw a punch at his lower jaw. The last thing John saw before his senses left him was the face of one of the remaining two persons by the window: a young man, short in height with dirty-blonde hair and pale ivory skin. He didn't have the same crazed look in his eyes as the others. His was full of uncertainty, even a touch of fear. John couldn't hold onto his state of awareness any longer and slipped into the darkness.

Chapter 5

“Alright, rookie, are you ready for the time of your life?”

John looked up to see Matt O’Brian, his first trainer for the fire academy school. Matt was a short Irishman with a permanent scowl on his face, he had a buzzed head adorned with black stubble. John could feel his heart pounding. The thumping in his ears was distracting.

“Yes sir,” John replied.

He reached down and picked up a large gray duffle bag full of medical supplies, clothes, toiletries, and his handheld gaming console. Matt briskly walked over to him and pulled the bag away from him.

“What, bring your whole apartment with you? We are only doing a thirty-six hour work day and you came prepared for the end of the world,” O’Brian sneered.

John pulled the bag away from him.

“Sorry. I….. I tried to bring everything I might

need," John apologized.

"Well, I hope you weren't planning on spending a lot of time relaxing. Your learning ain't stopping just because you're out of the academy."

John followed him through the front doors. He was overwhelmed with everything before him. The whole place smelled like bleach cleaning materials, along with a hint of rubber.

"Now for the tour, I suppose," Matt said as he pointed at the front desk that was being run by a young, brunette lady with just the right amount of makeup. John shyly waved hello as they passed by. Matt led him up a set of stairs and down a narrow hallway. As they passed the first door on their right, Matt informed him that it was the fire chief's office and to never go in there if the chief was not there. At the end of the hall, John saw a bronze-colored pole that dropped deep into the center of the garage. Looking down he saw people cleaning the fire engines and holding clipboards.

"Don't get too excited, little man, you have to pass training before you get to take a turn on riding down the pole," Matt said, looking back at him.

John tried to hide the excitement he felt finally being where he had worked so hard to get to. John noticed there was a closed door to the left of the pole.

"Hey, where does that lead?" John asked. Matt looked annoyed.

"If you'd stop drooling I'll tell you."

They turned a corner and continued down the hallway. Matt pointed out a classroom where John's training would take place, along with several other office doors.

Matt led him up another flight of stairs that opened up to a large shared room. Several sets of bunk beds stood against the wall. The room was equipped with a kitchen, weight-lifting equipment, and a 4K TV that was mounted on the wall.

"Holy hell, rookie, did nobody teach you how to shine your boots? An armless monkey could shine boots better than you."

"I didn't... I didn't know they didn't come shined out of the box. I'm sorry." John stammered. "Is that what you are going to tell the widowed mother who just lost her husband? That you looked like garbage because of the boot company?"

John started to get frustrated.

"You're supposed to train me, not talk down to me!"

"Listen here, princess, don't blame me because I'm

the first person to be honest with you. If you want to make it here, you have to act the best, live the best, and be the best. What we do here is save lives, and babying a rookie takes away from our ability to do that."

Matt pointed at a bed and told him that this would be his bed for the night. He was expected to keep it made unless he was in it. Matt walked over to a bookshelf and pulled out two large books: "EMT 1" and "Fire 1."

"These are the first two certifications you will need to start. If you fail either course you are out. I suggest you use any free time to memorize every sentence of these books." Matt handed them over to John.

John could feel his adrenaline starting to tank and a wave of exhaustion came over him. He thanked Matt and plopped down on the couch with "EMT 1" in his hands. He cracked open the book." Chapter One: How to Survive Trauma." John felt his eyes start to doze as he read through the most complicated jumble of words he had read since high school. With one last fleeting attempt to keep his eyes open, John began to softly breathe and fell asleep. A screeching alarm made John's head pop off of the couch cushion.

"Holy shit, this is how you react to an alarm. Get up

let's go," Matt yelled.

John, trying to get his bearings, looked at the clock that read 03:48 in a neon blue glow. The high-pitched squeal rang through his head, so loud that he could barely hear himself think. Matt walked over and yanked John to his feet by the back of his collar.

"I said let's go. Now. Move!"

Matt had to yell just to be heard over the alarm. John had a spike of adrenaline that awakened all of his senses. Firefighters were all jumping out of their beds and running out the door. John lurched toward the door, his legs not completely on the same page yet. He stumbled, stepping right foot over left, and tripped into the wall. Matt pulled him off the ground and pushed him out the door.

John ran down the stairs to the second floor, at the landing John used a wall to counteract his momentum and went down the next hallway. Coming around another corner, he found himself facing the fire pole at the other end of the hall.

"Don't you even think about it rookie, you'll break your ankles without some training!" Matt screamed. "We already have one emergency to deal with, we don't need two."

With each sprinting step, John got closer and closer

to fulfilling a lifelong dream.

How mad could he possibly get?

Five feet from the pole he jumped in the air with his hands outstretched, ready to connect with the pole. John's neck snapped forward hard, using John's momentum Matt pushed John out of the way of the pole and landed on top of him. "I told you, no. If you want to make it anywhere you need to start listening". John with bruised pride got up and followed Matt down the second set of stairs, through a door leading to the garage.

"We are riding in Car One, the paramedic truck over there," John got in the car and off they went. The feeling that John was going on his first call was exhilarating, the sirens spun over the top as they navigated the dark streets.

"Where are we going?" John asked Matt loud enough to compete with the noise of the sirens.

"Someone called in a cardiac arrest," Matt replied.

The truck pulled to a stop in front of a white, two-story home with a neatly trimmed pine tree out front. A short, older woman came running out of the front door and across the grass of the front yard sobbing.

"Help! It's my husband. He fell over and won't stop mumbling. I think he is having a heart attack."

Matt jumped out of the car and opened a metal side

latch that contained several medical bags. He grabbed one and threw it into John's arms and grabbed two more. They briskly walked through the yard and into the house with the sobbing wife, she looked to be about forty-five or fifty.

"Just up the stairs to the right. He's in the bedroom on the floor," the woman said, choking the words out between sobs. Matt and John found the man on the floor, pale and clammy, his whole body was drenched in sweat.

"John, you start with the CPR. I'll get the rest of the equipment." Matt reached on his hip and grabbed a radio. He started giving details of the situation to the incoming ambulance. John knelt at the man's side and put his left hand over his right, interlocking his fingers. He leaned forward and began pushing down on the center of the man's chest.

"You're not pushing hard enough, you'll hear his sternum crack when you are doing it right," Matt told him between radio transmissions.

John leaned his weight forward and pushed harder with each pump. A disturbing *CRACK* came from the man's chest, and John could feel bone give way underneath his hands. John felt nauseated, the pressure and the stress finally taking its toll on him. With each push, he felt himself get more fatigued and lightheaded. All outside noise had gone silent and his peripheral vision had blacked out. The only thing he could see was his hands moving up and down on the man's chest.

How long have I been doing this? It all feels like a bad dream.

"John!" Matt yelled, grabbing John by the shoulder.

John was unphased. He continued chest compressions, waiting for the man to sit up and take a deep breath of life, like you see in the movies.

"John. STOP." Matt pulled back on John's shirt causing him to fall backward onto his butt. "John, he's gone. You can stop."

In a daze, John looked at the man who had a certain glaze to his eyes that told him he had failed. His eyes trailed to his unpolished boots, Matt's words ringing in his ears. "What are you going to tell the widowed mother who just lost her husband?"

It was nighttime. John's first observation as he slowly pried open his eyelids was how dark the room was, the moonlight shown through the shattered window. An overwhelming rush of pain washed over his head like a river. Opening and closing his dry mouth a few times, John rotated his bottom jaw, a loud popping noise sounded off where a fist had connected, hard. His eyes took a moment to focus as he blinked repeatedly. He pulled his hand to his face to wipe his eyes and assess the damage but was met with resistance on his wrist. John turned his head and squinted at his arm. Only now did he see the rope tied tightly around his wrists, both sides were fastened to support beams on either side of him. His hand still bothered him from the little present the oak tree gave him. Paddling his feet back and forth, he felt for any connection to the ground, feeling nothing but empty space. John had found himself suspended a couple of feet in the air.

Hang on… where's my clothes?

At some point while he was unconscious they had removed all of his clothing, save his black boxer briefs. John felt the cold radiating over his skin.

At least they had the decency to leave those on me. But why bother taking clothes in the first place?

"Hey, Van, looks like your guy is coming too," said a woman behind him. From what John could discern, several people were grouped by him. John rotated his head as far as he could, ready to tell her how he really felt, but all that came was a raspy mumble of unintelligible sounds. He was in no shape to speak let alone do anything, his thirst was overwhelming.

The door which had been locked via padlock earlier, creaked open and a figure holding a dim candle entered the room. Donned with the same tan robe and green sash with the hood pulled down, the figure drew closer to John. He recognized him as the short, young dirty-blonde man from before. The man — which John wasn't sure was the technically correct term for him, *he still looked young enough to be under eighteen years old* — dragged his heels on the wooden floor and slowed to a halt just in front of John. The young man didn't have any symbol on his forehead like the ones he saw the night before.

"Here," the man said. He pulled a green and orange sports-style water bottle from a pocket on the inside of his robe. He raised the pressure nozzle up to John's mouth, John pulled his head backward and pursed his lips doing anything he could to avoid the contents in that bottle.

"Relax, it's just water. Not a lot, but more than you've had in the last twenty-four hours."

Is that how long I've been out?

Considering it was the middle of the night, he assumed it had been even longer. John figured he was already at the mercy of these people, so he relented and opened his mouth to welcome a reprieve from the dryness. The man squeezed the water bottle and a stream of water shot onto John's parched tongue. It was more water than he was expecting, and he felt like a dog drinking from a water hose as he tried to gulp down as much of the water as he could. Van stopped the water flow and put the bottle back into his robe pocket. Van then removed an old, military-style canteen attached to a sling that sat around his shoulder. John hadn't even noticed it until now. He had a feeling that it was more than just water. Van reached his right hand out and yanked a shard of glass from John's forehead. John could feel an itch from the paper-thin wound.

"So, your name is Van?" John asked, voice still raspy.

There was no harm in trying to learn about his captors, especially if it could give him a way to talk his way out of this situation.

Van's face changed slightly, taking on an irritated expression.

"I told you not to say my name around him. Especially not THAT name." John assumed this comment was for the female still positioned behind him.

"What? You want me to address you by your full name? Mr. Jacob Van Johnson. It's not like it'll matter soon anyway. Lighten up. Plus, until you take your first rite, you're a nobody to us." she replied with condescension.

Van rolled his eyes as he unscrewed the cap from the canteen. He lightly slapped the back of the canteen and a black blob came pouring out in a single circlet of oil, the smelly aroma of oil and kerosene filled John's nostrils. The memory of the floating oil blobs in the park rushed to the front of his mind and he began to struggle against his bindings. John's sudden burst in aggression caused Van to flinch backward, throwing a few drops of the black, flammable liquid into the air. This drew a laugh from the woman. John, again, picked up on the mockery toward Van.

"Careful there, Van. He might bite." The faint glow of the candle was enough for John to see fear and anger construing Van's face. Van steadied himself before throwing a punch at John's face. The woman's laughter grew louder. Van's knuckles landed right where John's jaw was already sore. The punch itself felt fake and full of restraint. John had been hit harder by kids.

Van, shrugging off the chagrin that boiled inside him thanks to his counterpart, grew confident and moved to John's right arm, using the rope to stabilize himself. He dipped his finger in the floating blob hovering out in front of him again, this time removing it with the oil soaked onto his fingertip. The mixture was cold on John's skin as Van began to write something on his arm.

"Newton's first law: an object will not change its motion unless a force acts on it." Van recited in a ceremonial voice. It was hard to make out, but John could see the same words had been written on his skin. A growing dread settled over him as the realism set in that he would be a human sacrifice. Van awkwardly climbed across John's torso, and the ropes, to John's left arm. He repeated the process, this time reciting Newton's second law.

"The force on an object is equal to its mass times its acceleration." The smell of John's condemnation began to burn inside his nostrils. If his head wasn't already pounding from the beating he received, he was sure the odor would have done the job instead. Van pulled himself under John's arm to his back and said,

"When two bodies interact, they apply forces to one another that are equal in magnitude and opposite in direction." The cold feeling was almost a stinging sensation now. The woman chimed in.

"Now, don't forget the seal on his forehead." Van dipped his finger in the concoction again and began to draw on John's head. Van mumbled out loud, almost as if he were struggling to remember this part.

"F equals G… multiplied by "m one, m two"... all over "R two," he uttered.

"So, you went with Isaac Newton to dedicate your rite to. Typical, but fitting," she said, moving closer, reviewing Van's handiwork.

"So, you're just going to kill me is that it?" John blurted out. "For what? Why go through all this trouble to off people in some sick fashion? You just want less competition for resources."

A husky, pompous male voice piped in, "Though I am big on showmanship, I will tell you that we are doing this to save the world. Your puny, uneducated mind wouldn't understand. We are saving the savable and putting the useless to good use."

"To what end? You just light people on fire and throw them up. How the hell does that save anybody?" John looked at Van with frustration. "You, Van, do you really believe in any of this? Are you so fearful that you're actually considering this?"

"I-I'm saving the world," Van stammered.

"When ten years have passed, and nothing has changed, will you accept the fact that you're just a cold-blooded murderer?"

Van looked shocked and uncertain for a split second. Shaking his head from side to side, his expression went blank. John knew he was getting in Van's head. Using John as a counterweight, Van pushed himself toward the floor. Van grabbed the candle and pressed it down hard on the floor, the odd, circular flame positioned below John's feet.

"You don't want the candle to get too close. You'll start the fire too soon." Van told himself aloud. The little bit of hope that had been building in John vanished, resentment and rage taking its place.

"Come, brothers and sisters, let us go prepare the artifact." Van pulled his hood over his head and pushed toward the padlocked door and the other two followed. This was John's first look at the woman and the other man. The woman was wearing the same robe as the rest of the cultists. She had her hood down, exposing her long, blonde hair, bright enough to almost be another source of light in the dark of night. She had narrowed eyes that made John feel as if she could peer right into his soul and reveal any secret.

John noticed that the plump man was wearing a robe different from the other two. It had many scientific formulas stitched in gold thread all around it. He had something pinched in between his arms but John couldn't get a good look at it. Without the candlelight to give perspective, the room had become pitch black. John's eyes hadn't adjusted and his mind told him that every shadow was Van ready to finish his work.

I thought staring out at the forest at night was unnerving... but, it's way worse when there are no noises to tell you the world is still alive. I would trade the rest of my food just to hear crickets and birds again. Why is this kid the one being pressed to kill me? He looked scared. I don't think he wants this any more than I do.

One of the many skills John had learned during his firefighting days, as well as his numerous backpacking excursions, was knots. Not only did he have the most common, useful knots memorized to make an emergency shelter or connect two pieces of rope into a longer one, but he also made it a point to practice and apply one new knot each camping trip. Aside from noticing that the rope being used to restrain him had obviously been used on previous victims, stained black with blood and oil, he recognized that they were secured to his wrists by bowline knots. The bowline is strong and won't come undone very easily. They must have had plenty of time and not worried he would wake up soon. He could feel the wiggle room on his right wrist that brought him a shred of faith. Lucky for John, the

Atomists had also removed the soiled, makeshift bandage he had wrapped around that same palm.

John clenched his teeth and took a deep breath. He began to dig his fingernails into his palm. He smashed his fingers together as much as possible, then opened his hand as wide as he could stretch it. He repeated this process over and over, scratching at the wound each time he closed his fist. However bad he thought the original damage had hurt, it was quickly replaced in his mind with this new searing, ripping sensation. The pain was enough to draw an audible curse from his lips.

"Dammit!"

He could feel the warmth of his blood beginning to soak his hand. He knew that without gravity the blood would not simply run down his hand and in between the rope and his wrist. He made sure to thrash his whole arm around to try and catch as much of his blood onto the rope as he could, hoping this was not all for nothing.

John, with one last strong pull, yanked his right hand with all of his strength. The knot that held around his wrist tightened so far that he could feel that his circulation had been restricted.

I'm exhausted, and there's no shot I can get out of

these ropes. I have to find another way.

John could feel his heart pounding in his chest and on his reopened wound. The strain he had used caused his muscles to flex and spasm involuntarily. John waited in the darkness for his captors to return to finish their insane project.

Seconds turned to minutes, minutes turned to hours. John felt a radiating pain from his shoulders and arms, his muscles had grown tired and sore. His hand had long been numb. This felt like an eternity. He was almost hoping one of those goons would knock him out again just to get some rest.

Maybe I've died and this is my hell for leaving so many behind. I don't deserve any better than this.

A tap on the wall near the door in front of him brought him out of his state of self-reflection. The door swung open with a squeal. There stood Van, centered in the doorway holding John's axe.

I don't know if I am ready for this. Maybe this will be preferable to dying as a fireball sent heavenward.

Van pulled himself into the room and readily secured the padlock.

"Listen I don't know how to go about this but I need your help. These people want me to hurt you. I.... I just can't do it. They caught me in a storeroom office while I was sleeping and told me that I could join the cause or die for the cause." John stared at Van, remembering the pain he had caused him.

"No," John said flatly.

"No? What do you mean no? It took me hours to give those two the slip. I am telling you that I'm helping you get out of here and you tell me no."

"I don't know what kind of game you're trying to play, but I've been through enough to know when I'm being lied to. You tie me up, draw all over my body, and even now you are standing in front of me holding my axe. Does that scream "I should trust this guy" to you? Quit patronizing me and just get it over with." Van moved closer and lifted the axe with both hands high above his head. John closed his eyes waiting for the swing.

Thwack. Opening his eyes he saw that Van had brought the blade of the axe down on the rope that was tied to the beam. *Thwack, thwack, thwack*. John felt the constant, pulling pressure on his left arm loosen with the last swing. He pulled his arm in toward his chest, his bicep throbbed with pain as the blood started to return to its natural place. Van cautiously pushed himself in the direction of the other side of the room. Both men locked eyes, sharing a semi-distrustful glance. Van swung the axe down on the knot attached to the beam securing his right arm, only this time, there was no relief for John's aching body. The axe had lodged into the wood. Van pulled back hard but it didn't budge. Just then, three booming knocks rang out from the door.

"I knew he was making a run for it," a man yelled from the other side of the door. John recognized the voice as the fatter man's.

John intensely looked at Van, "Boy, if you're going to do something, now would be the time." Van planted both his feet on the wood beam and pulled. At the same time, John worked to untie the knot around his right wrist. The axe came loose as the pounding on the door continued harder with each hit.

Through the door, John heard the blonde woman sneer, "I can't wait to finally put hands on the twerp. I'm going to go up and over so we can pin them in." Van pulled on the axe once more, freeing it from the wooden beam. He swung down with all of his strength, this time hitting his mark. The rope snapped, allowing enough slack for John to untie it from his wrist. A fresh wave of pain and the feeling of needles consumed his wounded hand as blood rushed back into it. Van slowly paced his feet against the ground walking toward John. Face to face, he dragged him down to floor level. For a moment Van and John held each other's gaze, both trying to determine how much trust they could put in the other.

"How about we call a truce and figure this out later," offered Van. John nodded and reached for the axe. Van flinched and pulled the axe back, paused, and then handed it to John. Another round of resounding strikes drew the men's attention again. They noticed that two of the three hinges had been broken. Each knew that the last hinge wouldn't put up much of a fight. John pushed himself toward the front door with Van following close behind. As they reached the door, the padlocked door behind them broke open, the plump man pulling himself through the doorway.

"Professor Weston, just let us go. We aren't hurting you none," Van pleaded at the man. As John stood on the threshold of the doorway he heard a scratching noise above him. John looked up to see the blonde woman crawling down the wall head-first.

"We need to leave now, Van", John yelled.

The plump man propelled himself toward the bar, catching onto the edge and pulling himself down behind it. He stood back up holding what looked like a rusted shotgun.

By the front door of the bar, John noticed a faded-out red fire extinguisher hooked to the wall. He grabbed the front of Van's robe with his good hand and the extinguisher with his other.

"Jump!" John instructed Van.

John heard the clear rack of the shotgun from behind him while the woman was getting to the edge of the front door. John knelt the best he could in zero gravity and jumped with everything he had, aiming to clear the looming trees of the park in front of them. John and Van sailed upward uncontrollably into the sky. John watched as they sailed over the trees, their altitude increasing exponentially.

"I'm afraid to die!" Van clung to John's arm while he began to scream. Van started tugging on John in hysteria, making both of them twist and turn while sailing upward. They had passed over the park completely and they were now careening over the shops and homes on the opposite side. John pulled the pin from the fire extinguisher, pointed the spout toward the sky, and squeezed the two metal handle pieces together. White powder erupted from the nozzle, changing their course back toward Earth. Van continued to paw at John like a panicking wild animal. Van's hand scratched down John's face. John felt a seer of heat followed by pain. He reached his hand up in a balled fist and brought it down hard on Van's forehead. Van immediately went limp.

John transitioned his grip to Van's arms and wrapped them around his neck, then continued to use the extinguisher to propel them both downward. Once they had nearly reached the ground, John spotted an open window of a two-story building.

I really hope that building isn't occupied or we are done for. John couldn't make out the sign over the front doors. *At this point, I'd hide in a freaking morgue.*

Pointing the nozzle of the extinguisher down, their speed slowed with their descent. He pushed Van through the window first, taking a long look behind them to ensure they were not somehow followed before ducking inside.

Chapter 6

Light crept into the room as the sun made its way over the horizon. Bright rays hit John's eyes through the crack of the closet door. John had finally let exhaustion take over about two hours before the daylight woke him, leaving him feeling groggy and irritable. After he and Van had entered through the window the night before, John found an unlocked broom closet. It was hard to determine what the room was previously used for, the only hint being a strong smell of fresh paper. John could see faint outlines of several desks and computer towers. John dragged Van's limp body into the closet and set him in the back corner, then positioned himself near the door where he could keep an eye out through the door.

He looked at the corner where he had left Van, only a floating wooden-handled mop lingered in his place. He quickly looked around and above him, he had vanished. The panic that set in pushed out his tiredness momentarily as he fondled for his axe. Grabbing its handle, he realized that if Van wanted to kill him or take his weapon, he had already passed up the opportunity. John drew a deep breath to help him gather his thoughts before pushing the door all the way open.

What am I doing with this kid? Last night he was going to kill me. Why did I try so hard to save him? I should have left him in the bar.

The room was larger than he initially thought. John assumed it to be some call center back when it was in use. He estimated that the range of the room was at least half of the building floor. With the dawn of the new day, John could better see the gray, melamine desks crowding the room. There were colorful cords strung across the room, still connected to computers and wall outlets. Scattered around the desks were some uncomfortable-looking swivel chairs, outdated computer monitors, papers, and manila folders all in various levels of suspension. Interestingly enough, the terrible paintings and stock photos lining the walls in frames were still there, stuck in place by the nails they were hung on. One that caught his attention had a cat hanging on a branch and read "Hang in there."

John looked out the open window through which they had entered last night. Squinting past the light shining in his eyes, he could see the edge of the park in the distance, about five blocks away. Memories of the previous couple of days flooded his thoughts, bringing back the anxiety of the fact that he and Van were likely being hunted right now.

A flash of movement to his left caught his attention. As he turned his head, he caught a glance of the tail end of a tan robe disappearing around the corner of a tall, all-glass building on the other side of the street marked with the Atomist symbol.

Was that Van?

John stared in that direction for a few more seconds before closing the window and turning his attention back toward the room.

"Van?" John said in a voice just above a whisper.

No response. John began navigating his way through the multitude of office supplies and furniture toward a narrow hallway in one of the corners of the room. He reached the hallway and peered down the hall. An opening at the end looked as if it opened into a similar large room as the one he was currently in. In the middle was a door on the left wall. He drifted his way down the hall and caught hold of the door frame. The door itself was wood with a frosted glass window in the center. He opened the door and inside was a break room containing a refrigerator, two microwaves on a countertop next to a sink, an island, and a small TV mounted in one of the top corners. He couldn't help but take a moment to scavenge through the cupboards lining the wall above the sink. They had been cleaned out, save a few plastic utensils and paper plates. Opening the faded-white fridge he held his breath in anticipation, finding something in a fridge was like winning the lottery. Nothing.

Figures.

John exited the break room and continued down the hallway towards the next office area. He stopped himself on the corner of the wall and peered around, scanning the room before making his presence known to anyone who might be waiting for him. The tan robe caught his attention first, making his heart begin to race with anticipation. It wasn't until Van lifted his head, turning his gaze from something he was holding in his hands to the window he was facing, that John recognized the back of his head.

"I was thinking you'd gone off on your own," John said. "Still wearing that robe, huh?"

Van elected not to answer as he attempted to discreetly slide whatever was in his hands deep into his bag before turning to face John. John decided not to pry about what it was, but it put him on his guard.

"Thanks," Van said, pointing at his head, "for the headache. Seems a bit unnecessary." His voice was loaded with sarcasm and annoyance.

"Unnecessary? You were going to send either yourself or both of us into orbit the way you were thrashing around," John said, half of a grin appearing on his face with the memory of giving Van a hammer fist on the head.

"Whatever. So what's our plan now?"

"Our?"

"Yes, our. I'm stuck with you now. I can't go back to them, that's for sure."

John paused for a moment, debating how he should respond to Van.

Should I threaten him to leave me alone? Or let him tag along for now? I do sort of owe this guy my life.

"I'm going to need a little convincing as to why I shouldn't just cut you down right here. You got me out of that situation, but I can tell you're not exactly calm under pressure. That's bound to get us both killed."

Van's brow furrowed and John could see his jaw clench. *He sure is a hot head*, John thought to himself.

"How about the fact that I know this town better than you do? I know the routes these guys coming after us like to take. And I've got two good hands, unlike you at the moment," Van retorted.

John clenched his right hand, the reminder bringing the pain of his injuries back to the forefront of his mind. He thought about an old joke his father used to tell him when they would go camping: You don't need to be faster than the bear, you just have to be faster than the other person. The thought of tossing Van to the cultists as a last-ditch effort made a wave of guilt wash over him. At this point, he was willing to do what he needed to get out of this forsaken town and away from the band of crazies that wanted him dead.

"Crap. I forgot to mention, I'm pretty sure I saw one of your old friends just down the street," John said, suddenly remembering why he was in such a hurry to find Van in the first place. Van nodded.

"Yep. I've seen a couple of pairs roaming nearby. They haven't bothered with this building yet. It never contained anything useful, so it's probably not a priority for them to come looking here. I've seen them enter a couple of other buildings. I think it would be smart to try and travel through those buildings as much as possible. Stay out of sight and not have to worry about them double-checking the same spot."

John didn't want to admit it, but it wasn't a bad idea. And, if he knew these people's habits like he said he did, using Van, at the very least, to get out of this city was not the worst idea ever.

"Fine. We'll travel together for now. Don't get used to my company though," John warned.

"Whatever," Van said. He sure did like to use that word. He kept reminding John of a punk kid, one whose attitude probably would have made him a loner in high school and a problematic student.

"We're going to go down to the floor level and exit from there. You'd be surprised how little these people look down when on patrols," Van explained.

John thought that seemed a little backward, but he wasn't going to question it. He had always made a point to stay closer to the ground in case an erroneous movement sent him upward he would have more time to react. John nodded and the pair made their way to the stairwell to begin their descent. How many stairwells had he climbed just like this one? His coworkers and he had spent so much time and effort staying in shape to make sure they could climb level after level. It all felt like a lifetime ago to John, now that going up was as easy as going down, and neither made him sweat profusely or breathe heavily.

Once at ground level, they entered the front lobby of the business and glided silently to a fire exit in the back. An ear-splitting bang rang out from above them. Simultaneously, John felt something whiz past the back of his neck, a small gust of air smacking his skin. John and Van looked up to see two figures about five stories above them halfway down the block. The two sat as silhouettes, positioned between the sun and where John and Van were perched. Even so, it was clear that these figures donned robes, and John was willing to bet on what color they were. One appeared to be braced against the wall of the building while the other held onto the railing of a balcony just behind their cohort. One of them made a motion with one arm that John recognized as the chambering of another round in a bolt action rifle, the obvious barrel of a rifle joining the other silhouettes. John's senses finally took over the rush of adrenaline and panic that had frozen him in place and pushed Van in the direction away from their attackers. As he jumped off of the light pole to follow Van, another crack of a gunshot sounded, along with a ping as the bullet hit the metal pole. John did not bother to try dragging Van along with him this time.

"If you can't keep up they will gun us both down,"

John yelled. He checked over his shoulder to see Van in close pursuit.

"Get behind the bakery!" Van directed.

Without hesitation, John redirected himself off of a trash can cemented into the sidewalk, soaring across the street towards a small, red-brick shop with "Clay's Bakery" painted in white on the front window. John grabbed the corner of the bakery and stopped his momentum to scout the alleyway he was now entering. Not two seconds later Van burst around the corner, landing with all fours on the building on the other side of the alley. He continued on down the narrow passage, bouncing from wall to wall while dodging the dented beer cans and trash bags that filled the space. John found himself surprised, even impressed, with Van's agility.

"Come on!" Van shouted without looking back. "If you can't keep up they will gun us both down." He repeated John's words with a cynical tone.

Hope he knows where he's going, John thought as he sprung after Van, not entirely comfortable with letting him take the lead.

Van mumbled to himself, "Take a right, then a left, and another left."

John was about to speak up when Van made a

closed-fist hand gesture that told John to stop. They stopped at the entrance of the alleyway, each checking the street ahead and behind them.

"You guys have guns and you didn't think it would be a good idea to snag one before we left?" John questioned Van.

"No, I didn't," Van snapped back. "I was in a hurry and just acted."

"Well, where are we going now? I'd rather be moving right now than sitting here waiting to be found."

"It's not going to be that simple. When going out in pairs, there's usually a smaller person who will provide over watch. Stick to the tops of the buildings, be the eye in the sky." Just saying the words made Van check above them in every direction again. "The other is usually a lot bigger, more suited for going hands-on, and tries to directly pursue the target."

John looked around at the floating garbage around them; the two dumpsters at either end of the alley, a couple of folded-up tarps. He knew they didn't have much time before their pursuer would be on top of them. He grabbed for a tarp, hastily unfolded it, and pushed one end into Van's hands, whose confusion grew apparent to John in his expression.

"Spread it out. They can't have an eye in the sky if they can't see," John explained. Van took a second longer to offer an apprehensive glance before following John's lead in creating their trash canopy. The pair began placing garbage all along the alleyway, leaving enough room to maneuver, and fight, beneath it. They made a point to put different objects and different heights to make it more inconspicuous to their assailant. The floating junk did not offer complete coverage between them and the rooftops. It did, however, obstruct any clear line of sight from anyone who wanted to get a bird's-eye view of them.

John wasn't sure what he would have done had one of the cultists turned the corner while they were in the middle of their setup. He was a little surprised, and a little worried, that they hadn't seen one yet.

"Van," John said intently, "We need to draw one of them in, go back to the street, and try and get one of them to follow you. I will stay here and surprise them when you come around the corner, we can work together to overpower him."

Van looked like he wanted to argue. Seeing as how he could not think of an alternative at the moment, he simply nodded and bound down to the other side of the alley towards the street. John drew his body around the corner onto the sidewalk, grasping his axe in one hand, and the edge of the building with his other. He scanned the rooftops in front of him, watching keenly for any flinch of an arm or glint of a scope. He had only searched from his nine o'clock to his eleven o'clock when he heard a mix of two voices and the sound of feet and hands smacking off of brick. He took a glance around the corner of the building down the alley, a hulking shadow was almost within reaching distance of Van as the two of them sprang towards John.

John withdrew his head and took a deep breath. He would never be able to put into words why, but seeing the man chase Van filled him with a fury, a new animosity, that took over his thought processes. Maybe it was the sense of camaraderie that had been instilled into him during his normal life. Maybe he was justifying, subconsciously, that there was only one way to do things in the apocalypse after all. John grasped the handle of his axe with both hands, staring at the blade as he cracked his knuckles with the force of his grip. John rotated the axe over his shoulder and swung with every ounce of force he could muster as Van flew out of the entrance to the alley. John's arms were halted to a painful halt as the blade made a distinct *thunk* as it connected and sunk through Professor Weston's skull. The golden atom symbol decorated across his forehead was now split in twain. A tremendous shower of blood exploded outward in all directions, giving an eerily accurate impression of a massive fireworks finale. A true splitting of the atom.

Weston didn't even have time to scream out in surprise or pain. There were no last words or final struggles. John brought the axe, and body, below his feet. He pressed down on Weston's chest and yanked the blade from its place, bringing with it an encore of blood and skull fragments. John raised his eyes to Van, who stared at the scene before him, mouth agape. He must have been mid-turn when John made his attack, as only his left side, from his head to his toes, was speckled dark red.

"What the—" Van was cut off by a newcomer bursting down through the floating garbage about halfway down the lane. As they landed on the ground, they struck one of the walls with an ice pick to hold them in place and looked around. John recognized her as the blonde lady from before. She had a wooden stock rifle with a sizable hunting scope slung across her back. She had been the eye in the sky, and Weston's second. She had come down from her sniper's perch, intent on finally apprehending the traitor and his new friend. She had lost track of the Professor under the awning of garbage and decided she should help after he didn't reappear soon after. She locked eyes with Van and immediately ripped the rifle sling over her head, raising the stock to her shoulder. John grabbed Van by the arm, still numb to what he had just done, and pulled him in the direction of the nearby freeway and out of sight of the woman.

"You said we were just going to overpower him not kill him, he was a good man," Van mumbled through his teeth.

"Let's go," John directed. Van offered no resistance, electing to allow John to pull him along. He, too, was numb. He never wanted any of these people dead, he just simply wanted to get away. He looked up at the man lugging him along, wanting to pull away from his grasp; wanting to go back to the previous night and change his mind on setting this man, this monster, free.

When the blonde woman excited the alley the heavy presence of red out of the corner of her eyes caught her attention. She looked left, then down at the motionless body, the expressionless stare of Weston's lifeless eyes. In her mind, she turned to face the two men, raising the rifle and exacting her immediate revenge on them. Her body was locked up, holding her prisoner to the grief consuming her completely, as darkness consumed the night. Tears began clouding her vision, but she could not get herself to blink them away. She gently pushed away from the wall, embracing the body, and let out the blood-curdling scream that can only be birthed from total anguish. John paused and turned for just a moment, looking back in the direction of the carnage. They passed by the set of buildings at the city's limits and left the nightmarish town behind.

Chapter 7

Portland, Oregon. The day of The Lifting.

NPR Radio.

“People keep fighting over this and I don't understand why. We don't have to separate science and church because they are one and the same. Hear me out brethren, we have had many prophets through the ages that we don’t acknowledge as such,” a gruff man stated.

“What do you mean by prophets?” the voice of a matured-sounding woman asked.

“This is an unsung truth that everyone fails to see. Galileo, Newton, and even Einstein were all made from the same cloth, and they all testified the truth that science is not a thought or an idea. Science is a real living entity and we are its people.”

“Just because they did great things doesn’t mean they are some kind of holy man,” another man's voice interrupted, more nasally than the other's.

"The people disregarded Isaac Newton and look what happened: Science created the black plague. For failure to recognize Albert Einstein, World War Two began," the gruff man said, conviction creeping into his voice now. The woman cut back in.

"Are you insinuating that every major world disaster is the direct result of an apostate-created world?"

"That is precisely what I'm trying to explain, and warn, the world about."

"We would like to thank Dr. Houston, a twenty-five-year professor of quantum physics and organic chemistry from the Massachusetts Institute of Technology. Next, we will hear from—" *Click.* Tommy turned off the radio, the sound of the cascading rain on the truck roof drowning out the noise of the rattling engine.

What a load of crap. Just another distraction to blind the people from our country's real problems.

Tommy pulled his white, rusted Chevy pickup into the parking lot of Karl's Grocery. It was just a ten-minute drive from the RV park where he lived. He liked to come here most nights for their dinner special in the deli department. Tommy wasn't much of a cook and found it easy to stretch his limited pension money — earned from his thirty-year law enforcement career — further if he took advantage of deals like this and five-dollar pizzas.

How is there never a parking spot open up front?

A young boy no more than eight years old bolted in the front of his truck close enough to slap his bumper. Tommy slammed his foot hard on the brake pedal, hoping his squealing brake pads worked better than he knew they should, the truck lurched to a stop. The rain was making it hard to see. Tommy stared over the front of his hood, his anxiety growing with every second the kid didn't emerge. He felt a breath of relief escape his lungs as the child popped out to the other side of the truck. The boy ran up the wet sidewalk and escaped the downpour under the roof of the strip mall neighboring the grocery store. Tommy watched the boy's mom, a young blonde woman, wave at Tommy, embarrassment written on her face as if to say "Thanks for not flattening my kid."

The Karl's stood to the left of a trampoline park called Bounce. It had just opened its doors last week and all of the young families in the area flocked to the new entertainment point. Tommy saw several parents and children funneling in through the entrance. The whole business was decorated with colorful, fun cartoons on tinted windows that made it hard to see inside if your face was not pressed against the glass.

Tommy pulled into a spot and killed the engine. He reached over and grabbed his umbrella from the passenger seat. The driver's door screeched as he opened it. He slid off of the driver's seat, landing in a small puddle as he touched the ground. Opening his umbrella, he briskly walked through the parking lot up to the front doors, avoiding any further puddles along the way. He paused for a brief moment when he saw a group of kids taking turns jumping off of the sidewalk into a sizable puddle that had collected around a pothole. He watched as one of the smaller kids leaped, pulling his feet up as high as he could, and then stamping down with all the force in his little legs.

I'd hate to be the one dealing with that muddy mess he's going to drag into the car.

Each child had their fair share of mud caked onto their clothes. The door cracked open to the trampoline park as a parent briefly poked their head out. An instant rush of noise pounded out, filling the air with the sounds of kids playing and laughing and adults talking. The door slowly drifted closed and the noise ceased. Tommy walked into the store and folded his umbrella, giving it a couple of shakes. A burst of cold air hit him as he walked through the second entrance door past all of the discounted food items. He turned right and was greeted with the delightful scent of glorious fried food. Tommy walked up to the counter to find Agatha, the usual deli attendant, waiting for the next customer.

"I don't get it, Tommy. Every week you come in and buy this crap for dinner. You know it's been sitting out all day," she called out.

"Are you kidding me? Deli meat beats a sirloin any day of the week. How else am I going to catch the eye of the best-looking attendant in town? Plus, it's half-price after six o'clock," Tommy replied. Agatha blushed a little and waved him off. To Tommy, she resembled a Russian egg doll, both in weight and in age. Her thick, old country accent was her most defining attribute.

"You do know, Mr. Tommy, it is only five-thirty? You have another thirty minutes til' half price."

Tommy, although aging himself, was still handsome in a rugged way. He had always been popular with women and was still suave enough to put on the charm. He pulled his hands through his long, pushed-back, dark-brown hair, making sure to flex his biceps as he did.

"Listen, little pretty man, all you have to do is ask, no need to tease me," Agatha said. Now it was Tommy's turn to feel flattered. He pointed to a large tray of dried-up chicken strips behind the glass window.

"I'll take all the chicken you got. I was out working on the boat again today and haven't had a bite of nothing," he said. Tommy had been working on restoring a small fishing tugboat for years as a retirement gift to himself. After one marriage and thirty years on the police force, he knew he needed a hobby to keep him, and his mind, busy. The problem with fishing boats, though, is for every one thing you fix two more things break. Agatha briskly wrapped up eight chicken strips, tossed them onto a tray, and slapped a barcode sticker on the side, her arms jiggling with each movement.

"Oh, that is interesting. What were you fixing today?" Agatha asked.

"Been putting a new coat of blue paint on her and I think when I'm done she will be ready for her maiden voyage. Well, really her re-maiden voyage. I just haven't decided on what to call her."

"Well, whatever it is it has to mean something," Agatha said. Tommy picked up the chicken and a handful of ketchup packets and thanked Agatha.

Something with meaning… he thought. *Maybe I'll call it the St. John. It's been years since I've seen the boy.*

Maybe I'll call him when I get home.

Tommy did not allow himself to dwell more on his sons, especially Colby. His oldest son, John, lived somewhere in Idaho, although he wasn't sure exactly where. The last he had heard he was going to go into public service as a medic or firefighter.

Tommy walked toward the check stands, picking up a bottle of water on his way through to the front. He chose the shortest line and looked past several people at the elderly woman lazily pulling her groceries out of the cart one at a time. She paused when grabbing a loaf of bread and gazed at it.

What could she possibly be looking at? Annoyed, Tommy skimmed through the candy choices for a desert to his kingly dinner feast. He looked back at the old woman.

"Do you think this has eggs in it?" she asked the checkout boy.

"We have been over this time after time Miss Appleberry, you can't hold up the line for questions on each of your items," the boy said with an impatient tone. Tommy looked back to the candy and picked out a chocolate bar. The woman directly in front of him in line rolled her eyes in such an exaggerated motion it affected her whole neck and head. She let out a sigh and moved to another line.

Tommy stepped up and placed his items on the conveyor belt. He looked up to see how close he was to being next and saw the old woman pull out a wallet-sized coin purse and start counting quarters. The check stand boy sat on his job-approved stool with a slump and let out a moan of defeat. Tommy heard Miss Appleberry start telling a story about how the whole area had once been apple trees, though nobody was listening. Tommy's mind started to wander as he watched the exaggerated motions the old woman made when she talked. Her head was almost alien-like how it bobbed back and forth.

If you put a football jersey on her you could pass her off as a life-size bobble head. But where would you keep such a large toy? Maybe a garage, or your man cave or something.

The old woman finally snapped her head up and declared that she would pay with a card after spending about five minutes counting out coins. Once she collected her groceries and walked toward the exit Tommy stepped up and paid for his food, including the basket of chicken strips that were going cold.

As Tommy was leaving, he paused in the median between the two sliding doors, checking to see if it was still raining. Grabbing out his umbrella, he noticed it was still damp from his short trip into the store. He pulled the Velcro strap wrapped around it and pushed the button to open it. Stepping forward with his umbrella pushed out in front of him, he walked out of the store.

I figured the rain would have died out by now, but it's coming down even harder.

The downpour was almost deafening as it pelted his umbrella. He looked out toward the parking lot, trying to remember where he had parked. The rain was so heavy that it was difficult to see the back of the lot. He felt two stuttered vibrations come from his pocket and pulled out his phone. He looked at the screen that read "No Signal."

That's weird. I wonder if it has to do with the rain.

All at once, the constant beating of the rain stopped in an instant. A cold chill ran through his entire body. The rain in front of him appeared to be falling in slow motion toward now. Tommy peeked out from under the edge of his umbrella toward the sky to see that the rain had stopped, each droplet holding its position mid-fall.

The sudden sound of a child splashing in a puddle broke the silence, making Tommy whip his head to the right. He saw a chubby, young girl standing in the bottom of the pothole, confused and bewildered. The water from the pothole was spread outward in every direction, refusing to return to the pavement. Too shocked to move, Tommy's vision dazed in and out. His hearing zoned in on the sound of cars crashing all around him.

What is happening?

Tommy looked to his left, toward the trampoline park, and heard the most sickening noise that would ever haunt his ears.

Thump… Thump... Thump.

His thoughts jumped to the multitude of families he had seen entering the park just twenty minutes prior and his stomach sank. Adrenaline started rushing through him for the first time since his retirement. He put his right foot forward to take a step.

Something is wrong. I need to get in there and help.

As moved to run forward he tripped. Without hesitation, he put his hands out to catch himself but they never met the ground. He found himself slowly drifting forward in a circular motion, head over foot in a weightless front flip. His basket of chicken flew out of his hand. He watched as the tenders scattered slowly in all directions. His body rotated until his hands were parallel to the ground. He reached out and stopped his motion, using the ground as a counterbalance.

Tommy looked back toward the parking lot. His stomach flat with the ground, he saw that the rainfall had created a layer of water about half an inch thick along the span of the asphalt. The droplets had created millions of miniature explosions, frozen in motion. Tommy heard a hand slapping glass coming from the trampoline park and twisted his body again to face the front doors.

The door drew a crack, releasing the screams that had been dulled by the doors and windows. A hand emerged from the crack and a young woman wearing a trampoline park uniform dragged herself through the crack. After fighting her way out of the door she sat – as much as one can in zero gravity – two feet above the sidewalk and seemed to fixate on a distant object that only she could see.

The thousand-yard stare. John recognized the look all too well. *She's in shock.*

"Uh… ahhh…" she started out slowly, mumbling, building up to a frantic, ear-piercing howl while tugging at her hair. Her body lurched forward as she vomited. The combination of bile and undigested pizza shot out in a cylindrical shape the width of her mouth. The vomit drifted in an exact projection in front of her until it hit the wet concrete, splashing outward just as the puddle of water had.

The smell of vomit hit Tommy and he had to fight off the urge to join her in the act.

I need to get home. I'll be safe there.

Pinpointing the spot where he had parked, he jumped in the direction of his car, severely overestimating the strength needed to reach his destination. He floated at an awkward angle, drifting past the other cars in the lot. Some of their alarms were going off, others floated silently, tilting one way or another. As Tommy reached his truck he put his hands out to stop himself. Tommy's body collided with the truck, unable to safely stop the velocity at which he had propelled himself. Tommy felt his right shoulder slam into the truck door and then his head. His vision blacked out as the sounds of the screams, banging, and catastrophe gradually gave way to silence.

Chapter 8

John stared down the main highway road, trying to determine their best mode of travel. John felt naked without his pack and clothes. Without anything to attach the axe to he simply had to carry it. There was no way he was going to let Van have his only weapon, even if it made travel more convenient.

"What do you think? We could just keep a slow pace and walk on the road," Van offered. Ever since their encounter with the Atomists while leaving the city, Van had not said much to John. When he did speak he kept it as short as possible, his voice tense as if he were having to forcefully push the words out. He was battling new, conflicting feelings regarding his travel partner. He felt vulnerable, yet protected. He was scared of John, yet angry with him. It was like he was seeing this man for the first time, having to relearn the details of his appearance and mannerisms. He was not even sure he wanted to keep traveling with him, yet he knew it was his only option at this point, considering what had occurred.

On either side of the highway were dead grass fields that wrapped over small, rolling hills. Along the right side was a telephone wire running parallel to the highway. The road was still in good condition, aside from some chunks of pavement missing here and there that now had weeds filling in the holes. John assumed they were made by vehicles clamoring into each other during The Lifting.

"I don't know… Do you think those wires have any juice left in them?" John asked. They both looked up at the wire, it hung twenty to thirty feet in the air. John pondered this for a moment. "Nah, after two years there's no way there's any electricity running through. They probably went dead when the power plants stopped working."

Van positioned himself below the wire and made a hop up toward the wire. John held his breath, waiting half expecting Van to go rigid and crispy. Van grabbed the cable with his hand and gripped it tight as his body spun one hundred eighty degrees to where his feet faced the sky. Van refused to acknowledge just how careless this was. John felt the tension between the two of them, thick enough that he could probably cut it with his axe. The heat of the sun beat down on his exposed skin, beads of sweat collecting on his cheek. John wiped his hand across his forehead, and with one flicking motion sent small, coagulated sweat globs off through the air. He looked at the daunting task ahead, wondering how far this line would get them, and to what possible dangers it could lead them.

"How far did you say it was to Oregon?" Van asked.

"About 500 miles."

I'm not sure how much longer I should keep letting this guy stick around. If he doesn't somehow get me killed, he may just try to do it himself. He cares more about those creeps than he lets on.

Slowly pacing his steps, John crept up to the nearest pole and shimmied his way up, being careful not to lurch too hard upward. Nearing the top, he reached for the wire and pulled himself next to Van. John expected the cable to be hot, but it was cool against his hands.

"Well, now what?" Van asked, looking at the line of poles that eventually disappeared into the horizon.

"This road goes west and that's the direction I need to go," John said bluntly. He pulled himself hand over hand down the coil toward the next pole.

"What's waiting for you west?"

John stopped and looked at Van. He was still unsure

just how much he could trust telling him.

“When I was young we lived out in Oregon. My mom had gotten leukemia, and the doctors told her and my dad that some ocean air could help her lungs. Dad sold our house and moved the family into a mobile home near the coast. The money from the house was used to pay for my mom's cancer treatments. Near the end of her life, we were left penniless and heartbroken. We ended up in Portland when Mom finally passed away. For a long time, I resented my dad, telling myself he let her die. He told me that he would never leave because a piece of him was rooted in that city.” John stopped talking and looked at Van, realizing he had shared more than he wanted.

“Sorry,” John said, "I haven't been around people for a while.” Van let out a chuckle.

“It seems like you needed to get it off of your chest. Who am I to stop you? I'm used to conversations about scientists and all the prophetic things they accomplished in their lifetimes." John continued pulling himself along.

"So, why do they call you Van? I heard that lady say your name was Jacob.” John asked. Van was now leading them across the next set of power lines. He took a moment before responding.

“My mom and dad named me Jacob Van Johnson. I

was given my middle name because I was born in the van on the way to the hospital."

"Where are your parents now?"

"Dunno. I lived with my dad after they got a divorce. Once a month I got on an airplane and flew to Los Angeles for a week to visit my mom. I was waiting for my flight in the airport when all of this started." John stopped and looked at his hands. The coils from the power lines had been pinching and pulling at his hands. He had been switching hands with his axe, giving his shoulders and fingers breaks, but the roughness of the lines had still done their damage. His wound had not had a real chance to fully heal yet with everything that had happened.

"Hold up," John said. He showed Van his torn-up palm. "This isn't working. The cable is reopening my hand." Van scanned the area. He could see a town several miles away off the highway and towards the north. In the other direction, he could see a tree line. His stomach growled, reminding him that it had been almost two days since he had eaten last.

"Listen, I have an idea, but I don't think you will like it," chided Van. "I still have some twine rope. We could wrap it around your waist and I could pull both of us."

Judas Priest, I'm not completely disabled, man. He

could easily push me off into the air without a second glance.

"No," said John. "I will manage on my own." Van gave him a queer look and continued pulling himself hand over hand, head first down the line.

"Who are those other two cultists to you, anyway?" John asked.

"First of all, we're not a cult. The one whose head you split open was Professor Weston. He was the head of the Atomists in Fernwood City," contempt crept into Van's tone. "Ashley is the blonde. She's pretty on the outside, but she reminds me of a lot of the mean, popular kids in high school."

"Why do you call him Professor? How did you end up with him? I thought you said you were at the airport?"

"He's actually Ashley's uncle and the rest of us just caught on to the name. Coincidentally, he holds a higher ranking in the church with the same title. His job is to help newcomers fulfill the initial rites before entering into the service of Science," Van explained, now seeming distant as he spoke.

"I don't understand. Are you saying they pray to science?" Van stopped moving along the cable and looked at John.

“Did your mom ever read the Bible to you when you were a kid?” John nodded. “Well, in the Bible, when God's people started praying to idols and wouldn’t follow the commandments, God would turn away from them and create famine and disease. It talks about Adam and Eve eating the forbidden fruit and being thrown from the Garden of Eden. At one point, someone went to catch the Ark as it fell, God's greatest treasure and God killed him. We believe that Science is that same God, one that has given many things to his prophets. Time and time again man has turned its back on Science, ignoring basic key truths we have been given. So, like the God of the Bible, Science turned its back on us for the sins we have committed.”

“So, in layman's terms, you send people into space because you think it will appease your god and he will turn gravity back on?” John asked sarcastically.

“No… and yes.”

“So you were going to kill me in hopes that you gain favor with Science?” Van kept climbing along, avoiding John’s eyes.

“You were supposed to be my first rite into the church so I could get my Acolyte’s Mark and be welcomed into the fold,” Van said softly. “But I couldn’t do it. When

I finally looked at you, I realized I was a coward. How am I supposed to save the world if I can't even pass my first rite?"

John decided not to answer and left them in silence. His stomach growled.

Man, I wish I had something to eat. How hungry do you have to be before you eat someone? I don't think I could ever be tempted enough. John looked up to the sky. *If I get that bad I will just save the cult some trouble and send myself to this Science being. How long would it take me to die if I just went straight up?*

"Do you see a bird or something?" Van spouted back.

"No… No, just thinking," replied John. As John and Van slowly pulled themselves along like a sloth crossing jungle vines, he thought about what he might say to his dad after all this time, after all that had happened. There was no guarantee that he was even alive, but John chose to not think of that possibility. It helped keep him going. John and Van traveled in silence down the wire for what felt like an eternity. Each pole looked the same, making John feel like he was in an endless time loop. With no landmarks to go off of, it was almost impossible to determine how far they had traveled.

“Hey, Van, what do you make of that?” John pointed to a small gas station standing resolute on the crest of the next hill ahead of them. Van stopped and studied it for a moment. The windows of the gas station had rod iron covers and the doors were nailed so tight that John didn’t think anyone could get in there without a wrecking ball. A small roof covered the front door and two rusted unkempt gas pumps, one of which had its gas pump floating like it was abandoned mid-use.

“If it’s all the way out here it’s possible that it hasn’t been touched yet, I guess.”

Arriving just above the station, John stopped at the nearest pole and noticed the most peculiar thing he had seen in years. A large, flashing red “Open” lit up the window.

“How in the hell do you think they manage that?” John wondered out loud, nodding at the sign.

“I didn’t want to point this out, but are the hairs on your arm itching?” Van said. John looked down at his arm and noticed he had built up a static charge.

“Hello up there,” a man's voice, oddly cheerful, came from the gas station below. Van visibly jumped at the surprising sound of another person’s voice. “You probably don't want to hang on to those. They're live. You’re lucky gravity is a reason why people got zapped on those. Why don't you come on down here and we can talk shop? You are the first customer that has come around in weeks."

John and Van exchanged wary glances. John aimed his body at the ground near the gas pumps and nudged himself forward with his toes. Upon passing the canopy over the pumps, he could see a short, old man silhouetted in the window of the gas station. John grabbed hold of a pump, keeping his distance from the old man while inspecting the area for any sort of trap.

"Who are you?" John questioned.

"Name's Artemis. Arty from my friends, but they're all dead now. Anyways, what can I get for you folks? I got a new batch of freshly made jerky yesterday."

Van softly landed next to him and they stared up at the open sign flashing. John felt like he was taking crazy pills.

"Did this guy not get the memo that the world ended?" John mumbled to Van quietly.

"Well howdy you two, can you hear me? Y'all want some lemonade?" the man snickered. "Just kidding, I haven't seen a lemon in years. They only grow in temperate zones and the mailman don't bring them this way no more."

"What… How… are you in there alone?" John

asked. John began noticing more details of the man as his attention was drawn away from his surroundings. He had white hair under his tattered ball cap. His unkempt beard matched in color, surrounding a bulbous, red nose. The old man could not have been more than five feet tall.

"No, sir, you are never really alone when you have so many visitors." the old man said chipperly. So, fellas, what can I do for you? And just so you know we don't do money, jewels, or gold; worthless, the lot of it. Oh, but I see you have acquired a fine piece there indeed," He said, pointing at the fireman's axe in John's hand. "There's a lot a man can do with that kind of tempered steel."

John tucked the axe under his arm and pulled himself past the two gas pumps up to the bar windows. John tried to look past the old man but only saw heaps of garbage bags.

"Old man, it looks like all you peddle is junk. Where do you get your food and water from?" asked John. He took another look around.

Nothing..... There is nothing out here. Where are his people?

"You don't need to worry yourself none about how I get on in life. What will it be? I have clean water, fresh red jerky… In fact, let me strike a deal with you. I know a man who would give his left foot for a fine tool such as that. Final offer, I have some clothes and a nice leather backpack. I will even fill it with some provisions for you's gents."

"Fresh meat? Probably people meat," Van said in a hushed tone.

"Alright old man you have a deal, but no meat. I want canned goods," said John.

"Ohhh, sonny, you push a hard bargain. Alright, final, FINAL offer good sir." Artemis ducked down below view for a moment. The sound of cupboard doors closing and items being rummaged filled the silence. After a moment he popped back up like a whack-a-mole and pushed a backpack and pair of dirty, blue sneakers out of the window, needing a little force to squeeze it through the bars.

"You are a very trusting man, Artemis. What's to stop me from just leaving now?" John probed.

"Hehehe. Well, you see, young sir, Lucille here takes care of the thieves for me." The old man pulled up a pristine AR-15 rifle. "You see, boy, I don't like to toot my own horn, but I'm a pretty damn good shot. Although it does take a bit of squirreling around to stop my momentum so I don't go spinning around like a top."

John grabbed the pack and unzipped it. Sure enough, inside the pack was a liter water bottle full of the clearest water he had seen in over a year. There was also a neatly folded button-down plaid shirt, jeans, and a pullover hoodie stuffed in the bottom of the bag. On both sides of the backpack were open-top pouches that held several food cans with calcified gunk growing over them. John, though thankful for the goods, was reluctant to hand his axe over on such a whim. He had used this axe to save his skin more times than he could count. It was like an extension of him at this point.

I really need these supplies if I'm going to make it to Dad... John reasoned to himself. *I'm sure I'll find something else to use within a couple of towns.*

John held onto the blade of the axe, handing it through the bars, handle first, to Artemis.

"Oops. Almost forgot. I'm not a man who, in good conscience, can leave two perfectly nice strangers like yourselves defenseless. So, here," Artemis said, pushing a painted-over jar out of the window. John examined the jar, confused. He went to open the lid to examine the contents when Artemis stopped him, putting his hand on John's.

"Nuh uh uh... I wouldn't open up that lid unless absolutely necessary. I also wouldn't shake the thing too much," Artemis warned. "To satisfy your curiosity, I will tell ya's that it's filled with a bunch of metal shrapnel and black powder. “John inspected the white string poking out of the lid. Turning it over, he noticed a small lighter was taped to the side of the jar.

“You’re giving us a freaking bomb?!” John exclaimed. “You just hand these out like candy on Halloween?”

“Well you can never be too careful in these parts, buncha weirdos roaming about. Hehehe,” Artemis replied. John felt uneasy. What John once suspected to be the beginnings of senility on the man’s face was now madness. His smile was forced and wide and the whites of his eyes appeared bigger and brighter than before.

“Do you know how far the next town is?” Van asked, apparently not catching on to the creepy aura Artemis was emanating.

“The next stopping point is west another ten miles just into the forest. The bright, wooded town of Briarton,” Artemis informed them, using a television announcer-like voice.

John looked at Van sternly.

“We should leave, this guy is really giving me the willies.” They both looked back to the window and the man was gone.

“Yup, let’s go,” Van agreed. The two of them

pushed off away from the gas station and back to the road.

"May Science guide our way," Van mumbled and continued. John wasn't sure if he had meant to say it loud enough for him to hear, and he was not sure which would have been weirder. He hurriedly slipped his newly acquired clothes and shoes, stinging as they brushed against his reddened skin. They caught hold of a guardrail on the opposite side of the road and pressed on, continuing their westward journey.

Chapter 9

A large, sun-worn billboard sat on the side of the road, against a stretch of pinewood trees. It displayed a forest with a cave at the center.

"Cave of Wonders. One and a half miles" Van read out loud. "Do you think it's worth stopping at?" Van looked over at John who was forcing down a can of mystery meat. They had stopped for lunch, taking advantage of the shade of a lone tree.

"The old man said there was a town in the woods. I think it's worth a look. If anything, we might find a map of the area," John said.

"You trust that crazy old geezer?" Van asked.

"Crazy… You're no less crazy than he is. Every person I have met traveling west has tried to make sense of the world and justified all of their poor actions. As I see it, you're crazy, he's crazy, and I'm maybe the craziest of us all. Whether he's lying or not, the Cave of Wonders should give us a good sense of direction." John tucked the now-empty tin can into his pack and secured it to his back.

"I think we should cut off the road into the trees 'til we make it to the cave," Van said.

"Yes," John agreed, "but, we need to be careful not to stray too far from the road or we might lose our bearings."

Using the guardrail as a counter, they pushed off toward the trees. John estimated the distance from the road to the tree line to be about the length of two football fields. He felt a twinge of stress sink in. He didn't like the feeling of extended free floating. Going from one object to another nearby was one thing, but jumping for something in the distance, with so few saving graces in between, was another. As they soared over the dead grass and weeds John felt his nose twinge and tickle.

A sneeze? What will that do to my course? John worried. He tried plugging his nose but it was too late.

"Ah— achoo!" John flinched and looked at Van. A shower of spit and mucus shot out his mouth, yet no relief came. The itch in his nose got worse and a burning sensation began rising in his nasal cavities.

"Achooo!" John sneezed so hard he started to drift into a backflip. Head butting the air, John found himself now drifting at an awkward angle toward the trees.

Halfway there. I need to correct myself quickly.

A large, dead thistle weed stood out above the rest. Its dead leaves were barely hanging on and the thick base of the trunk had long, sharp-looking hairs. It resembled a small, sad Christmas tree. John extended his left arm as far as he could and grabbed the center of the weed stock. The dried hairs felt like hot needles on the palm of his hand. John pulled himself to a stop and let out a sigh of relief and pain. Looking down, he noticed his good hand already turning red. John frowned, annoyed with himself.

I'm going to run out of hands pretty soon.

He felt as though it may have been worth it to take a rough landing on a tree. Van went coasting by with a smug look on his face.

"Last one to the trees is a rotten egg," Van roared over his shoulder.

He's oddly chipper...

John pushed off from the dirt, making sure he angled himself parallel with the ground while keeping his eye on Van. Without warning, Van slammed into the first tree he came to, and the audible noise of air being punched out of his lungs shot out from his mouth.

"I–I'm alright. No worries," Van shouted back in

John's direction, wincing as he did. John at last met the tree line and stopped himself with considerably more grace than Van had.

"You know, if you're not careful a crash like that could easily break your wrists," John cautioned. Van rolled his eyes and pressed onward into the trees. John warily moved between the trees one by one, his tender cut reminding him to look more carefully at where he was going. Van showed no such mindfulness as he ricocheted himself between the trunks and branches, nearly missing all of several of his intended targets. John grew anxious watching the young man bound around like this. Van called out to John. John locked onto Van again just in time to see him throw a small pine cone in his direction. He threw it hard enough that it caused him to lose his balance in the air. John caught it, eyeing it over to look for any significance this might have to cause Van to toss it to him.

"What am I looking at here? It's just a pinecone." Van floated to him, halting himself on a branch above John.

"I heard these are edible," Van said. Annoyed, John handed it back.

"Then go for it." John carried on through the woods and Van followed, keeping the pine cone in his hand but questioning if he wanted to try biting into it. After several minutes John stopped on a tall pine and pulled himself to the top, trying to survey the area. He was looking for anything that might give them an idea of how much further they needed to go.

A large mass of water, shaped in a near-perfect circle, hovering above a dried lake bed caught John's eye. It was larger than any building he had ever seen. The sphere was half the size of the lake bed in diameter, at least half a mile wide to John's best estimate. A thin mist held around the water like a physical barrier. The ground below had become a dried dust bowl, the ground littered with many dead logs, moss, and weeds.

"Whoa… haven't seen anything like that before," Van said. The two studied the sight before them in silence for a moment. "Do you think there are any fish in there?" John shrugged.

"It wouldn't matter. How would you get out of there once you dove in? On top of that, I would imagine the fish swim faster than you."

"Have you always been this big of a buzz kill? Besides, surely you can swim through the water just the same without gravity," Van challenged.

"I'm a realist," John stated, his matter-of-fact tone putting an end to the conversation. Just then, a small, speedy carp exploded out of the sphere and into the trees off to the men's right side.

What a waste.

"Hold on, look," Van whispered, pointing near the spot where the fish had disappeared into the trees. John squinted and held his hand above his brow. He could see shadows moving just behind the tree line. As his eyes adjusted further, he could see that the shadows were a small group of people emerging from the forest. This was a surprise in itself, but even odder was the gray, plastic object they carried. John was not able to see it clearly enough to identify it.

"Hello!" Van yelled. John hurriedly pulled himself behind a tree.

"What are you doing?" John angrily asked through his teeth. "We don't know who these people are."

"What are you afraid of? It's not like they're going to try to kill and eat us."

"I've been almost killed too many times recently to have a lot of trust in random people. Your time with your little cult has made you too comfortable, too trusting."

The group stayed where they were, talking among themselves for a moment, then turned toward John and Van. A woman who appeared to be in her forties approached through the air. She was wearing tattered blue jeans and a gray hoodie. Her face drew down with age and her skin was bronzed from overexposure to the sun. Her hair was tied in a tight ponytail that extended outward and held in suspension. She grabbed a branch and steadied herself two trees over from them, being cautious to keep some distance. The woman pulled a black and green crossbow she had strapped on her back and held it out in front of her. For a long time, the two groups stared at each other, waiting for the other to make a move.

"My name is Betty. What's with the robe getup, are you like a monk or something?" she said. A pinch of anxiety welled in the pit of John's empty stomach.

If she finds out what Van is, they'll never trust us.

"Something like that. I am part of a church, though, it's—"John interrupted Van from around the tree.

"What are you doing out here?" Betty flinched at his sudden appearance and pulled the crossbow up, her finger lingering over the trigger. Betty looked back towards her group that sat just below the water mass.

"Isn't it obvious? We are fishing. We stopped here for the night and saw a fish launch out of the water. We spent a whole day rigging a water hose wheel so we can safely get up there and back." Betty said. John dared to turn his gaze up at the water.

"How do you suppose they stayed alive this long up there? Do you know how many there are?"

"Dunno, but we sure could use your help. The more people that stay at the bottom, the better the chance we won't be pulled up when we wind the swimmer back down." John was still racking his brain, thinking of reasons why the water still stood there while every other pond he had come across was dried and gone. He then remembered the fish, and he pictured a nice filet of fish with a slab of melting butter on top. His mouth started watering.

"All the fresh fish we can carry along with more water than I have seen in months? You can count us in," Van blurted out. John nodded in agreement and the three of them pushed off in the direction of the group under the lake.

John stopped himself on a dead log roughly ten feet from the others as they made their approach. In front of him were three, very ordinary, middle-aged people. The first was a slim woman whose graying hair was chopped at the shoulder. The other two were men, obviously twins, and blonde with squinted eyes. One's face carried more wrinkles around the lips, giving away the fact that they had precisely had a smoking habit. He had a duffle bag slung across his chest, while the others had normal backpacks. All three of them donned tattered clothes and their hollow faces looked like they hadn't eaten in days. Their biceps had an odd sag to them that stood out to John for some reason. Betty paced around a log near John's.

"This is my sister, Kristen, and my twin cousins, Ronney and Jack," she said, indicating to each in turn. Jack was the one with the smoker's wrinkles. John introduced himself and Van and moved closer. He was able to get a better look at the device they were carrying that was now floating between them. It contained a wheel mechanism with a rope wound inside. They had been positioning themselves in a triangle around the device, ensuring it could not float away from them.

"Is that a thing people use to store garden hoses?" asked Van.

"Yes, it is," said Jack. "We needed a way to reel someone back in once they jumped in the water."

"How do you plan on catching the fish?" John inquired.

"I'm going to wrap this rope around my waist and jump into the lake," Jack chimed in while pulling a large fish net out of the duffle bag. "Then, I'm going to swing like hell and hope that I catch us some dinner."

John looked over at the twins and noticed that

Ronney's pupils were a flat oval shape. "What happened to your eyes?" Ronney looked around as if trying to pinpoint who was asking. It was then that John realized he could not see.

"A couple months after everything began floating my eyesight started going fuzzy. When it got really bad, Jack told me that my eyes were shaped funny. We can only assume that it has to do with being in zero gravity. I was obsessed with space as a kid. I remember learning that all kinds of weird things happened to astronauts' bodies in space," Ronney explained.

Jack float-stepped to the wheel, unraveled several feet of rope and then tied it around his hips. John was impressed with his knot-tying. *He knows his stuff,* he thought to himself, feeling a sense of fellowship sparking in this shared knowledge. Betty moved Jack and double-checked that everything was secure. Nodding, Betty looked around at the rest of them.

"You ready?" she asked. Ronney, Van, John, Kristen, and Betty huddled as closely as they could. Each person grabbed a piece of the rope adding to the collective weight.

"Alright, Jack, after a couple of seconds we will give a hard yank on the rope and then slowly reel you in once you are out of the water. But, try not to jump too hard or we may all go with you," Betty explained.

Jack held the net with both hands, looked up at the massive bubble of water, and jumped toward it headfirst. The reel whirled round and round as the tote rope unwound. Jack's feet had not yet entered the water completely before he started swinging his net wildly. John watched as the water mass absorbed him in an instant. Countless terrified trout and carp launched themselves out of the water's surface toward the dried lake bed. It took every bit of self-control John had not to abandon his post and start scooping in as many as he could. Betty started to count down from ten out loud.

"Four… Three… Two… One. Pull!" Betty yelled. All five of them gave a hard yank on the rope, and both of John's feet left the ground. Betty had planted her feet in the hole of a dead log, half-buried in the dirt, and helped pull him back down. Jack's limp body sharply pulled from the water, like a chunk of fruit being ripped out of jello.

"Something's wrong. He's not moving," Kristen blurted out. In a panic, Ronney fumbled for the wheel, finally grabbed it, and started winding fast. Jack's body started drifting downward while Ronney was drifting up.

John instinctively grabbed hold of Ronney's legs.

"Make a chain, we have to get him down fast," John yelled. As they drifted upward each member grabbed hold of the others' legs. At the bottom was Betty wedging her feet on a large log. Ronney made it to Jack and put his face closed to try and see through his hazy vision. Jack had a water mass that had filled his mouth and extruded outward around his chin.

"He must have breathed in some water. We left him in there too long," Betty cried. One after another the group was pulled down, finally getting Jack back to the Earth. Betty grabbed hold of Jack's shoulders and tried to wipe away the water from his mouth by inserting her fingers into his mouth and scooping outward. If gravity still existed the water would have flowed out of his mouth. But now the surface tension of the water clung to his mouth and face like a permanent water mask. With each swipe, a small amount of water would break away and the remainder would recollect in his mouth, continuing to suffocate him.

There has to be some air left in his lungs.

"Move out of the way," John commanded. Betty quickly shifted to the side of Jack. John, with as much force as he could muster, uppercut Jack in the stomach with his good hand. As his fist pushed into Jack's midsection he felt something inside the man crack. The pressure of the hit forced all of the air from Jack's lungs, finally propelling the water from his mouth and sinuses. Jack lurched forward instantly in a coughing frenzy. Jack buckled over and vomited, sending a projection of yellow/red liquid out toward the ground.

"Oh, Jack what happened? Are you okay?" Ronney asked. Jack took a few minutes to catch his breath. John could see a large, bright-red semi-circle on Jack's cheek. Upon closer inspection, he saw a multitude of round, red marks of varying sizes covering his body. Jack stopped coughing and looked at Betty.

"When I got close to the edge of the water I could see tons of baseball-sized bubbles. When I dove in the bubbles started to burn me, like they were filled with insanely hot air. I tried to swipe at them with the net but that only made them smaller and they landed all over my body. I screamed and sucked in water by accident," he said. Jack looked down at his chest. "It hurts to breathe, but I'm alive." John looked around to see many fish flipping and flexing their bodies in midair.

"We need to get as many of these fish as we can before they get too far. Jack, you need to stay put and catch your breath. Ronney will stay with you," Betty instructed.

Everyone spread out to gather the fish that spanned outward from the lake bed. John reached his first fish which was lodged among some dead branches. He gripped the trout with both hands, convincing himself it needed to be cooked before digging in with his teeth. He carefully put the fish into his pack and looked for the next one.

He scanned left, then right, and noticed Van a short distance away picking through some bushes. Van picked up a monster fish that surely weighed five to ten pounds. He pulled the fish to his face and muttered something too quietly for John to hear. Van hurriedly looked around and threw the fish underhanded toward the sky.

What the hell is he doing? John thought, dumbstruck that he would throw away food like that. John pressed off from a log and drifted toward Van.

"What was that? Did you just throw that fish out on purpose?" John asked. Van stared as if looking at something in the distance.

"No," he replied shyly, "the fish slipped out of my hands. Don't worry, I'll get the next one."

"Bullshit it slipped," John responded in a sharp whisper. "I watched you throw it. I thought you were done with all that preachy science crap. How could you just senselessly throw away something that could feed you for almost a week?"

"You still don't understand. Science made that fish. Science held that water in suspension and allowed the fish inside to stay alive all this time. Don't you see that we have to pay a levy to science for him to continue showering blessings down on us?"

John reared his arm back and punched Van square in the mouth, propelling him into the nearest tree.

"You are an idiot, and I'm done protecting you!" John roared. He left Van floating there, his face was contorted in pain and shock. After searching for half an hour, John spotted the group reconvening on the opposite side of the lake and went to join them. Betty and her family were standing in a circle taking turns carefully suspending fish in the center of them.

"This whole ordeal was more exciting than I wanted it to be… but, I think we made out with a fair amount of food." Betty looked over at John. "Where is Van? Wasn't he with you?"

John looked behind him just as Van slipped to the left of him, holding one single rainbow trout. He could feel John's eyes practically burning holes into the side of his head as he placed the fish on the pile.

"Looks like all together we got eighteen fish," Betty said. "I know that we all just met but I think it would be smart for you guys to stick with us. I think we can safely say that we trust you enough to break bread with y'all. On our way through we found a cabin not too far from here that we thought would be a safe place to rest for the night. Won't you join us?"

John reluctantly looked over at Van and they both nodded in agreement. The group gathered up the fish in their packs and followed Betty into the forest.

Chapter 10

"We need to get as many of these fish as we can before they get too far," Betty said to the group. Van looked left, then right, scanning the area for any movement. The sun reflected off a large trout several feet off the ground, its rainbow-silver scales glimmering. The fish's large tail whipped back and forth as it struggled for air. Van pushed off toward it, determined to retrieve the biggest fish for himself.

While floating through the air he was reminded of a lesson that Professor Weston had taught him. He was sitting in a dust-filled room waiting for Weston to bring him his meal for the day. He handed Van a fresh apple that the group had found earlier that day before taking the biggest bite he could out of the juicy piece of fruit. He pushed his head out of the single window in the room and spit the bits of apple into the air. Van asked him why he would waste such a sweet gift as an apple. Professor responded with one of the most profound things he had heard that stuck with him still today: "If we aren't willing to sacrifice a rare gift like this to Science, then we aren't meant to save this world."

Van steadied himself against a large rock covered in dirt and dead, green moss. He reached up and pulled the fish down, holding it out in front of his chest. The trout was a beautiful specimen; silver with soft stripes of green and red and little black dots randomly scattered its body. Van gripped it with both hands and found that it was so big his fingers didn't wrap around the body enough for his hands to touch each other.

Professor Weston's voice sounded out, as if he were standing side by side with the man: "If we aren't willing to sacrifice a rare gift like this to Science then, we aren't meant to save this world."

But, it's a waste... why would science give me a gift like this only to ask for me to sacrifice it?

"Does that mean you aren't worthy? How else can anyone really show their true worth if not for sacrifice?" Weston asked. Van looked at the fish.

How does one sacrifice even an ounce of such an amazing fish like this?

"If you can't give some, then give all," the voice resounded. Van's hands shook as he traced the shape of the atom on the fish's forehead. He pulled the writhing fish close to his face so he could look at it eye to eye. A distinct, unpleasant odor exuded from the fish.

"Science, I give this to you. Forgive my misgivings and give me the strength to carry out your will," Van uttered. With one sharp push, the fish left his hands and rose into the sky. Van watched until he could no longer see it before checking over his shoulder. His stomach flopped as he saw John coming his way.

"What was that? Did you just throw that fish on purpose?" John asked. Too nervous to face John, Van stared off into the trees instead.

"No. The fish slipped out of my hands. Don't worry, I'll get the next one."

How could he ever understand the truths that I've been shown? Van pondered.

"Bullshit it slipped," John said in a sharp whisper. "I watched you throw it. I thought you were done with all that preachy science crap. How could you just senselessly throw away something that could feed you for almost a week?"

"You still don't understand. Science made that fish. Science held that water in suspension and allowed the fish inside to stay alive all this time. Don't you see we have to pay a levy to science for him to continue showering blessings down on us?" Van yelled back. He had barely spoken the words before he felt John's punch connect with his mouth. His vision wobbled as he was propelled into the tree logs behind him. The shock of the impact wore off quickly, replaced with a throbbing pain.

"You are an idiot, and I'm done protecting you!" John yelled at him.

Van watched as John pushed away and left him to be alone, touching his face and checking for blood. A strange slapping noise snapped him out of his gaze. Van looked down and found a meager-looking fish stuck in the middle of a shrub.

"With sacrifice comes great blessings," the voice of Professor Weston charmed. Van grabbed the fish with his right hand, the tips of his fingers wrapped around the spine and touched his thumb.

I am happy to receive such a gift even after all of the wrongs I have done to my fellow brothers.

Van saw that the group was coming together once again and went to rejoin them. Each one of them had several fish to present and share with the party. With a little reluctance, Van laid his small prize on top of the pile.

Betty led the group through a series of thick tree patches, needing to stop and wait for everyone to catch up a few times. The sun started to dip on the edge of the horizon.

"Come on, we have to get to the center before the sun goes down," Betty called out. John knew from experience that it was unwise to travel in zero gravity in the dark. John pushed forward, gliding several feet off of the ground from one tree to the next. Maneuvering through a patch of trees, John could partially see an outline of a building through the woods in front of him. Looking behind him he saw Jack helping Ronney from tree to tree, with Kristen not too far off behind them.

Where is Van? He usually never has his mouth shut.

John used a branch as a centering point and nudged off, landing on the tree next to Betty. Van appeared quietly from below. He had been using the forest's undergrowth to make his way through, avoiding the group, and John, as much as possible. Betty pointed to a two-story cabin ahead, confirming their destination.

"There it is. That's the ranger station we found before stumbling upon the lake." Betty looked longingly at the building as if it had been her home. The cabin was equipped with a wraparound deck on both sides. The real owners had stained the outer walls, rather than painted them, giving it a homey, outdoors feel. The cabin stood in the center of a clearing alone and resolute. Betty stepped off of the tree and bound for the cabin with one foot.

Gutsy. We must be at least six hundred yards away.

John watched as each one of the group followed suit, each one safely landing on one of the deck levels and then disappearing around the house. Not to be shown up, he took a moment to aim then pushed off. While drifting along, John was able to get a better look at the valley they were in. The clearing with the cabin was at the center of a bowl-like valley where mountains peaked up on either side. John could see a long-dried streambed that probably came from the lake. It was the sort of picturesque area John had spent countless weekends relaxing in before The Lifting. The only thing stopping him from living out the rest of his weightless days in such a spot was the fact he could not reliably get food, even from hunting.

John stopped himself against the side of the cabin

wall on the second story. Using the handrails of the deck, he pulled himself around the cabin to find the rest waiting near the front door.

"Dammit all! I don't remember what key it was," Betty said as she fumbled with a big ring of keys.

"You've been here before?" John asked.

"Yeah. When we found this place we had to smash through a window to get in. But, after looking around a bit we found an open lock box with all of the building's keys, including the master set." Betty held up the keys and rattled them as if to prove her story to John.

"I told you it was a dumb idea to lock the door. Who else would possibly be out here?" Kristen said to Betty. John almost laughed at the irony of that statement. Betty gave a long stare at Kristen then continued trying for the right key.

John looked over at Van who had been staring at him. Van flinched and looked away quickly. John's eyes narrowed.

What was that about?

"Got it," blurted Betty and opened the double doors all the way. John pulled himself around the right side of the door frame, parallel with the deck, and onto the outer wall of the entryway. He was met with a stationary sign that read

“Welcome to the Cave of Wonders.” In front of him was a miniature display of the cave with information on each of the different portions that were available to the public. On the edge of the display was a filthy, dark-red button. The white lettering reading “push me” was nearly completely worn off. John landed himself over and pushed the button, not actually expecting anything to happen. And yet, the display was brought to life by small lights illuminating the cave openings.

A cheery woman’s voice began playing a prerecorded message: “Welcome to the Cave of Wonders, the largest cave in all of Idaho. Discovered by early settlers in the late 1800s, this cave was used for mining and provided hundreds of jobs to a boosting locale. Push any of the other red buttons you see and learn more about the fascinating history of this great landmark.”

John looked around the outside of the display and noticed several more red buttons, some of which were dimly lit now, awaiting their turn to be activated.

“Power… does this building have power?” John said out loud. He looked in the direction of Betty. “This shouldn’t work. Why is there power?”

Next to Van was a large panel of light switches. He tested a couple of them one by one, pausing momentarily after each switch. Random lights in the ceiling flickered on and off. A feeling of overwhelming anticipation welled in John's mind.

Think of the possibilities having power would bring.

John moved on to the next red button that sat just below a green and brown-painted mountainside and pressed it.

"The Salmon River Mountain is a popular place for camping, fishing, and mooooouuuttttt—" the same chipper voice from before became weak and distorted; the speech slowed and the words became incoherent. The lights that Van had left flickering dimmed, then turned off altogether.

"Well, that was short-lived," Van stated. John pushed the button again but this time no message played.

"We need to clean these fish before they start to rot," Betty called out. "There is a kitchen on the other side of the display through that door."

"I'm going to go look around while you guys start on that," John said. Kristen and Betty disappeared through the door. John pulled himself down a hallway to his left, checking each door handle as he went down. Every one of them was locked. He eventually came to a door with a plaque above it that read "Communications Center." John, his interest more piqued than it had been for the other doors, was disappointed to find this one locked as well. John, while holding the doorknob, stretched his body out as far as he could. With one quick motion, he pulled himself at the door, meagerly hitting it with his shoulder. He was only effective in causing dust to disburse throughout the air.

This would have been so much easier if I hadn't given up my axe. This would have been quick work.

John tucked in his legs and aimed them just to the side of the doorknob. With all the force he could muster he kicked his legs out. He heard a cracking of wood and the door had more give in it than before. He rated back again like a mule and kicked again. The door gave way under the pressure and slammed open. His body propelled backward, smashing into the opposite wall and knocking the wind out of his lungs. A new indent was made by John's shoulder colliding with the old drywall. The old drywall now boasted a new indent the width of John's broad shoulders.

"You know I have keys right?" Betty mockingly called from around the corner. John ignored her and entered the room. On the walls were topographical maps, lists of coordinates with instructions for directing a medical helicopter into the area, and a Morse code cheat sheet. There were two small windows on the back wall overlooking the valley. He then noticed a small, metallic box with many dials held in place by a power cord still connected to an outlet. Also connected to it by another wire was an old-fashioned hand microphone.

A radio! I wonder if I can use that to get in contact with Dad.

John had learned the basics in his time with the firefighters. He knew that with this he could talk with anyone worldwide. He dragged himself through the door and stopped on the wall with the outlet. The device looked like it had been used recently. The dials had already been set to a frequency and much of the dust had been wiped off of the device. He flipped the power switch on but the radio remained inoperative.

John pushed out of the room, clinging to the wall until he located the kitchen Betty had pointed out. He cracked the door open and saw Betty stab a small knife into the chest of a fish and cut it down to the tail. She gripped the throat with one hand and pulled the fish's stomach away from its body with her other and she flicked the bright red guts toward the wall. The stomach sailed through the air, hitting the wall on the opposite side of the room with a small, wet smack.

"Do you think we should keep the guts in case we

get desperate?" Kristen asked.

"Naw, we have more fish here than I think we can eat before it goes bad," Betty replied. John entered the room. All eyes turned to him.

"Ahhh, so chivalry isn't dead after all. Come to help the women with the meal?" Kristen asked. John, feeling a little embarrassed that he didn't think of it earlier, moved toward the mass of fish that was hovering above the kitchen island table and plucked a fish from the air. The fish's gills flexed open and closed in his hands as the fish made its last fleeting attempts at drawing water into its body. Its eyes stared blankly as its mouth opened and closed, struggling for life. He pulled a small knife from the knife block on the table and pierced the fish, slitting the gills and throat. The body flexed and its tail whipped left and right. John gutted the fish with ease and placed it in the sink with the others.

"How do you suppose we should cook these?" John asked.

"Well, I think starting a fire would be a good start. It's a good thing we are surrounded by wood," Kristen retorted. John grabbed the next fish to the gut.

"Have you checked all of the rooms in the cabin?"

"No. We were too worried about having a nice meal, we didn't want it to go to waste." Betty said. John told them about the room he found containing the short-wave radio.

"When you found the cabin did it have power?" John asked. Betty stopped what she was doing and looked at John.

"I remember seeing some of them black solar panels up on the roof. Haven't found any batteries though, since we didn't clear the place. If you can find the power box and turn it off it might give the building a chance to gain a charge." She paused for a moment, studying John's face. "Why is radio so important? The world has already ended. Who could you possibly hope to contact? There is no saving grace out there."

John finished gutting his second fish and reached for another.

"It's weird, but ever since everything fell apart I can't shake the feeling that I need to know if my father is alive. We left things badly, mostly on my part. Even if it takes me years, I will try to find him until I either succeed or I'm dead." Kristen wiped away some fish blood from her hands on a rag she had floating next to her.

"I can understand the appeal of wanting to stay with family. We have been through some interesting trials, but I know that no matter what we encounter I can trust my family to be there," Kristen said, giving her sister a slight nudge, accidentally sending her off balance for a moment.

"So how did you and Van come together then?" Betty continued. John stared at the dead animal in his hands, trying to decide how much to tell her. The thought of Van throwing a fish into the air made his blood begin to boil. As calmly as he could, John unfolded how he and Van had met. He could not stop himself from going into detail when he recounted Van drawing scientific symbols on him. John described their escape and travels along the grass plains. When he told Kristen and Betty about John sacrificing the fish the women gave each other a concerned look.

"I can't believe you are traveling with someone who tried to kill you," Betty said incredulously.

"I mean, I didn't have much of a choice. He did end up saving me. And he knew the town and how to get us out." John explained.

"Told you there was something funny about that town," Kristen told Betty, raising her eyebrows. "That could have been us turning into unwilling astronauts."

"I feel like I need to thank you," John said. "Thank your whole family really. I avoided most people for a long time, knowing that they only had a drive to help themselves. You're genuine, and I feel like I can trust you," John felt vulnerable. He blushed and looked at the floor. The group continued cleaning the remaining trout and carp in awkward silence.

"Well, that just about does it," Betty piped up. "Kristen, will you go find a nice log to burn?" Kristen wiped her hands clean on the rag, tossed John the ring of keys, and left the room.

"I didn't want to freak anyone out, but I'm thinking of my family when saying this. If you choose to keep that lunatic around, then you have no place with us," Betty stated matter-of-factly. She wiped her hands and left John alone in the room. A glob of chum meagerly hovered past John's face. He studied it, pondering Betty's words. John decided to head to the basement to track down the power box. The basement was spacious, dark, and cold. To John's luck, the box was located by the bottom of the stairs. A group of electrical boxes wrapped around the wall and under the stairs. John swiped the dust away from the label that read "Tesla."

Here's a power storage box.

John found a large, black switch on the side of the power station. The instructions posted next to it explained how it would change the source from regular power to storage power, along with a long list of warnings and do-nots. He flipped it and it was rewarded with a dull hum as the air conditioning unit on the other side of the wall turned on. John moved on to scouring the other power and breaker boxes, looking for anything he could turn off to save as much power as possible.

A/C... don't need it.

Click.

Displays... nope.

Click.

Satisfied with his choices, John closed up the boxes and made his way back to the main floor. The halls were now lit with the exception of a couple of bulbs here and there. The thick presence of dust was highlighted by the overhead lights now. He made a point to turn off as many of the switches as possible on his way through. As he made his way to the communications room he came across Van in another room that had no furniture. Van had turned on the light and ceiling fan, holding onto a fan blade as it picked up speed. John watched as Van, along with the fan, began spinning at a dizzying rate. Van quickly lost his grip and flew across the room, the side of his body slamming into a wall and creating a mini dust explosion. John grunted and rolled his eyes and flipped the switch off.

"We need to save power for essentials," John said

flatly.

He returned to the room where the radio stood and switched it on. As the interface illuminated, voices mid-conversation began coming over the speaker. John's heart leaped as he fumbled for the receiver microphone.

"Hello? Can you hear me?" John impatiently waited for a response.

"Who is this?" A rough voice, cackling with static, came over the radio.

"This is John, who am I talking to?" John pressed the talk button so hard that his thumb turned white. It seemed like an eternity before the man responded.

"This is Fred. We live in a town called Briarton." the man responded.

Briarton... isn't that the town the old nut job mentioned?

"How many of you are there?" Fred asked.

"I don't think I'm allowed to answer that question. I don't know who you are," replied John.

"That's a fair answer, John. I can't blame you for being a little careful. My family and I are the only ones that live out here in Briarton. Since The Lifting happened we've stayed at home… been surviving off of old food storage.

Are you passing through the area?" Fred asked.

"Hey everyone, come here!" John yelled behind him. He was afraid to leave the radio and lose his opportunity to talk to someone else. Betty drifted into the room.

"Are you still there Fred?" John asked.

"Yes."

"We are traveling west for the moment."

"Well, if you happen to stop by for a rest we have some food we could share, but not much. It's always nice to hear what's happening in the world outside of here." Fred said. John looked around at everyone in the room and they all seemed to nod in agreement.

"You can count on us stopping by, Fred. I think we are at least a week out from your location," John said.

Betty gave John a questionable look.

"John, you know that town is only a mile north, right?"

John put his finger to his lips, telling her with his eyes to trust him.

"Sounds good, folks. We will keep an eye out for you," Fred agreed. John turned off the radio and looked at the others.

"Why would you tell him we were so far away?"

Jack asked.

"So we can be safe tonight, for one," Betty piped in, understanding John's line of thinking. "And so we can get a peek at them before we show ourselves to them."

John looked out the window at the sun that was setting in the sky and wondered why they would ever leave such a place.

Chapter 11

Van sat poised in the glow of a burning log. The raggedy group of survivors eagerly huddled in a circle, warming themselves by the lit chunk of pine, which was prepared with several holes around its circumference to allow airflow. The log did not billow smoke, nor did the flames dance like Van was used to. A normal fire reached for the sky and drew in any air it possibly could to feed itself. Without gravity, the fire had a rounded edge, making it more difficult to provide oxygen for it to keep burning. The slow ball of flame made Van think of a miniature sun.

The party had reserved themselves to the small library. It was filled with maps and outdoor hiking guides. A stuffed moose head was mounted to the wall, giving an almost sinister look in the glow of the flames. Betty, who had been fetching the freshly cleaned fish, returned with an armful. She let go of them carefully and grabbed two more logs for the fire. She slowly placed one log after another on top of the fire, growing the flame enough that Van could feel the heat on his face now. Jack, also feeling the heat, flinched and backed away from the fire. Large boils had started forming over his burn marks from the lake. Van watched as Betty grabbed a small trout and brought it close to the flames. Using her thumb and forefinger she twisted the tail, sending the carcass into a gradual rotation for even cooking. Van could smell the acrid stench of lake trout turn to a more desirable, mouthwatering scent. The skin and scales of the fish bronzed against the fire. One by one, the fish were carefully positioned just outside of the fire in a slow rotation.

"Are you okay, Jack? Your burns are looking really bad," Betty worried.

Jack extended his arms out in front of him, examining the blisters scattered around his body. A couple of them had popped and the puss was suspended on the outside of the wound. Betty made her way around the circle of people and pulled a small jar out of her bag.

"This is an herbal cream that might help. I found it in a drawer at the nurse's station." Betty, with the care of a mother to a son, brushed a mint-smelling cream on his blisters. Once she was done John displayed his right hand, showing off the unhealed gash. A blood blister had formed around the wound and a tinge of yellow was seen within the blood. The cut had deep indents where John's nails racked across it when trying to escape his captors.

"You got something for this by chance?" John asked. "I'm worried it might be getting infected."

"What you really need is some stitches."

Betty scratched the blood bubble and wiped away as much as she could manage. The smell of rotten blood mixed with the aroma of fish. Betty reached into her pocket and pulled out a short, slim bottle with a red cap on it.

"I'm going to put some glue on it and try to get it to close," Betty explained in a soft voice. It was comforting to let somebody else tend to him for the first time in years. He could not remember the last time he had allowed himself to be so vulnerable. Betty squeezed a healthy glob of glue onto the cavernous cut and pinched the two sides together until it held on its own then topped it off with a slab of the same cream she put on Jack's blisters.

She turned her attention back to the fish. The skins had darkened and turned crispy. Betty, using a long stick she had ripped off of a tree, pushed each of the fish away from the fire and divided the portions among the group. As she passed by the fire a peculiar shape caught Van's eye. Professor Weston was leisurely sitting on a tall-backed red velvet chair. Weston's face had a grotesque, open wedge down his forehead at about a forty-five-degree angle, dividing his right eye from his left. What was once a prized symbol to the man on his brow was now the display from a horror scene.

"Oh, young brother, she will try and give you the share, but you know which piece you should take," Weston spoke with a refinement of royalty. Van, too stunned to speak, hesitantly looked around the room to see if any of the others were aware of Weston's presence. "You know what is so satisfying? For two long years, my body hasn't relaxed. No lying on a bed or resting in a chair. But this… this has been truly marvelous." Weston ran his hands across the smooth soft exterior of the arm. "You could have this, you know. This place is our reward for such diligence to the cause."

Betty passed John to where Van was sitting and tried to hand him a large portion of fish. He pointed at the smallest carp in the pile.

"I think I just want that if it's okay with you?" Van said. Betty gave him a queer look.

"I bet you haven't eaten this good in a long time. Besides, you earned your share by helping us out. You don't want it?"

Van hesitated, looking back and forth between the delectable fish and Weston, still relaxed in the chair, watching him intently.

"I'm… just not that hungry," Van said as he pulled the small fish from the pile.

"Good. Good, my boy," Weston grinned.

Van looked over where the Professor was sitting, but he had gone. In three quick bites, Van put the fish down from head to tail, bones and all. Van felt an eager tension in his stomach that made his feeling of hunger intensify. He wanted more. His body demanded it.

"So, now that we've all filled our stomachs, why don't we go get to know each other a little more?" Kristen suggested. "I'll start. I'm Kristen, Betty's sister. I used to work as a secretary for a law firm. I was at work arguing with my boss when The Lifting happened. I threw a pen at him, and when it hit him it bounced off but didn't drop to the ground. That's when all hell broke loose." Kristen looked over at Ronney whose gaze was fixed on the fire. "Ronney, you're next," she chided.

Ronney hesitantly looked around the room searching for someone to look at. "Ronney, and my brother, Jack." He jabbed his thumb toward Jack next to him. "We both worked as mechanics in a small shop we owned, just outside of Livingston, Montana. We were replacing a stubborn engine build when our tools, and ourselves, started drifting around the shop." The following silence signified that he had said all he intended to. Next was John, who put his hand up in a waving gesture.

"I feel like I'm at an AA meeting but here goes nothing. I'm John. I was an active firefighter in Boise, Idaho. I worked at Station 62 which was built in a quieter part of town. I was cleaning one of the engines when a car sailed through the upper floor of the station. I've been wandering my way to Oregon for two reasons. I hope that being near the ocean means more food or fish. I'm also looking for my father and that is the last place I knew of him living." He didn't feel it necessary to explain the other horrible sights and sounds that still haunted him from The Lifting, just as he was sure the others had omitted. Betty inched forward.

"I'm Betty, the oldest sister in the family. I was visiting our mother in the old folks home when it started. The power went out and I could hear all of the heart monitors in each room sync with the same dull tone, becoming loud enough it felt like they were screaming at me. The day that gravity stopped, so did our mother's heart."

Betty held a distant stare and glanced at Kristen who looked surprised.

"You never told me that story," Kristen said sadly. "I always knew that she died but I didn't know you were there." She maneuvered around the fire and held Betty in a loving embrace. Another moment of silence. After the sisters had let go of each other, Van felt all eyes land on him.

"Hi. I'm Jacob, but I go by Van. I uhhh…. Never really had anyone to look after me. My mom and dad were always fighting until they got divorced. Once a month my dad would dump me at the airport for a flight to LA where my mom lived. My mom never knew how to act around me so she would always just buy me a new video game to occupy our time together. I was in the airport when everyone started floating around the room." He briefly paused, reflecting on that day. "I watched a plane that was parking, crash into the terminal opposite ours and it caused a big explosion. I was alone for a really long time..."

Van looked down at the floor trying to hold back tears, his hands shaking. He looked up and Weston was in the corner of the room examining a book.

"Don't you talk about us, boy. They won't

understand," Weston warned.

"I met a couple of people who helped me and brought me in until I met John," Van finished hastily. He averted all eyes, avoiding John's disapproving look.

"You forgot the part about the cult. You've gone this far. No need to leave the biggest piece out," John said sternly. Betty hesitantly looked at John, as if to tell him to stop, sensing the tension that had just been created. John himself knew this would only create tension. Part of him wanted to stop himself, but most of him did not care. Maybe, subconsciously, he believed that resorting to this was the only way to be free of this burden. Maybe he just wanted the others to empathize with him after having no decent human connection for years. Whatever it was, he knew he wanted to be with these people, and that did not include the man-child that was Van. "Tell them that you and your friends trapped me in a bar," he pushed on, the rage and volume of his voice climbing. Tell them about how you planned on lighting me on fire and sacrificing me. Or is that just too much to share?"

Van looked into the eyes of each person finding confusion and alarm.

"I— I... everyone I've ever met has left me. My mother, my father, everyone! The only people who ever really gave a damn are now dead. I know my mistakes are many, but don't act like any one of you is perfect in this godforsaken world," Van said with tears in his eyes, embarrassed. "I need to go outside and take a leak." He stumbled and pushed toward the sliding window door that stood adjacent to the fire. He pulled it open, rotated his body around the middle of the door, and slid the door shut.

The full moon splashed the large forest in front of him, making the shadows abysmally black in comparison. The pine trees seemed frozen in place. The outside air held a quiet reverence much like standing on holy ground. Van wiped the tears from his eyes and flipped them off to the side. He scaled the cabin wall up to the rooftop and planted himself next to a rusted weather vane that was decorated with a cawing rooster.

"So far so good."

Van flinched at the sound of the voice. His head spun to the side to see Professor Weston sitting next to him. Van didn't want to be so close. The skull fragments and brain matter had a more venomous look when mixed with the moonlight.

"I need you to go away. I'm trying to stay with these nice people," Van said.

"Nice? You are a chosen one to help fulfill what is

required. Don't you see, my son? I stand before you without restraint," Weston hopped to his feet and stood firmly on the rooftop. "Jacob, you have to complete your rites, including the final rite. With the help of Sister Jessica, I was able to complete my final rite and look at how I've been blessed. Don't you remember your rites?"

"You only taught me three. Nothing about a 'final rite.' The first rite of Sacrament is where you take a piece of your food and give it to science. The second is the rite of Lifting, and the third is the rite of Donning, where you put on the robes to be a Professor." Van said

"You are missing the final, and most important rite: Self Sacrifice. A final act of giving to Science. You recite a very sacred prayer and give your life for Science." Professor Weston explained slowly.

"That's literal suicide. You always told me that we were to inherit the world after The Lifting was over. You said we were to lay the rites throughout the land and that science would then bless us."

"Don't you see it before you right now? I have been blessed. I have inherited all. It's not too late for you to return to the fold and continue your path."

"I don't know how to feel about that, truthfully. You are asking me to eventually commit suicide for a greater cause?" Weston wrapped his arms around Van and squeezed him, bringing fresh tears to Van's reddened eyes. "How can you forgive me when I have strayed so far? I'm the reason you're dead."

"You didn't kill me; the usurper below us did. At this very moment, he is plotting how to be rid of you. How to kill you. But, you must know, my boy, that you set my final rite into motion. I never would have obtained what I have now without you and your courage," Weston reassured him.

"So… what do I need to do? How do I come back after so much descent?" Van asked. Van looked over toward Weston, ready to receive whatever instruction he was given. And yet, Weston was gone. He frantically looked around the rooftop, then the trees.

I need to be with my own people. I need to make this right, Van thought. *I wonder how long it would take to get back to Fernwood... If I only had a phone—.*

The radio. The memory of the radio just below him in the cabin interrupted him mid-thought.

I can't go through the door. The group would notice and get suspicious.

Van elected to stick to the outside and find the window leading into the communications room, hoping he would find it unlocked. He pulled his body along the rooftop, being careful not to thump or scrape along too loudly. He elected to go down the wall feet first as he worked his way down to the window of the communications room. With a light tug, Van tried to pry the window open but it did not budge.

I really hoped it unlocked.

Trying a second time, he pulled much harder. The window argued loudly as it stuttered open. The wooden frame and window edge had grown snug over time as they swelled. Van watched the door intently, his heart pounding in his ears, waiting for someone to barrel in. After waiting for what felt like an eternity, he rolled his body ninety degrees and pressed himself through the gap and into the room. He halted a second before going to the radio.

Why am I so scared to commit to this? John has been nothing but a self-righteous jerk ever since I saved his ungrateful ass.

Van, with newfound determination, pushed his way over to the radio and grabbed hold of the equipment, stopping himself in the wall with his feet.

Ah, crap... Do I even know how to use this?

"I believe that is the book that you will need," the Professor said, pointing at a thick three-ring binder floating just behind Van. He was now standing on the floor, leaning on the wall by the window. Van reached over and grabbed it out of the air. He turned his shoulder so the moonlight illuminated the pages as he looked through the tabs sticking out of the pages. Even so, he had to bring the book close enough to his face that his nose was nearly brushing the paper. He flipped to the page that had the "Radio Coordinates" tab. Upon inspection, he found an extensive list of cities in alphabetical order. He skimmed through the pages further until he reached the F's. Each city appeared to have either one or two radio coordinate frequencies.

"Hurry, Van, they will be getting suspicious of your absence," Weston muttered.

Chester. *Got it!* There were three different radio coordinates labeled under the town. The first set had "Chester Fire Station" next to it. The second read "Chester Police Station." The third set of coordinates was handwritten in pen. To the left of the numbers, written in sharp scribbles "ARTY GAS STATION."

Why would his name be on this list? We must not have been the first to find this place after all.

Van tried to remember what locations in the town his fellow Atomists had made home.

"Sometimes I don't understand you, boy. I'm here

to help you and you still insist on doing this all on your own," Weston said with a sneer. Van looked over at Weston, doing his best to avoid looking at the obvious, gory injury.

"Fine. Which one should I put in?" Van asked in a hushed tone. Professor Weston, quicker than Van's eyes could hope to keep up with, vanished from the corner of the room and reappeared by Van's side.

"Well, the fire station of course. Why would anyone want to stay at a police station? They are such negative, dank places," Weston retorted.

Van grabbed the dials and gently spun each one to its correct position. With the correct sequence of numbers displayed, he took hold of the microphone and held down the talk button. Nothing happened.

"I don't understand. What did I do wrong?" Van asked, looking up at Weston.

"Were you born an idiot or is that just your nature? Do I really have to do everything? I'm starting to think I am wasting my time here. You are a piece of dog crap with no real purpose." Weston yelled.

"I'm sorry. I'm trying my best," Van cowered.

"Well, if this is your best then mankind is doomed, and you with it!" Professor Weston's voice took on a strong, sinister tone, filling every corner of his mind with the intensity of a sonic boom. “IDIOT! DOOMED, DOOMED IDIOT. YOU'LL NEVER SUCCEED. RID THE WORLD OF YOURSELF AND SAVE US ALL THE TROUBLE. DOOMED, BOY!”

Van grabbed his head. Weston’s voice screamed out of every corner of his conscious mind. He struggled to focus on anything else; anything for the screaming to stop. He could hear running water and a powerful hissing noise. A child’s giggle was followed by car horns blaring from all parts of the room. White noise from an unseen TV grew louder.

“YOU'LL NEVER FIGURE IT OUT. I SHOULD HAVE LEFT YOU WHERE I FOUND YOU.”

Van’s head almost vibrated from the noise. He looked at the multiple cords floating around and noticed the silver end of an auxiliary plug among them. The microphone was unplugged. He took one of his hands away from his ringing head, snatched the plug out of the air, and plugged it into the back of the microphone. The noise ceased as instantaneously as it had started. He felt dizzy and disoriented. He wasn’t sure if anger or sadness had a firmer grasp on his heart. He did his best to shrug it all off and grabbed the radio, mashing the talk button this time.

"Hello. Hello, this is Brother Van." He spoke into the mic. Open-air static sounded over the speaker for a few seconds, then disappeared. Van sat in silence for several seconds, shooting a glance over his shoulder toward the door.

"Brother Van?" A deep male's voice responded. "We had given up hope that you were even alive. We have been searching for you since you left. Where are you?"

"I'm in a cabin, a station of some sort, just a few miles off of the third exit out of town. I wish to return and, with your help, I have several people ready for departure," Van said excitedly. A squeak behind him made him lose his grip on the equipment. Van turned toward the door and his heart shot all the way down to his feet.

John distanced himself from the uncomfortable warmth of the fire heating his sun burnt forehead. His stomach bulged a little from gorging on the fish. He wiped the juice away from his mouth eagerly and licked his hand.

"Do you think we ought to go for some more fish

tomorrow?" John asked Betty who was finishing her own meal.

"Well, based on the amount that we got, it's not too far-fetched that there could be more. How long do you suppose fish stay good out of water?" Betty asked.

"No way am I doing that again," Jack insisted as he gingerly picked at one of the blisters on his leg.

"Jack is right. We'll have to find a better way to get the fish moving. All he did was splash around a bit and the fish went running." Kristen said.

A high-pitched screech called out over the grumble of their conversation.

"What was that?" Ronney asked, visually checking each window and door. John looked at Betty.

"We didn't search all of the rooms. I don't think we are alone." John then heard a squelch that he recognized as radio noise. He quickly bound away from the fire and around the corner of a wall. Scaling down the wall past each shut door getting closer and closer to the communications room. He pushed the door open and passed the threshold of the door to see Van with his back turned to him, gripping the radio.

"—your help, I have several people ready for

departure," Van finished, but John had heard all he needed.

"No!" John yelled as Van was turning to face him. Gripping the sides of the door frame he launched himself toward Van, resembling a large boulder being released from its elastic sling. John sliced through the room with no concern for his speed and crashed into Van, his shoulder meeting Van's solar plexus. He grabbed onto the speaking microphone which Van still clung to.

"Help!" Van yelled out with as much force as possible, the wind having just been knocked out of his lungs. John grabbed the cord connecting the receiver to the microphone and gave a sharp yank, effectively stopping the transmission. Betty appeared in the door frame.

"What are you doing!?" Betty asked with alarm.

"He contacted the Atomists. They're coming here. For us," John said while trying to keep a hold on Van. Van saw the opening and punched John in the stomach. John felt a fleeting suffocation as his abs recoiled from the hit. Betty pulled the crossbow over her back and head and pointed it at John and Van as they wrestled through the air. The distinct twang of the string rang out as she loosed a bolt. Van let out a shrill cry as the silver, razor-sharp head of the bolt dug itself into, and completely through, his right calf muscle. It finally stopped as it became firmly lodged in the pinewood floor on the other side of the room.

"Gah! Y—you don't understand! I have to atone—argh!" Van yelled out in agony. The pain intensified as his mind focused on it more and more, the adrenaline from the fight wearing off. John took the chance and socked Van across his jaw, hard enough to leave an imprint of three of his knuckles for several seconds as blood returned to the area. The blow sent Van sailing across the room toward the bolt stuck into the floor and John pursued. Betty was trying with every bit of strength she had to pull the arms back of the crossbow but was unsuccessful.

Van pushed on John's chest as they made contact again, John's mass sending him backward even faster. John looked behind him and prepared to land as gracefully as possible on the opposite wall. Van, having now hit the wall, reached for the bolt. He tried to dislodge it from the floor with the desperation of a cornered dog, but the carbon fiber shaft had a slick coating of Van's blood. With both hands, he planted his feet and desperately pulled at the two-foot weapon, freeing it from the wood. He locked eyes with John once again, waiting for the next attack. He felt it difficult to focus on fighting when he could feel his heartbeat through his wound, each pulse delivering a fresh wave of anguish.

John planted his feet on the side of a bookcase

bolted into the wall and launched himself at Van again. This time he flipped forward, pulled his feet in, and aimed them at Van as he rocketed through the room. The bottom of John's donated shoes planted themselves into Van's chest, who was unable to raise his arms in time to deflect the attack. Van lost his grip on the bolt as his body crunched against the upper portion of the window. He buckled over from the pain and shock, trying to catch his breath. The window had spider webbed from the impact.

Not wanting to give Van a chance to recover, John grabbed the bolt and leaped at him. In a fleeting reaction, Van raised his hand in an attempt to slow John's assault. The bolt slammed into Van's hand and pierced through the skin and out the other side. The force drove Van's hand to the wall and the bolt pinned it up against the scratchy wood log. Van screamed out, an intense throbbing pulsating within his hand. He reached over and weakly tried to dislodge the rod from his hand.

A metallic click from behind John caused him to stop his blitz. He looked back and saw Betty pull the trigger once again from the crossbow. In the blink of an eye, another bolt disappeared from the bow and punched into Van's side just below his ribs and stopped on the wall behind him. Van coughed a mouthful of blood, too weak and in shock to scream at this point. His free hand danced between each bolt as he despondently tried to free himself from the wall. John swung his fist again and knocked Van unconscious. Small blisters of blood started to well around his abdomen and hand where the shafts kept him pinned.

"I tried to get a cleaner shot," Betty said. Her voice was melancholy, almost guilty. "Should we stop the bleeding?"

"He just tried to sentence your whole family to death…. He's getting what he earned… We, on the other hand, need to leave… before the rest of those lunatics get here," John said between panting breaths. "They tried to kill me… they won't hesitate to take you and your loved ones out."

I should just end him. Twice now that he has tried to make me his sacrifice. Not heeding his own advice, he took his time staring at Van, rage boiling over within his heart. *I could strangle him, make it less of a spectacle than it needs to be.* John went to put both of his hands around Van's neck, smearing imprints of his blood-covered hands on his throat.

Betty placed her hand on John's shoulder.

"John," she pleaded tearfully, "don't make yourself do this. Don't give up your humanity for him." Hesitantly, he let go of Van's throat. Van's lungs sucked in air. His breathing was uneven and labored even in his comatose state. *Bled out then... and rot in hell.* John turned away and followed Betty out of the door. The rest of the group sat in the hallway, watching in horror at the aftermath of the battle.

Chapter 12

Seaside City, Oregon. Two years after The Lifting.

Tommy held a flat metal scraping tool in one hand and a black suction tube in the other.

I always hate when it's my turn to clean the water filtration tank, he thought begrudgingly.

He sat in a large, metallic, box-shaped tower that was covered in salt crystal buildup. The mountain of a contraption was used to convert salt water from the sea into drinking water for the residents. Aside from the tools in his hands, Tommy wore a bright yellow harness with a cord attached to it for his retrieval once he was finished. Using the metal scraper, Tommy went along the outside of each wall racking off any chunks he could find then vacuumed them up with the tube. A long, slender rod stood at the center of the box, extending from one wall to the middle of the open space. He found a particularly nasty buildup that looked like it was left over from the last cleaning. Several large, square opaque crystals had grown to the size of fuzzy dice you would find in a car hanging from a rear view mirror. Using the blunt handle of the scraper Tommy dislodged the salt and put the large pieces in his pocket.

This will be good for my collection at home.

He scraped the last bit of salt, fed it to the hose, and gave the walls a thorough double-check.

"Alright, pull me back. I'm done in here," Tommy called out towards the opening hole of the container. A strong tug yanked at the back of the harness and he drifted up and out through one of the side walls. "Who was the last person to clean that?" Tommy asked. Two people stood side by side, holding the other end of the rope. The one on the left, Maureen, shrugged her shoulders, her long black hair floating in suspense. Maureen had the appearance of a Halloween witch mid-flight on a broom, each strand its personality.

"It was me. Why?" the stout man on the right said with a sad, bulldog expression. Frank's cheeks drooped off the sides of his face. His neck resembled that of a rooster cawing side to side. Without gravity keeping his jowls down they danced around every time he shifted his head too quickly. Tommy reached inside his pocket and pulled out a handful of the fist-sized salt crystals.

"If you're not going to do your job then you might as well put in for a different task. These have been growing for at least three months. Any further and this could have easily damaged the heating rod," Tommy chastised. The light from the morning sun reflected off of the blocks, causing a rainbow to vibrantly coat the wall of the tank.

"Lay off, Tommy, don't pretend that you are the only one that cleans this thing." the man quipped back at him. The two scowled at each other for a moment, then the scowls turned into smiles. Frank yanked on Tommy's harness, sending him sailing off to the sky. The rope went taught and Tommy's body struck like he had hit an invisible wall.

"Very funny, old man. Pull me in so we can get on with our day," Tommy yelled. Frank, as aged as he was, had arms like tree trunks. Frank's body had hardened through the years of construction and hard labor.

"Hey, how does this thing work anyway?" Frank asked as he reeled Tommy in.

"The bottom tank is filled with seawater. The seawater is heated by the rod. Normally, water boils and the air pushes up. But, since there's no gravity, the heated steam bubble stays trapped on the heating rod because of the surface tension of the water. We use a driving tube that pierces the heated air and pushes the steam through it to the next tank that sits above it. As the tank builds in pressure the cool metal creates a condensation effect and the clean water collects on the outside wall of the tank." Tommy moved over to a large pipe hanging from the upper tank that had been painted red. "Once you have enough pressure we open this pipe and the clean water is projected out of the tank." Tommy thought the whole idea was crazy, but all it takes is a couple of engineers to save humanity. Plus, it had been doing exactly what it was designed to do so he couldn't complain.

"So, what's next on our group list today," Maureen asked. Frank pulled out a piece of lined paper from his back pocket.

"Looks like, collectively, we have three tasks for the day. I'm glad you guys proposed doing them together. The first was to scrape the water filter tank. Second, we have to go harvest the tomatoes from the greenhouse before a couple of hours of guard tower duty."

The town had an acre of land set away just for the greenhouses. A dozen buildings sat side-by-side on the opposite side of town. Maureen, Tommy, and Frank drifted toward the main road. As they got to the town's main street,

Tommy looked for the safety wire. Yet another smart idea from the big brains. The town utilized a traveling system that allowed its inhabitants to move freely without the fear that they would step too hard and send themselves to a heavenly grave.

A braided wire was woven through a D-clamp brace, allowing the user to attach a carabiner to the wire. Each clamp was about twenty-five feet from the other and ran alongside the streets' sidewalks. They were then free to move in the direction of the wire that held them grounded and the clip slid along with them. In the town of Seaside, everyone who was a bona fide citizen of the town was given a harness and clip to free up their movements. Sometimes the smaller kids used the old water irrigation sewers to get around. The parents always felt that that way was the safest mode to get around town so they allowed it. Clipping onto the wire, the three started traveling down the hill to the opposite side of the town for their next task.

"Did you see what the city engineers planned on working up next?" Frank asked as they sailed down the line.

"Are you talking about the tunnels?" Tommy asked.

"They are working on mapping out a series of tunnels that you can take from one central location to any point in the town," Maureen said with excitement.

"I know you are kind of new to the town, Tommy, but did you know we were working on a subway system that was set to go all the way to Portland?" Frank asked.

"No, I didn't know that. Where's the tunnel at?"

Maureen pointed at a large steeple seen above the rest of the town. "They had the station built under that building. They had about one hundred feet of tunnel framed before they gave up on the project. They said it cost too much taxpayer money, even though they already took it from our property taxes."

Frank looked back at Tommy as they pushed along. "The engineers said that because they don't have to worry about the dirt caving in around them they can easily carve carefully placed tunnels to each end, making it easier to get around town."

The three slowed themselves to a stop just out front of a sign that read, "Green Gardens" spray painted in dark green. They unclipped their harnesses and pushed toward the nearest greenhouse. The smell of fertilizer drifted in the air around the buildings. Tommy pushed his way through the sliding glass door and into the nursery. Several rows of tomato plants filled the glass building, a sporadic spectacle of reds, yellows, and deep greens.

"Do they want us to pick all of the tomatoes?" Frank grumbled.

Maureen, tip-toeing her feet on the ground, moved to where several large bags of mesh bags with zip strings hung on a nail by the door. Fans had been fastened to the walls. Large purple UV lamps sounded off a miserable hum resembling that of a small town grocery store's lights. "We're supposed to water them and pick all of the tomatoes for the town feast tomorrow," she replied. All three of them started with the harvesting, cautiously pulling on the plants' bristle-covered branches. Each vine was secured in place just above the planter boxes with a series of wires. The roots hung loosely below the stocks, completely exposed without soil. Making quick work of it, Tommy went over and stashed the three large sacks that were now gorged with ripe, delicious tomatoes.

"Next is the watering, Frank. Have you ever done this before?" Tommy asked. Frank pulled himself down the line of garden beds to reach Tommy and Maureen.

"I know I'm old but I'm not an idiot. I bet I've planted more gardens than you've ever seen in your life." Frank said with a touch of cynicism. "What you two don't know is that after dousing the roots with the water we have to draw as much of the water as we can off of the roots," Frank added.

"Why is that?" Tommy asked as he picked up a plunger filled with a mixture of fertilizer and water.

"Most plants aren't meant to sit in a constant state of moisture, they get sick. When I was settling into my first house I planted a garden. I had always thought that more watering was better for the plants. I watered them 3 times a day. I wanted to give my garden every luxury I could. After a week the plants all turned yellow and died from over-watering."

Frank pulled in close to a plant and slowly pushed a string of water, about as thick as toothpaste coming out of the tube, onto the roots. He then very gently pulled on the black metal plunger handle, pulling in any blobs of liquid while avoiding the roots as much as possible. Tommy started on his first plant, pushing more liquid out than he meant to. He pulled in the blobs and found that a thin layer of water still stuck to the roots.

"Hey, Frank, what do I do if I can't get all of the water?" Tommy asked. Frank joined him at the table.

"No problemo, man, you don't have to worry about that." Frank pointed out the industrial gray fans all around them. "Each one spins in a perpetual motion," Frank twirled his finger in a clockwise circle in front of Tommy's eyes.

"The whole point of the fans is to move the air around causing the water to dry up from the roots," Frank responded. He returned to his row of plants and continued carefully wetting each set of roots.

"I don't get it," Maureen said, abruptly changing the subject. "Why would we want to celebrate the planet losing one of its primary key elements? Most of us lost our family and friends that day. Why celebrate The Lifting when it ruined our lives?"

Tommy shifted over to the next plant. "It's all how you look at it. I don't see it as a celebration of death and destruction. I see it as a celebration for those who survived. Like the Fourth of July. We celebrate the victory of life and also retain a reverence for the fallen."

Maureen stopped and looked solemnly up at Tommy. "I would trade a lifetime's amount of fresh produce for my children back." Tommy felt his face flush. His cheeks felt the creeping warmth of embarrassment. All three of them remained in silent contemplation as they went through the arbitrary task at hand. Tommy was the first to break the silence. "You know, I've heard a lot of theories as to why gravity stopped working. Why do you guys think it happened?"

"Well, that's a dumb question, Tommy. Don't you know that the government has been messing with shit they don't understand for years? Have you ever heard of the super collider?" Frank asked. Maureen and Tommy both shrugged their shoulders. "Out in Europe a bunch of smart people made a machine that caused two atoms to spin in a circle in the opposite direction. Once the atoms hit a certain speed they forced those two atoms to collide, creating a massive surge of energy. I think while they were meddling they turned on the machine and tried to create a surge and accidentally condemned the world."

"Hard to believe the government is to blame... seems like an easy scapegoat," retorted Maureen. "Before everything went kablooey the president would come on to the TV all the time and he was a dumb dumb for sure. He could barely form a complete sentence let alone accidentally destroy the world. I think it was a super black hole. Our world sits in a large galaxy that is but a spec in the universe. I think our part of the galaxy has started to drift into a black hole, causing a quantum distortion in the natural laws of Earth."

"How did you come to that conclusion?" Tommy asked, doubtful of Maureen's knowledge of anything involving the world quantum or physics. "Well, I used to be a master in reading the stars. People would come to me to read the stars for them so they could know how to proceed with their lives. I noticed that a little at a time the stars started to move or go out altogether."

Frank rolled his eyes. "You think that you can read the stars?"

"I used to, but everything has changed now. Orion usually peaks out in the early hours of the night around late September. The last time I did a reading with his power in the sky I noticed he was missing his bow. I knew that had to be a bad omen."

Tommy moved down to the other side of the tomato plants, finished the first row, and moved on to the next one.

"So which is it, Tommy?" Frank asked pausing to look up at Tommy.

"I can tell you that my first knee jerk was that it was the end of the world. I never went to church much but the doom and gloom I saw that day at the grocery store seemed to be the closest thing to the rapture that I care to see. However, I have come to believe that it is just yet another hurdle that mankind must go through to progress forward."

"How do you suppose that is?" Frank asked.

"Noah had the flood, the Knights of the Round

Table had the black plaque. In the 30's they had dust storms that nearly brought the whole country to starvation and financial ruin. I think that we, right here, right now are meant to walk through this challenge to better our race. You can't argue that the generations of children seemed to be getting worse, and more entitled. A scientist once placed a colony of mice in a massive cage with no interaction with humans. The mice went through many stages. One of the stages was interesting because it resembled the era when World War Two was over and all of the returning soldiers returned and filled their houses full of kids. The mice went through an explosive breeding stage that bolstered the population. The last stage the mice displayed before the colony died was the grooming stage. The mice didn't care about food, water, or sex. The only thing they cared about was their appearance. Most of the mice starved to death because they took too much time cleaning their coats. I can't help but see the comparison between bulimic teenagers and mice who starve to death for looks. I would say that humankind was drifting to its destruction and the Earth decided to intervene."

"Yeah… the Earth is sooo smart that it decided to turn off gravity. I like my theory better." Frank said as he put his plunger on a hook, studded against the wall. "I'mma bid you all farewell. My shift on the tower starts in 20 minutes and I don't want to be late. Don't want to be responsible for someone's ultimate demise or anything," Frank grinned as he waved at the two and exited the greenhouse.

"Maureen, I'm sorry you lost your family. I know that even though Frank has a weird way of showing it he means well." Tommy said. He made his way over to Maureen who had a tear stuck in the tear duct of her eye. He hugged her like he used to hug his sister whenever she was sad. They finished up the watering and parted ways. He left the greenhouse, secured his clip to the safety wire, and started toward home.

He steadied his body, stopping in front of a sun-worn boat along the way. He unhooked his carabiner and pushed toward the sad, rectangle RV home next to the boat. Opening the door, a glimmer of shimmering light coming from the direction of the RV skylight caught his eye. He pulled out one of the large salt blocks he had kept from earlier and meticulously centered it in the skylight, transforming the space into a natural disco. Scaling along the side of the RV cabinets, Tommy tugged on a drawer where he kept his more personal belongings. He grabbed a wallet-sized photo of his son, John, from near the back of the drawer and returned with it to the skylight. He took the cube and licked one side, then took the picture of his son and pressed it hard on the newly wet crystal. A strong flavor of the sea stung his tongue. Gazing at his handy work, he brought the salt back up to the light. The picture of the small boy resonated and had an outer glow like a natural frame of light. Tommy hung there motionless for several minutes, staring at the picture, pensively wondering what his first words to his son would be if he were ever able to see him again.

Chapter 13

Van's body remained motionless, stapled to the wall as the group retrieved the remainder of their belongings. John stood resolute in the corner of the communications center, eyeing their wolf in sheep's clothing. One thing was certain: if he heard even one thing out of that traitor's mouth he would have no hesitation to finish the job. Everyone elected to stay mostly silent while getting things ready to leave. They moved with haste, knowing that they were now the targets of a murderous group of crazed cultists. Jack was the first to break the uncomfortable silence.

"Does anyone have room for the fish?" he asked.

"I can fit most of it, I think," offered Ronney, feeling around his pack to see how much free space was available. "Are there any plastic or garbage bags around to put the fish in first? I don't really want my backpack smelling like that permanently."

"We can find something, yeah," assured Kristen.

"Everybody's got some water?" asked Betty.

The lot nodded solemnly in affirmation.

John could not decide which thought was worse to him; leaving Van to bleed out slowly – or, potentially, he would even survive somehow once he came to – or going back to slit his throat and be done with it. The latter option felt like cold-blooded murder. The former, in John's mind, would at least allow him to sleep at night. It was the same as the woman he had found in that apartment.

Am I a coward? A hypocrite? I may not be the direct dealer of death, but I definitely can't consider myself innocent.

"John!"

John had his torturous thoughts interrupted by the sound of Betty's voice. It took him a moment to realize that she had been trying to get his attention as the rest of the group was watching him with concerned expressions, all of them packed and were ready to go.

"Sorry, guys, I'm ready," he apologized as he zipped up the top zipper of his bag and slung it on his back. Only once tempers had settled from the fight in the communications room did John realize just how exhausted he was. He had been looking forward to his first decent night's rest in however long he couldn't remember. It was starting to affect his thinking, and he was sure that he would start hallucinating soon enough.

I could light the place on fire on our way out... make sure it's all over with. Would that make the rest of them even more upset? Would they pursue us, though?

John thought better of it, not wanting to jeopardize his new companions unnecessarily. As of now, he saw no real reason that they would choose to come after the group. Van had left them of his own free will.

Hell, they may just kill him once they find him for betraying them.

The five of them headed out the front door and closed it on their way out. The sun had not yet made its way over the horizon, but the faint glow that precedes the sunrise had begun to bring back those long, eerie shadows through the trees.

"Sure feels like a waste. Do you think we can return here soon?" Kristen asked as she gazed at the prestigious cabin.

"I think once they see this cabin they won't want to leave," Jack said.

Betty helped fasten a line from Ronney to Jack to

ensure that he wouldn't accidentally get hurt or worse. By their best estimate, while studying the map of the area they had found, they needed to head north-northeast, which would lead them to the top of a ridgeline overlooking the town of Briarton.

They had no guns, only Betty's crossbow which was down to four bolts. The only items they were able to take from the cabin for weapons were the kitchen knives, of which each person brought two. The ladies donned new jackets with park ranger patches on the shoulders that were found in a closet in one of the rooms. The same closet also contained some semi-folded blankets that they begrudgingly decided to leave behind since they had no good options for packing them on such short notice. They were, however, able to fit a couple of hand towels into their pack. John had remembered seeing a few extension cords and thinner towing straps in the basement during his venture down there. There was enough for each member of the party to have one of either. The final treasures they laid claim to were a flashlight still in its packaging, complete with two AA batteries and binoculars in a dark-green leather carrying pouch. John was chosen to carry the binoculars while Jack kept the flashlight, to help him navigate while towing his brother.

The vastness of the forest appeared incredibly more sinister knowing that there may be someone lying in wait for them in its depths. Even knowing that the Atomists couldn't have caught up to them yet, John's heart beat harder and his eyes dashed left and right as they moved. Using the faint sun rays as a guide and their map knowledge – since there were no compasses to be found at the cabin – they headed off in the direction of Briarton.

"We got a bit of a lucky break finding those binoculars, eh? I can't wait to use them," jokes Ronney in a feeble attempt to lighten the mood. The only reaction he received was a small grin from his brother. Silence accompanied the rest of their journey, save the occasional direction from Jack to his brother.

John was surprised at how quickly they arrived at their destination. The sun was barely beginning to warm the back of their necks as they cautiously approached the edge of the ridge overlooking Briarton. The peak of the hill was met with a sharp cliff that stopped several hundred feet below.

They all scrambled up a large pine tree that rested just before the cliff drop-off, they're heads were exposed while they surveyed the town. As he pulled up the tree he found himself annoyed. Even though the tree seemed dead it still had an excess of sap hanging off of it. John flexed his hands watching the skin stick as the sap released its grip.

Surprising to John was the size of Briarton. It was made up entirely of modest-sized homes; not a store, gas station, or public service building to be found. The southernmost home sat just below the ridge. Each small plot of farmland looked like it was meant for livestock grazing. John could see many small typical red-and-white barns placed throughout the farmland facing away from the group's position. The humble town spanned not quite a mile north and was just a few blocks wide, forming a rough crescent shape. There was just one road that led out of the town, twisting and turning through the woods out to the northwest, presumably leading back to the highway.

"Cute place," observed Kristen. "I don't think I would have loved having to leave town any time I needed some groceries or gas, though. Seems like a hassle."

John gently lowered himself down from the tree top to the ground, the smell of dried pine needles surrounded the air. Lying on his stomach, propping his elbows up on a flat rock that jutted out of the dirt. He pulled the binoculars from the case in his backpack, placed the strap around the back of his neck, and brought the eye cups up to his face.

His odd movements while getting in place caused his legs to elevate higher than his head.

Betty moved down the tree stopping just above John. Securing herself to the trunk with her tie down strap she lightly placed one of her feet on the small of his back to help keep him from drifting away.

He spun the focus wheel with the forefinger of his good hand – *I'm getting better at using my left hand for stuff* – until the fuzzy edges of the houses below became crisp. He did a quick sweep of the town for anything obviously strange or any movement that might catch his eye.

"Nothing so far," John said out loud. He moved his gaze back to the homes closest to them, this time moving his gaze more deliberately, stopping briefly every few houses to study them. Betty spotted one of the barn's doors flung open.

"Oh, there!" said Betty. John flicked his binoculars to the sudden disturbance in time to see a black garbage bag tossed into the nearby fence, followed by two skinny young men scrambling out of the barn. As quickly as they could they urgently crawled around the doors to get them shut again.

"Something's in the barn," John informed them. "They don't want whatever is in there getting out, that's for sure."

"Maybe they're keeping chickens or some other animals for meat," suggested Jack.

"Yeah, it makes sense," agreed John. The brown-haired boy retrieved the bag and followed the blonde one back to the house. Another middle-aged man's head popped out of the cellar doors at the back of the home to meet them. He was somehow even skinnier than the younger men and sported a white t-shirt, battered blue jeans, and a neon-orange cap turned backward. His face and neck were covered by a short, scruffy beard. *Fred, maybe?* The man began to gesture at the boys and barn erratically, apparently yelling at them in turn. The boys followed the man into the basement, heads lowered like whimpering dogs. The town grew still once again.

"Now what?" asked Jack. Each person took a moment to think.

"We ought to wait and watch a little longer. At least most of the day," John said.

"You guys care if I catch a nap then? I can't help much in the way of scouting after all," Ronney groaned, pointing to his eyes.

"It would probably be good for all of us to try and sleep. Let's take turns watching," Betty said. "Ronney, you,

Jack, and Kristen get some rest. John and I will wake you to switch when the sun is about at its peak. I want at least two on watch to make sure we don't all fall asleep by accident."

"No argument here," agreed Jack as he pulled out his extension cord and found him and Ronney a shady spot to secure them to a trunk. Kristen followed suit. Within minutes of closing their eyes, all three were lightly snoring.

"So, what do you want to talk about?" John asked, lowering the binoculars but keeping his eyes on the houses below.

"I've noticed that people don't seem to bother giving their last names anymore for whatever reason," Betty said thoughtfully. "Our family's name is Felter. Not that it makes a difference, really."

"Ridmore."

"Ah, well it's nice to meet Mr. Ridmore instead of just John," Betty said with a smile. John blushed, feeling a connection to Betty.

"I knew a Felter back in my hometown. Any relation to Beckett?"

"It doesn't ring a bell, no." An awkward silence ensued, neither knowing what to talk about next. John was out of practice when it came to making small talk. To say he was a little rusty was, at best, a massive understatement.

"Do you want to talk about Van? Get anything off your—" Betty started.

"No," John cut her off. It took him a moment to realize how rude he had just been, so he followed up the interruption. "But, I do want to thank you again for being so kind to me. I'm not sure I'm a man deserving of much kindness, and I sure as hell didn't think I'd find any in the apocalypse." Betty laughed lightly.

"What can I say? It's nice to have another person on board who knows how to take care of himself and can contribute to the group. Ever since Ronney lost his vision, Jack's had to do all the heavy lifting." John couldn't help but laugh at the irony in her terrible pun. And he continued to laugh with her for minutes on minutes. They laughed so hard that his stomach began to ache. W*as it the exhaustion? Or was it years of stress and loneliness? He wondered.*

John would never care to try and distinguish, because, in all truth, it was probably an unhealthy dose of each. The pair did not say anything for the rest of their watch, enjoying the view and each other's presence in this small instance of serenity.

Once the shadows were at their smallest, they woke Jack and Kristen to take over the scouting. John drifted over to a nice shaded spot, wrapped the extension cord around his waist, and did his best to lay horizontal on the ground. It was a comfort thing, really, to try and simulate the act of lying down before going to sleep. Regardless of the peace he had been allowed, his usual constant bombardment of disquieting thoughts and what-if scenarios roused his thoughts. He could not block the image of Van pierced to the wall from his mind before drifting into a deep sleep. He did not dream any dreams, for which he was thankful as he was sure they would not have been pleasant ones. They never were anymore.

Chapter 14

John awoke to chatter coming from the rest of his companions. Betty was already up and packing away her own strap. His eyes felt heavy, imploring him to keep them off the clock a little longer. He pushed the temptation aside and began to untie himself. Tired as he was, the nap had worked wonders for improving his alertness and clearing up his brain fog. The sun was still a couple of hours away from retiring behind the trees.

"The only things that's moved all day was those two boys again," Kristen informed John once she noticed him stirring. "They took some chains to that barn but just tossed them in the door. They almost seem scared to go in there."

The five of them deliberated on what their next move should be for a little while. They had only seen one family inhabiting the hamlet. The rest of the homes showed no signs of life.

"If everyone feels comfortable, I think it's time we

made their acquaintance," Betty decided. Each gave their approval in turn. They formed a single fine line as they made their way to the near end of the ridge, wrapping around the right side of the town and down a path leading down the ridge.

"Should just one or two of us go and meet this guy? Keep our group size a secret?" Ronney asked.

"If it's one family here I don't see the harm in all of us going. May make them less likely to try something stupid if they see that we're a bigger group," John said. No one offered a rebuttal. The party kept their file formation as they moved past the first row of houses and over the street. The houses lining each side of the road were still in considerably good shape. Many had short, white picket fences that lined the outer limits of their front yards and hand-crafted mailboxes painted varying colors. It reminded John of a storybook's perfect town where children should be playing and riding their bikes, and you could leave your front door unlocked and your garage open. The desolation gave it a creepy aura that made his skin crawl as if he were being watched at all times. The others must have felt the same. They closed the gaps between each other in their line and nervously kept their heads on a swivel. The road took a bend to the right that led them to the farm homes.

John paused outside of the off-white, one-story house in which they had seen the family. It had a front porch wrapped in broken, white vinyl lattice. His suspicions of being watched were almost undoubtedly confirmed when the man they had seen in the cellar opened the front door and drifted out to the front railing of the porch, followed by the two younger men. After a brief moment of sizing each other up, John offered the first words of introduction.

"Hey there. My name's John. I spoke with Fred on the radio. He told us to come here," John said carefully. The man spat a wad of gunk into the dirt below him.

"Yep, m'aware," the man replied.

"Is that chew you got there? I can't believe you were able to find some," Jack said, unable to control his outburst while nearly salivating at the thought of tobacco.

"We make our own chew 'round here. Damn simple to do, really," the man said proudly.

"Ah, man, what'll you take for some of that?"

The man stared at Jack coldly, giving John the same skin-crawling sensation he had felt earlier while moving through the neighborhood.

"So… are you Fred?" John pried, starting to feel

uneasy.

"That'd be me," Fred answered, spitting out another chunk of goop. "And these're m'boys, Brock and Trevor." He pointed to each in order as he said their names. Brock was the blond one and Trevor had the brown hair. Each had rather large, pointy noses and their eyes seemed a little too close together. Before John could introduce the rest of the group, the distinct, fear-inducing sound of a shotgun racking a shell came from behind them. "Not that you're gonna need to be rememberin' names 'round here," Fred smirked as his eyes shifted focus to the back of them. The five followed his gaze and turned to see another group of what John estimated was fifteen men and women in a near-perfect semicircle, some closer than others. *How were they so damn quiet?!* A few were carrying guns, a mix of handguns, shotguns, and rifles. The rest wielded other weapons, including pipes, bats, and a few large hunting knives. Ronney twisted around within the rope around his waist attaching him to his brother, squinting and craning his head in all directions trying to make sense of the thick jumble of blurs around him.

"S'wrong with that fella?" Fred asked, looking at Jack.

"He's blind," Jack replied quietly. John could tell he

wanted to be angry with the strangers and curse them and ask all sorts of demeaning questions. John looked at the gathering mass, studying their faces; some giddy, some nervous, some downright angry-looking.

"Welp… I'm guessin' ya won't mind him not bein' your burden now." Fred nodded at one of the men nearest Ronney, who shifted his grip on the bat he was holding and struck Ronney in the side of the head with the butt of the handle. Ronney cried out in surprise and agony, curling into a ball as he grasped his head. Jack turned and lunged at the man just as another attacker grabbed the rope around his waist and the collar of his shirt and drove him headfirst into the ground. The rest of them converged on John and the others. Three of the larger men targeted John. As they pushed off from their mailboxes and fence posts he worked his way into a crouch. The closest one to John stretched his arms out in front of him, preparing to tackle John. John responded by going horizontal. He braced his hands against the pavement and kicked upward, hitting the man's chest with the sole of his shoe with as much force as he could. Hot, rotten breath and spit pelted his face as the man's breath left him. The man started gaining altitude as he continued forward, sailing over the top of Fred's house and onward into the air and above the trees, eventually disappearing as a speck against the darkening blue sky. The two attackers that followed grabbed onto John; one on his upper body and one around his legs. John threw his elbow into the back of the man holding his torso. The man grunted, tightening his grip. He fought his way up and started to wrap around John's arms as well. After a few more minutes of struggling, John had no more fight in his tired muscles. He looked around and saw that the rest of his companions had already been subdued and had their hands and feet tied together with rope and other cloth. They left Jack and Ronney attached. Two men and a woman pulled them down the street and disappeared behind a house on the opposite side of the street from Fred's place.

"Where the hell are you taking them?" Betty choked out through her tears and sobs.

"That's not for you to worry 'bout," Fred shot back. He looked at John. "You're a bit of a scrapper, huh? I think we'll break you first." He nodded at the rest of the townsfolk. They pushed John, Betty, and Kristen around the side of the house and toward one of the barns. The man on John's right, not much bigger than Fred, jabbed him in the side just below his ribs with his fist. His pointed sharp knuckles dug hard into his kidney causing John to immediately hunch.

"That's for Seth, you sum' bitch," the man snarled in his ear. John looked up at the barn as they drew closer. They took an unexpected turn and wrapped around the opposite side of the barn, the same barn they had been watching from the ridge. They had affixed sturdy metal brackets to the outside of the door, lying across them was a warped wooden two-by-four securing the door. A woman moved ahead, removed the pieces of wood, and opened the door.

Looking into the dark barn was like looking down the basement stairs knowing something was waiting. What made the hair on his neck stand up was the smell that flushed out of the doorway. It reeked of those same old smells that were burned into John's memory from his normal life: blood and death. Another scent – animal dander, urine, and feces – stung his nose.

Are they keeping animals in here?

They were pushed through the opening and John shut his eyes tight to force his eyes to adjust to the darkness faster. He slowly opened his eyes and looked to his left toward the front door of the barn. There were dim beams of light shining through the cracks of the wall boards from the low, evening sun. A loft circled the back three-quarters of the barn above him. The right side contained stalls while the left, where the light crept in, was empty space save a few floating chains, rusty hand tools, and small, dark clumps of what John assumed to be the scat. Above the barn door was a horizontal wooden beam that had been screwed in between two vertical beams of the barn's wall. In the middle of the horizontal one was a massive eye-bolt screw, larger than any John had ever seen in his local hardware store. There was a chain attached to it that extended up to the loft over the stalls. Upon the clamor of the wave of people filtering through the side door, whatever was attached to the other side of the chain moved, creating more slack in the chain. John squinted, looking for any movement, expecting more trapped people. Two small half-circles, deep orange-gold, came aglow as the creature crept forward and into one of the rays of light.

"What the f–!" John began to exclaim. The pain in his side from the punch made him stop and catch his breath. "A cougar?!" *How? Why? For how long?* John was so stunned and terrified that his mouth could not keep up with all of the questions entering his mind.

"See, here's the thing," the man who had struck him explained, the joy in his voice apparent. "You ain't gettin' out the side door once it's locked. The only way out is them front doors. But, our girl up there, Missy–"

They freaking named it... they're insane.

"–is always lookin' for a snack. Hell, she's snagged two of our own who wasn't careful enough during feedin' time. So, even if ya'lls get untied, you ain't gettin' out. But don't worry, the chain's short enough that she won't get to ya in the stalls."

"That's the reason you're putting us here? To be that thing's meal? Or do you just want prisoners for fun?" A gross, snarling grin grew over the man's face. John, Betty, and Kristen were moved to the stalls where more chains with handcuffs on the ends had been anchored to the concrete floor.

"Oh, ya'll are someone's meal, whether Missy gets you or not..." The man let his words sink in. Along with the others John was violently forced into a stall. Thick rings strung from the back of the stall to a pair of rusted handcuffs. With both hands the man threw him hard at the wall, the second he hit a fist slammed into his rib cage. John tried gasping for air that wouldn't relieve his pain. Only once the restraints had clicked, the cold metal stinging his skin, did John make sense of the man's statement. A new wave of panic washed over him. His fight or flight senses kicked in and he thrashed around his makeshift cell.

"You're sick! You're Demented!" Betty shrieked. Kristen continued to sob hysterically, reaching a point of hyperventilation. They had understood their fate as soon as the words left the man's lips.

"Ah, one more thing," the man said, grabbing a dark rag from one of his pockets. He shoved it in John's mouth, being careful to avoid John's biting teeth. The rag tasted like a mixture of old oil and orange peels. His peers mimicked him and quieted the females in the same fashion. "Ya'll be good and simmer down. You ain't dying right away. Gotta keep the meat fresh as long as possible." The mob backed out of the barn through the side door. The man who had been talking was last to leave, shooting John one more ugly smile before closing the door. The sound of the two-by-fours sliding into place really drove home the debilitating reality of the situation.

John eventually lost the will to fight against his bonds as the streams of sunlight thinned and then faded entirely, enveloping their prison in pitch darkness. Kristen had stopped sobbing, and there had been no noise from Betty yet. The predator above them had moved a handful of times, scraping its steel leash along the floor. Each scratch of its claws had John's heartbeat speeding up. At one point he looked up and made eye contact with the beast. John anxiously waited for it to pounce, although there was not much he was going to be able to do about defending himself in his current state.

It must have tested the limits of its lead and know it can't reach us here.

The thought brought enough comfort to allow him to fall asleep for a little while.

"John!" It was pitch dark when Betty's fierce whisper brought him back to the real world. "John!" His mind stayed half asleep as he forced his eyes open a crack.

"Hmm?" he moaned.

"Are you seriously asleep? How can you possibly sleep right now?" Betty sounded equally astonished and disgusted.

"It's been days since I had more than a couple hours of sleep… What's up?"

"What's up?" Her tone didn't change. "Our whole situation is what's up! How can we get out of this? Where the hell are Jack and Ronney? Are they even alive?"

Chapter 15

The room held the stillness of an empty museum. Undisturbed dust saturated the air. Van's limp body was held fast to the wall by the two bolts while the blob of dark red ooze grew on his side. The outer casing was gelatin in nature; solid, but cold to the touch. His body was in overdrive attempting to heal the sizable intrusion but was unsuccessful in bringing the bleeding to a halt. The noise of shattering glass from the floor below caused him to stir. Van's eyes snapped open and he looked around the room. His first instinct was to move. He was swiftly and painfully reminded of his status as he kicked his feet against the wall he was pinned to. Hysteria began to set in as he looked down to find the alien blood clot growing from his stomach and remembered the events from the night before. With his free hand, he took a swipe at the blood balloon.

"I wouldn't do that if I were you," Weston said as he leaned against the outer wall of the room. "That nasty bubble is all that's keeping you from bleeding out. You cannot die without completing your work." Weston's face looked worse, his head wound had taken on a rotten appearance that gave him a more cadaver feel.

Van made an attempt to reply but his tongue stuck to the roof of his mouth and felt swollen. His thoughts formed slowly and were disorganized. Van could hear the creaks of opening doors echoing throughout the cabin. Was the group still lingering here? Or had the Atomists found him? He wasn't sure which faces he preferred to see right now; the outcome of either may be equally fatal.

"The first step to forgiveness is facing your faults," Weston cupped his hands to his mouth. "We're up here. Hurry! He is bleeding."

"Stop that! I need… to think of how… I'll explain this," Van feebly whispered.

"Listen, boy, I shall spell this out for you. You need to amend what you could not do in Fernwood. You need to take your failed candidate and finish what you started," Weston explained intensely.

"I can't… I tried but I just can't…"

"You do realize that all you have to do to communicate with me is think what you want to say? It does look like you are struggling to live, let alone talk."

A shadow filled the doorway. Jessica had her hood pulled over her head, her blonde hair spilled out the side and around her face like a lion's mane. A glint from her branded gold atom symbol flashed from her forehead. Tense silence held as the two locked eyes with each other. She checked down both sides of the hallway and methodically pulled the door closed to the room. She briefly glanced at the radio equipment before turning her attention back to Van.

"Doesn't she look perfect?" Weston admired as he appeared by her side. "Athletic form with that menacing look that threatens to light you on fire if she willed it."

"He was the only one that brought me meaning." Jessica let go of the door and slowly drifted toward Van. "He was the only one who heard me. After all of the abuse and beatings and hate. He was the only one who cared and you took him away. Your selfish cowardice killed him. You deserve the same fate as him."

The animosity and resentment in her eyes almost grabbed at him. Van raised his hand to put up any defense he could. Jessica gripped his hand and pinned it to the wall and grabbed the bolt bored in his abdomen and twisted, drawing a squeal from Van. Quick to move, Jessica wrapped her other hand around his mouth before the sound could pass his lips.

"You don't even deserve to be given to the sky." Van looked at Weston who stood smiling, greedily awaiting the outcome. "No, no, don't look away." With no warning, she drove her thumb hard into Van's right eye.

"GAHHH!" Van's cry was muffled by her hand still cupping his mouth. "I did it… because Weston told me to!" he wailed into her palm. His own wave of anger and defiance brought him enough strength to thrust his stuck hand forward and off the bolt. He balled up his fists and threw them into Jessica's chest, propelling her backward. His eye remained closed as it started to swell with blood. Exhaustion constrained him once again. Consciousness was attempting to escape his control. *What do I do?*

"Tell her something you shouldn't know," Weston giddily suggested. "Tell her about the final rite. She will have to listen then."

"He told me about the final rite. He still talks to me," Van said slowly.

"I don't believe that, you snake. Why would he give you the glory of giving him the final rite?" she gnashed back.

"You're not doing very well, my boy. Tell her something personal... Oh! I have it. Tell her you know about

Sean." Weston said.

"Weston talks to me. He told me to tell you about Sean," Van relayed. Upon hearing that Mr. Hyde turned into Jekyl and her sneer disappeared.

"That's impossible. No one knows about that. I only talked to Weston about…"

"I told you, he comes to me sometimes and tells me things. He is the only reason I'm still alive. I need your help. I know you're mad and I know you don't want to believe it but we need to get John and send him up." Van tried to open his wounded eye, only seeing fuzzy shapes and colored specks before closing it again. "I need your help pulling out this bolt, first of all." Van nodded down at his hip. A thick glaze of blood coated the shaft.

Jessica looked scared now, almost broken down, like a beaten dog. With wary eyes, she approached Van. *What could have caused such a strong, mean woman to break?* Before his brain could register her motions she ripped the bolt out of his side. He was caught by surprise and let out a yelp. Several faces crept into the doorway.

"You found him!" one man cried. Jessica whipped around, scowling at the newcomers.

"I told you to leave him to me when we found him,"

she replied.

"Move out of the way!" A strong, burly man's voice announced behind the crowd in the hallway. The crowd of robed figures created a path for a short man with gray hair to come through, each with their own stamped mark on their forehead. His small body barely fit in the professor robes that were given to him, had gravity not stopped he would have been tripping over himself.

"Professor Lynn…" Jessica regarded the man with respect, yet a hint of defiance lingered in her tone.

"You don't make the calls here Jessica. When Professor Weston ascended to the sky I became the new regional professor and you will respect that," Lynn said, reading clearly the rage she was attempting to mask in her face and voice. Van watched as Weston paced over to the short man and examined him like a rare insect.

"So, this is an odd turn of events. Never would I have guessed that he would succeed me. I wonder if he still has what it takes to make the final lifting," Weston reflected. Van couldn't help but wonder if anyone else could see Professor Weston.

"No, Van. I know what you are thinking and the answer is no. Only you can finish what you started and I will be here every step of the way." Professor Weston chimed. Lynn pulled his way into the room and over to Van, who was still bleeding from his multiple wounds and getting dizzier by the minute.

"Where did they go?" Lynn asked. His voice was calm and somehow demanded attention.

"They said there's a small town… across the ridgeline. A community… with food and water. I need your help, Professor. I was ready to perform my first rite when I was tricked," Van told him.

"Tricked? You betrayed us for a stranger. Van is the cause of Professor Weston's death. I watched as they split his face open with an axe!" Jessica yelled defensively. "We need to put this card down. He doesn't even deserve to head for the sky."

"I will not repeat myself again, Jessica. I make the calls, not you. Leave before you say something you cannot take back," Lynn instructed. Jessica exhaled her frustration, kicked off of the wall hard toward the door, and left, leaving Lynn and the others watching her closely as she did. "Now, I believe we need to bandage some of your wounds. Melody, will you bring the first aid pack in and help fix him up while we talk?" An older woman pushed through the wall of robes, stopping herself behind Van. "Let's start with the important questions. How many were in the group with you?"

"Five. Two women and three men. The one with a huge cut on his hand is John. He is the one I am meant to issue to Science. When I called for help they caught me… beat me… stabbed me…"

Melody removed several large, padded wads of cloth from a pocket in her robes and pressed them against Van's calf wound, removing any coagulated blood that had dried. She tore open the package of a sterile bandage roll and began wrapping it tightly around his legs to halt the blood flow.

"Melody was a nurse in Boise," Lynn said softly while watching her work. "When we met and taught her about Science, she embraced it wholly. I believe she resembles a rare form of Science that is hard to describe. There is beauty in the art of healing and medical care. Who did you dedicate your first rite to, Melody?"

"Madame Curie, who was a world-renowned chemist, used the revelations of Science and gave us the knowledge of X-rays. During the ugly time of World War One, she mended all of the soldiers. When she conferred with Science she was able to bless not just those of her time, but everyone after her as well," Melody described. She pulled herself around face to face with Van. From another pouch on her person, she drew a small white and red tube with a sharp needle attached to it. Before he could object she planted the needle near the wound he had on his side and pressed the plunger down. Instant relief washed over Van like a warm blanket being pulled over him.

"A little good old fashioned World War Two morphine. Next is a special kind of cloth called "Quikclot." It is a strip of bandaging that stops the wound from bleeding any more. Fair warning, it's going to hurt." She said calmly. Pulling a dull white cloth from its package, she began aggressively packing large amounts of the stuff into Van's side on both ends, hooking her thumb up into his flesh to jam as much material into the space as possible. Van's stomach lurched. He could not feel the sharp pain as expected – *Thank science for morphine, eh?* – it was the thought of someone's fingers pushing into him that made him squirm. The morphine continued to spread its numbing effect, making everything feel dull and exquisite.

"Alright, pay attention now. I must ask some necessary, yet uncomfortable, questions. Did you cause the death of Professor Weston?" Lynn asked. Van's slowed heart rate was calming. The question did not even phase him.

"I was afraid. I was afraid and couldn't go through

with the rite, so I told John whatever he needed to hear to get me away." Van chuckled, now loopy from the medicine. "Once we were out of town, Professor Weston appeared to me. He told me that I had a purpose and could redeem myself. You have to help me, Professor."

"He has lost a lot of blood, Lynn. I believe we need to wait – probably through the night, at minimum, so he can rest. He is no good to us if he bleeds out." Melody chimed as she finished up the bandaging. Van nodded off as the morphine drug took full effect. Lynn let out an annoyed sigh.

"I think you might have overdone the dope. How long will it be 'til he wakes up?"

"I couldn't tell you. Using morphine on someone so young isn't recommended. We'll have to monitor him through the night," Melody said as she headed out the door.

Van came to in an unfamiliar room. The walls were decorated with all forms of dead, stuffed animal carcasses. A white and black bird held its wings out as if mid-flight, flaunting its massive wingspan. A deep, steady throb radiated in his head accompanied by a drumming pang in each of his wound sites. Dried blood tickled and itched his cheek. He pulled on his hand to scratch his face and found it was stuck. The room was near dark with all but a reflection of light coming in through the window. His body was held secure by something he could not see, allowing only his head and arms to move freely. Shuffling his shoulders side to side he felt as if his body was tightly secured around his neck and chest. Like a flashing warning sign in his mind, an inclination that he was not safe induced panic.

"Help. Weston? Anyone?" he cried. He ran his hands up and down a cool, slick material, trying to discern what held him, creating a wisping noise as his fingernails brushed up and down. His head felt fuzzy and his thoughts incoherent.

That medicine is still wearing off...

He wasn't sure how long he had been out, but his mouth was as dry as sandpaper. As the panic grew stronger he started pushing and punching at the plastic material. His body started to flush with sweat. "What is this? Please, anyone!" A door behind him creaked open and he heard someone breathing as they came closer to him. Fingers wrapped around his arm in a firm grip. "Please, don't hurt me." Van cried.

"Settle down. I'm trying to help you." Melody's voice spoke softly in reply. "I'm just making an adjustment." A small flash of sparks, like a child's sparkler, flashed across the room. Melody struck a flint and steel rod against a dried piece of wood. A meager flame rested on dried wood but rapidly expanded and wrapped around the log. The darkness of the room faded, revealing Melody. She looked rather relaxed. This did nothing to calm Van as he continued to writhe. The pain from his injuries grew with each jerking motion but he did not care.

"You need to look at me," Melody said as she pulled her face close to his. Her eyes looked like black pits in the light of the fire. She pulled on a string near the top of his head, along with a few others across his body that he had not noticed yet. The hood that was tightly secured around his head loosened and his hands were free to pull up to his face. In a surprising gesture, Van wrapped his arms around Melody. The firelight gave the trophy room a sinister look as the flames licked the wood and gently illuminated the stuffed mounts.

"Thank you. I thought I was going to die. I feel like that a lot lately…" Van said tearfully. He felt her body lurch and heave.

Is she laughing?

"Have you never been in a sleeping bag before?" Melody asked, clearly humored. Van looked down and saw that he was wrapped in a dark blue plastic sleeping bag. His face became hot with embarrassment and he released his embrace even faster than he clung to her.

"You passed out from the blood loss so we put you in a sleeping bag to keep you warm. We have been checking up on you every couple of hours to make sure you haven't died. Jessica insisted that we needed to just send you to Science, but Lynn is keeping her in check. For now… After you passed out, Professor Lynn and her went into a different room and argued for hours. I think you should keep your distance from her." Melody pulled out a needle similar to the one from before, accompanied by two small white pills. "I need to give you another dose or the pain will soon become unbearable. These are antibiotics. They are the only two I have so I hope you are worth saving." She popped the pills into his mouth and then pushed the needle into his arm. He felt the pinch of the jab, then the dulling sensation as the medication slowly took effect. Van's lips contorted as he began to drift off again.

"Hello, Melody." A disturbing mixture of Van's and

Weston's voices echoed from his mouth. “I told you all, I will show you the way. This boy will be a prophet in the world. Science has deemed it so.”

Chapter 16

Boise Airport (BOA) - The day of The Lifting.

Jacob sat in an off-white plastic folding chair at terminal A11 waiting for his connecting flight to LAX. Jacob was only sixteen but he had more real-world experience than most adults, or so he thought. Pulling his backpack to his lap, he searched for anything to pass the time. Before he left home he had tried to give himself a large array of things to occupy his mind during the mind-numbing wait of the layover. His flight itinerary said that he was going to be stuck there for two and a half hours.

It's stupid airlines can get away with that, he thought to himself as he rummaged. *It can't be that hard to organize some planes.*

He was reminded, as he looked at the clock, that his flight wasn't set to show up for another hour and a half. A middle-aged man sat two seats down from him snoring, a small bottle of liquor in his drink holder. A grotesque odor radiated from him, causing everyone to give him a wide berth. He grabbed a large textbook from the bag for his physics class.

Like I'll ever use this in the real world.

Setting the musky book to the side, he continued to rustle through his pack to find his Gameboy that was buried deep at the bottom. He turned it over in his hands, checking to see what game he was dedicating the next few hours to. He had left a copy of The Legend of Zelda seated in the back of the handheld. His mother had bought him a plethora of these games. He always hated how she would not call or text, but felt as though she could fill in the gaps with stuff.

I would trade all the video games to be able to hear my mom ask me how my day was.

Jacob inspected the crack that ran from one corner of the handheld device to the other. The gruesome memory of the beating he had received from his father when he caught him with the games the first time briefly shoved its way to the front of his memory. His dad had ripped the device out of his hands while plastered one afternoon and threw it down the stairs. He always got so mad whenever Jacob brought up his mother.

Jacob ran his finger up the side of the Gameboy

turning it on. Upon seeing the red light glowing on the side telling him the battery was low he flipped the switch back down. He began his search for some new batteries from the shops lining the terminal. He entered a bodega shop and made his way past several pantries and businessmen in suit coats who were all actively arguing over their cell phones. Sometimes he felt like that kid from the movie, "Home Alone" when he was in the airport. When he would wander around the terminals looking for food people would give him funny looks. He knew they were wondering where his parents were, either ignoring or being ignorant of the pin that the airport had given him and clipped to his shirt that told the airport workers that he was a minor flying alone. He walked along a wall of books that were labeled best sellers or good reads. Several rows were dedicated to a self-help book sponsored by a celebrity. Just past the books Jacob found what he was looking for in between the single serving cold medicine and the nausea pills.

Thirteen bucks for four batteries? These better last until I die.

He brought the item up to the counter. A dark-skinned man sat behind the counter with an apathetic look on his face that screamed, "Take what you want, I don't get paid enough to try and stop you." The man rang up his purchase and lazily dropped the package in a thin plastic bag and handed it over the counter. Jacob thanked him and left the little store. Returning to his seat where he left his backpack, he pulled the back cover off of the electronic, replaced the batteries and flipped the switch once again. Two *dings* sounded off as the Game Boy symbol flashed across the screen.

Jacob spent the better part of the next hour staring at the pixelated world in the palm of his hand.

How much easier it would be to live in a video game.

All concentration was broken by an announcement over the speaker system by a soft female voice.

"Attention, all passengers: Flight 5687 to LAX has been delayed. Again, Flight 5687 to LAX has been delayed. Please review the updated departure time on the nearest schedule board."

Jacob checked the flight number on his ticket. *Of course... Now what?* He put his game back in his pack and moved over to the windows to watch the planes take off and land. A banana-yellow plane with "Spirit" on the side was landing just outside the view from the terminal windows. He watched as the front end of the plane tilted up as the front wheels touched the ground. A loud screeching sound could be heard as the brakes were activated.

The terminal Jacob sat in faced a separate loading terminal where a white airplane with a thin blue stripe down its side pulled in across and started to rotate clockwise to park. His phone vibrated in his pocket. A revolting sensation welled within him, as if his stomach had suddenly decided it wanted to eject its most recent meal.

Ah... bathroom. Now.

The sickening feeling rose from his stomach to the top of his shoulders as his feet left the floor. He snatched a side rail in a death grip, fighting the growing urge to vomit. He willed his legs to return to the ground yet they didn't respond. Panic and fear disabled his ability to think, then he started to involuntarily shake as shock started to set in.

Shattering glass and crumbling walls made Jacob snap his head up to see the plane that had been turning now digging a path through the opposite terminal. Its left turbine, which was still spinning, pushed through the terminal windows with ease and continued its rotation. Jacob could not pull his eyes away as shreds of seats, suitcases, and red mist spewed out of the back of the wing, accompanied by a deafening grinding sound. Though the terminal was distant, he could distinctly make out the shape of a person holding onto a load-bearing pole in the turbine's path of destruction.

A pop, then an explosion, rattled the windows as the rogue plane finally stopped. The turbine had finally struck something hard enough to break it. Pieces of the plane hit the glass in front of Jacob like steel hail.

It wasn't until the plane had finally stopped that Jacob noticed the roar that had erupted throughout the airport behind him. A mass of people, moments ago waiting for their flights, were now thrown into a hellish nightmare. He looked over his shoulder and a young lady, no more than twenty-one years old, spinning slowly, frantically trying to grab at anything within distance. Jacob awkwardly pushed off of the handrail, acting on a sudden urge to do something heroic like Link. He found himself flying at the woman much faster than he had meant to, stopping himself on her shoulders with a thud.

"Don't touch me!" she yelled. Terrified, she tried to pull herself up onto his shoulders, akin to how one would do if they were drowning.

"Calm down, lady. Stop moving!" Jacob shouted back. The woman held his shirt with one hand and aggressively gripped the right side of his head with the other. It felt like a hawk's talons were burrowing into his skull. He reached up blindly and found her face. He swatted at her face to try and get her to let go but not hurt her back.

The hair–pulling continued and he finally could not take it anymore. He started throwing his thumb around, eventually landing its mark. He jammed it into her eye, causing her to let go of him to bring her hands to her face. In that instant, Jacob pushed her roughly, causing both of them to float in opposite directions from the other.

Jacob drifted past the snoring man who now resided four feet above his seat and was, to his bewilderment, still very much asleep. Jacob's body collided with the airport window. He turned just in time to see a multitude of planes trying to land on the runway. A 747 slammed onto the tarmac, creating a fiery explosion. He saw the orange flash just before the shock wave from the explosion hit. There was something off about the fireball that now engulfed the plane in that it didn't simply pillar upwards as expected. A series of miniature, bubble-like explosions crawled up the plane's cabin as the fire caught up with the airliner's fuel line. The blast hit the terminal window. The rest of the intact windows simultaneously burst inward. The pressure caused a vacuum effect, drawing everyone and everything out the other side of the terminal and across the tarmac.

One Year Later.

Jacob held two large bottles in his hands. The bottle in his right hand had been filled with several servings of dirty water. He studied the small pieces of dirt and debris as each swirled uniquely within the liquid. In his left hand was a homemade water filter of his own design. He had started by cramming in layers of dirt, rocks, and loose grass. For each layer of dirt, he had put a layer of chunks of burnt wood. At the mouthpiece was a thin piece of a t-shirt wrapped over the opening.

Pretty sure I saw Bear Grills doing this… If I pour the dirty water into here it should clean the water.

Once the water had worked its way through the contraption he tipped the bottle down and brought it to his mouth, half expecting the water to come pouring out. He added a little pressure by squeezing the sides of the bottle, and a thick, cylindrical shape of water started to form around the mouthpiece as it made contact with the soil. The dirt was absorbing the water but wasn't directing it to the other side. He pulled out a roll of duct tape from his pack and with two swift wraps conjoined the two bottles with a healthy amount of the adhesive. Squeezing the bottle with the water again, a clear liquid built up at the mouthpiece of the other bottle on the outside of the cloth. With a little excitement, Jacob applied more pressure on the water bottle and was rewarded with a baseball-size ball of water, crystal clear and ready for consumption.

A small grove of aspen trees surrounded him, giving a pleasant abundance of shade. He watched as a line of ants walked up the side of the tree nearest him.

How is it that they can still survive on anything, but I have to filter my water?

Jacob remembered when he learned the hard way that he had to clean his water before drinking it. He had spent most of the following week in excruciating pain, a reminder that would last his lifetime. The audible groaning of his stomach brought his attention back to the ache of hunger surging within him. He hadn't eaten more than a few scraps in at least two weeks. His ribs had begun protruding. The pain radiated while gas forced its way through his body. It took a few minutes to subside, allowing him to focus his thoughts again. He pursed his lips and with forced restraint started to sip at the water. On just his second swallow he noticed that his stomach felt full already.

Has my stomach really shrunk that much?

He forced the rest of the water down then tucked the two bottles away in a small blue backpack and pulled it to his back. There was a crack of a branch above him somewhere and with no hesitation he bounced over to the nearest aspen, huddling down and scanning the trees.

"I didn't mean to scare you," a voice called out from the top of the trees. Jacob looked about, trying to pinpoint where the sound was coming from. "I just needed to know that you weren't going to try and hurt me before I introduced myself. Can I have your word that I'm safe to come down?"

Jacob tried to find anything he could use for defense.

A stick, maybe, or a rock... Anything.

He hadn't seen anyone for months and had thoroughly convinced himself that he was the only human alive.

"I guess... But I'm not moving from where I am," Jacob called out. A plump man emerged from the green leaves, gracefully descending like he pictured an angel would. The light reflected around the man's head, causing him to have to shield his eyes.

"You look a little worse for wear. My friends call me Professor Weston. Can I interest you in some lunch?" Weston asked. He finally settled onto the ground among the overgrown dead grass.

Professor?

Weston reached into a strap backpack he had on his back, producing a sandwich covered in plastic wrap. Jacobs' mouth salivated at the thought of eating such a rare delicacy. Weston unwrapped the plastic to reveal the most picture-perfect sandwich he had ever seen. Two large cuts of bread with blackened edges, a generous section of deli meats, an impressive slice of tomato, and overflowing leafy greens on top.

"They always pack me too much to eat. Worrying about me all the time… You would think I was the Pope or something," Weston joked. He sloppily pulled the sandwich apart, "I cut your choice. My brother and I used to have that rule so we weren't unfair with the portions." He held out two mostly even pieces of sandwich. "So, go ahead and take whichever you'd like." Jacob hesitated, sure that there were others waiting to move in and take everything he had. As if to nudge him along in his decision, his stomach piped up again with an awful rumble. He pulled himself from the cover of the tree and eyed Professor Weston before cautiously pushing toward him. Either a hand or a foot made contact with the ground or a tree at all times in case he needed to react quickly. He grabbed a fist full of dead weeds to halt his motion a couple of feet from the Professor.

Weston reached out and handed Jacob the bigger half of the sandwich and began eating. Jacob had been on his own for a while now. His independence had started ever since he realized he could not rely on either of his parents to totally have his back. He was just the chest piece in their back and forth game of trying to spite each other. He wanted to not worry so much about the grownup things; to be able to rely on someone to teach him what he was supposed to do. The attentiveness from this stranger had made him feel more connected to anyone that he could remember.

"Where did you come from?" he inquired.

Weston pointed through toward the other side of the grove. "Past that ridge is a little town where my friends and I live. Our beliefs are a little unconventional… but you are more than welcome to join us. You don't have to be alone." He popped the last bite of his sandwich into his mouth. "What should I call you?"

Do I tell him my real name? The name that holds all of my resentment and anger. I hate Jacob. I hate that he couldn't make his mom and dad love each other. I hate that no matter how hard he tries he would only be the forgotten burden of a failed relationship. I have a chance at a total fresh start.

"My name is Van."

Chapter 17

"You don't get it," Melody said with a quiver in her voice.

"What I don't get is why you are so worked up about this," Lynn chimed back. The room held a stillness that played tricks on the mind. The two had removed themselves from the rest of the group and hidden themselves in a small office. Melody reached above her, grabbed a small book out of the air and threw it at Lynn.

"Back in Fernwood I spent a lot of time with Weston. He appreciated my work and my expertise. If we weren't held by the restraints of Science I feel like we could have made something more together. I know his voice and that boy in there couldn't have faked it."

Lynn rolled his eyes. "What, you think he is possessing the young man? Is that truly what you think? He has come back to rekindle some lost love? Those are the kind of superstitious comments that get people talking about you."

"You can't argue that what we do as a whole isn't superstitious. I mean, we make sacrifices to a deity like all of the other religions we read about in books. Explain to me how sending people to Science is any more absurd than Weston talking to us?"

"I will tell you but it is a knowledge that isn't given lightly." Lynn pushed to the door and locked it, ensuring their privacy.

"Has anyone told you why sending people to Science is what it takes to save the world?" Lynn asked solemnly. Melody shook her head.

"I remember performing my first rite. Working in the ER and the labs gave me a resolute understanding that everything I did was to save lives. In my first week I felt like I couldn't get ahead. A young girl had come in; she had laceration as long as my arm across her back. I assisted in stitching her up and found that I couldn't leave her side until she was better. The chaos that revolved around me that day gave me cause to check on other people or to help other patients but I just couldn't. It was hard for a person like me to go from dedicating my time and energy to saving lives to ending them. I felt like a murderer." Melody held a distant stare.

Lynn pulled himself to Melody close enough that she could smell his breath. “We are told that the more people we send to Science the more in favor we are. I believe that is a blanket answer for those who just need something to believe in. I know there is more to that. If we are to repair the atmosphere we need to give it a jump start with several types of gasses. The amount of things that a person provides in the thin area helps build up the border between us and space.”

“But with that logic we could start cutting down trees and send them up instead. Then we wouldn’t have to live with all of the guilt.” Melody pulled away from him and sat gazing out the windows at the blackness of the forest.

“Yes, but we do not act wholly on logic alone. If we did, Science wouldn’t exist and all of this would be completely random; but it's not. When you went through your medical schooling you had the unique opportunity to literally read the words Science placed before us. He created volumes of books to help us better ourselves; to better our understanding of its will. This is just our trail to walk.” He took a pause to judge her reaction to his words. “How is a diamond made? Pressure. And that is what this is. Moving forward is never easy or comfortable. But the end result is always worth the struggle."

Melody looked at Lynn with uncertainty, trying to read his face. "That doesn't change the real question. What do we do with Van? If what you say is true, and it isn't really Weston, then he is crazy. If you're wrong then we would be stifling the words of a fellow Professor. Are you so sure that it is an impossibility that he would be able to speak through Van? Maybe this is how the Professors of old received their revelations?"

A soft knock rattled the door. "The Interim is about to begin on the radio if you choose to join us?" A man's voice said through the door.

"We cannot be late to hear the words of the master," Lynn said excitedly as he went for the door. "I think we keep Van close and make choices when we have more information." Lynn unlocked the door and left the room.

The group of Atomists joined in the study where a black hand-crank radio had been carefully positioned in the center of the room. In preparation to hear the Doctrinate speak they had placed items around the radio to represent the most basic elements, including two rings of water around the radio. Large rocks were periodically placed in the water rings, representing Earth. A ring of dirt, shaped like a flat disk, hovered under the radio display with small teacup candles decorating the outer ring. The whole piece looked artistic and deliberate. Lynn moved to the center of the room as the congregation eagerly awaited the words of the Doctrinate.

"I know we are all excited to hear from the Doctrinate. I want to thank Jessica for putting our altar together for this joyous occasion. This was fashioned after one of the most basic elements: carbon. Having said that, I will turn on the radio so that we may all bask in Science's revelations." Being cautious not to bump anything from the display, he reached through to the on switch and brought the radio to life.

"Hello and welcome to all those listening out there. As a means of announcement, I would like to give my findings and results on the project "Mass Exodus." As a brief recap, we used the small town of Abbottsville, a town just outside of Rexburg, Idaho. The hypothesis read: if one person being given to Science is to help restore gravity, then a large amount of people given at the same time will restore gravity in a large area. It took many districts' assistance to gather people from their houses in a safe manner. The total number of participants for the massive rite was one hundred-thirty seven people. It was recorded that the time the group was predicted to enter the troposphere, gravity was restored in the town for over a week. Several of our fellow Atomists were severely injured after falling from heights not sustainable under normal circumstances." The voice paused and the shuffling of a paper could be heard. "It was stated that the change in gravity was strong and retained an irregular shape. The return happened with such violence that a large amount of debris, such as cars and other large objects, caused a great deal of noise and damage to surrounding buildings. An adverse effect was also noted to have occurred to the followers of Science. Due to the loss of skeletal muscle mass over the course of two years they found it quite difficult to walk. They reported feeling as if they had forgotten how to maintain balance.

"Science has blessed us with more knowledge and we will take the findings and move forward with new hypotheses. Your efforts are not going unseen. For each person given, a small increment of gravity is sure to be restored. Thank you all for your assistance in showing Science that we acknowledge its power and love. We will now hear from several speakers that have prepared doctrinal dissertations relating to quantum gravity."

A whisper came from a man just in front of Melody, "Quantum gravity? Sounds made up…" The woman next to him shushed him sharply.

After about an hour of hearing from different speakers, the final speaker finished on the topic of black holes, spending a great deal of time talking about one particular black hole that was closest to the earth. The speaker stated that it was roughly 1,500 light years away, and that only thanks to the love of Science, and the work of its followers, it did not consume the Earth.

Professor Lynn slowly paced across the floor to the center of the room. "Now, we have to discuss our next steps. I see two options before us: the first is for us to return to Fernwood City and continue the good work that Science has charged us with. After hearing Doctrinate Houston talk of "Mass Exodus" I feel that we have an opportunity. If I am correct we have a town just a stone's throw away. Is that correct Van?" Lynn asked, looking in Van's direction.

"A man on the radio said that he and his family lived in a town on the other side of the ridge," Van confirmed, loud enough for the group to hear.

"You see, my colleagues, we have a chance to perform a side-by-side study that the Doctrinate himself witnessed and testified of the success. As a bonus, I am also told that our young Van has a need to take one of these people to accomplish his first rite. Like everything we do, it is left up to logic and reason. But, may I be the first to cast my vote. I believe we have both the man power and fire power to safely recreate their hypothesis, albeit on a smaller scale." Looking around the room, he found that all but two were nodding their heads in agreement. Both Melody and Jessica seemed like they wished to argue but knew that they were already out-voted.

"Unless anyone has any objection we will leave at first light tomorrow morning."

Flexing its retractable claws, the two-hundred pound mountain lion paced the upper floor of the loft. Its soft, brown fur gave a glimmer as stray sunlight filtered in through the cracks of the barn. Its black-tipped tail playfully twitched from side to side as it watched John with curious eyes. It stood up, facing the potential meal, and headed to the edge of the loft. Slowly dragging its fierce, muscular body off the edge of the loft, the cunning carnivore used its claws to stay grounded to the old wood. It walked along the underside of the loft and stopped just shy of the two large sliding doors, all the while its tail continued dancing to and fro.

John inspected the shackles that were biting into his wrists. Three press lines were bruised in a crossing pattern on his skin where the rusted cuffs had settled while he slept. The metal rubbed and scratched in the most irritating of ways, never offering even the slightest comfort regardless of what way he positioned himself. They seemed to press inward, cutting off circulation enough to make it impossible for John to ignore. A pair of voices caused John to jerk his head up. A dirty, rectangular window, halved by the stall separating him and Betty, allowed him to get a glimpse of the woods just outside the barn. John peaked out to see two men pass by. A flash of sunlight glinted off a familiar item strapped to one's back.

"My axe!" John blurted out, pulling Kristen and Betty's attention from their daydreaming. Betty pulled herself over to the dividing stall to where John could see her face from the bridge of her nose to the top of her head.

"What are you talking about, John?" she asked.

"Several days ago, Van and I were making our way down the highway and ran into a trader. He made a comment about my axe and how he knows people who would be willing to pay for it. I ended up trading the thing for food and clothes. He kept trying to get us to take some jerky, too…" John had to force his thoughts away from the uneasy realization he was coming to. He followed the shadows of the two men through the cracks in the wall as they made their way around the side of the barn. A second of hesitation as they stopped in front of the front doors.

John glanced upward at the cat, understanding now what it was doing; like a spider in its web waiting for a bug to land, the mountain lion hunched above the door frame. A dragging sound came from the door as the wood restraints were being removed. The lion's tail swayed left and right in excitement. The door cracked open. A head with dark brown hair started to enter the threshold of the door frame. The lion raised its right paw up and slapped down with its claws extended. The man looked up just in time to see the claws rake across his cheek. Howling, he grabbed for his face that was welling up fast with fresh blood. The lion stretched as hard as it could, extending its body out to a surprising length, but a tight shackle restrained it from going further.

"Oh stop your screaming. It ain't that bad. Go back to the house and have Fred fix you up." The second man angrily slammed the door shut and fastened the wood brace. John watched as his shadow made its way around the wall to the smaller man door on the other side. He cautiously moved his way into the barn. He had an old grocery sack in his hand. He was young and built like an ox; his muscle definition was prominent against his dirty yellow shirt. John noticed he was missing several fingers. An ugly scar, which John could only assume was given to him by the town pet, stretched from one side of his face to the other and his left eye was gray and cloudy. The mountain lion laid still on the ceiling, licking the blood from its paw, all the while keeping an eye on the stranger.

"We suspected that y'all were hungry and we did promise you a meal," the man said with a snicker. He rotated his body to be horizontal with the floor and scaled the stalls one at a time until he reached Kristen's. Spinning his body to face her, he reached inside the bag and produced a sandwich. He held it out in front of him in offering. The bread looked old but not molded. However, the meat patty had a pale-pink coloring that did not resemble any meat that she had ever come across.

"I'm not eating that," she said frankly, staring at the sandwich. She had spent the greater part of the night crying, her eyes bloodshot. "Where are my brothers?"

The man grew a sly smile. "You could say they are still providing for the family." The man grabbed the bread and meat and threw it in the direction of the lion. Kristen's body lurched and she vomited. “Oh, come now, let me give you a hand.” With a sneer he reached in the bag and pulled out a severed hand. The man laughed loudly at his crude joke. “What? Ya don’t think I’m funny? Well, if that’s how it’s gonna be then y’all waste away.” He grabbed several pieces of meat out of the bag and threw it in the mountain lion's direction, who snatched it almost gleefully with a snap of its teeth.

In the distance the sound of a rifle being fired caused the laughing to cease.

A man’s panicked scream cut through the following silence: “I’m shot! Guys—” A second boom echoed through the town, silencing the dying man. A raspy, shallow cough and gurgle, then nothing.

Then, mayhem.

Chapter 18

The cusp of the forest, typically dark and mystical, erupted with the glow and noise of gunfire. From the distance they were shooting, it sounded like hail slapping the soft dirt. John could hear men and women screaming, in fear and rage, as the barrage of bullets rained down on them.

"Get inside!" Fred was heard directing. Kristen, Betty, and John sat in their stalls, praying that a stray round didn't find them through the barn walls. The mountain lion, tense from the sudden affray, had pulled herself to the top of the door once more. The soft glow of the mountain lion's eyes penetrated, giving off the most sinister intentions. It had the right idea. They were all fish in a barrel as the situation quickly escalated into chaos. Anyone could lose themselves in the warzone and stumble through that door, providing an easy catch for the predator.

Like the silencing of spring rainfall, the shooting stopped. Only the thudding of John's heart filled his ears now. After what he thought to be about five minutes he heard the distinct sound of the side door opening. Though the barn was dark he made out the shape of Fred who was carefully pulling himself through, paying mind to the lion on the other side.

"This is yer doin', isn't it?" Fred said, stopping himself in front of John's stall. "I bet this whole thing was a ruse. So what was it you was lookin' for, huh? Food? Guns? What?!" Fred screamed. "No, no… I bet you was a scoutin' party, or maybe a distraction to get our guard down."

"You have only one option," John said coldly. "They will keep gunning you down unless you let us go. They'll decimate your entire messed up, inbred town."

"Ya don't understand the pressures a leader faces when the world's fallin' apart," Fred said as he checked over his shoulder for the cougar. As turned his body, John's axe, strung along his back and fitted into a modified rifle holster of dark brown leather and yellow stitching, waved at John almost mockingly. John couldn't tell if it was hunger, adrenaline, or the fact that he had almost died more times in the last couple of weeks than he cared to think about; the axe had an almost drawing glow to it, craving to be returned to him.

Another volley of bullets went off, causing both John and Fred to flinch. Slow and methodical, Missy crept out of the shadows. John seized the opportunity and grabbed hold of the axe with both hands. Fred lost his balance and his feet kicked up toward the ceiling. John planted both of his feet on either side of his shoulders and launched him to the other side of the barn. Fred slammed against the double door feet first. The fly was in the web and the spider was ready to pounce. With a quick, well-timed strike, Missy's paw struck down, the pads of her paw resting on the top of Fred's head. The cat flexed its retractable claws like fish hooks on the skin. Fred felt a sharp pinch on his head and realized where he was. Doomed. He reached up in a feeble attempt to push her away as Missy pulled upward, bringing his head and neck into view for the rest in the barn. Fred's scalp was palmed like a basketball. The cougar clamped its teeth down on his neck, rattling him side to side like a weightless puppet. Panic welled in Fred's eyes as he attempted to scream out, but the only thing to leave his mouth was an eruption of blood. As quick as it had started, Fred's life ended with the lion hopping back up to the loft in a single bound, prize in jaw.

John looked the axe over as if he had been reunited

with a friend. He felt remorse for abandoning the piece for such a cheap price. The axe represented the last of who he was before the world fell apart; a symbol that life used to be simpler and pleasant.

"John, are you alright?" Betty asked from the next stall over.

"I'm fine. I think I may have found a way out for us," John said, his eyes still locked on the scratched-up silver blade.

"Do you hear that?" Kristen asked. John refocused his attention and noticed that the firing had stopped. He went over to the window to get a peak as to what was happening. He saw the shadows of multiple bodies drifting through the air; lifeless, with intricate blood splatter strewn between. Each body appeared to have red roots growing from their gunshot wounds as trickles of blood leaked out.

"It has to be Van and the cult. They are probably coming for us. Or, at least me," John said through his teeth. "I'm sorry. I put your whole family in danger."

"Not the time, John. But you know, there will be a reckoning," Betty whispered.

John lifted the axe with both hands. He aimed at the most rusted part of the chains and swung down, creating a spray of sparks. The axe recoiled to the side, slapping the stall wall from the rebound force. Pulling the axe up for another go, he stopped before his next swing. Thudding footsteps coming from the roof. A flash of several robed figures upwards as they continued their assault on the town.

"They's up on the roofs!" a woman yelled from across the street. More gunshots went up and John heard glass breaking. He hastily started hacking at the chain with the fury of a desperate man. *If they catch us we will still be dead. We can't side with anyone here.* Finally, a rusted link gave way to the pummeling and John yanked the chain through the cuffs on his wrists. He sprung over to the next stall and, as quickly as he could, broke Kristen and Betty free. A much louder thud thundered on the roof. John looked up waiting for any movement, half expecting someone to come crashing through the ceiling. A shadow obscured the cracks in the wood panels.

"Door in the corner. Now!" John whispered. They moved through the barn to the door, catching pieces of old hay and dirt in their hair. John peered out of the door, axe raised defensively. Directly outside of the door faced a large open field. Nothing moved, no fuss to be heard. To John's left was the homestead for the farm. Its once white-washed walls were now a peeling mess. The roof looked like it had seen better days. Several holes were punched through. Most of the shingles had been blown off and would provide no protection to its occupants were it possible to rain anymore.

"Let's move to the house," John told them.

"What about Jack and Ronney? We can't just leave without them," Kristen insisted.

"We aren't leaving them. We need to get out of the line of fire. Most likely they are in one of those houses," John said pointing at the row of homes. "Right now we need to find a place to hide while everyone is distracted."

John pushed the door wide open and started towards the house in a crawl along the ground, staying as low as he could manage and digging his fingers into the hard dirt to stay grounded. The sound of a single round being shot was almost deafening, the bullet striking the ground just ahead of him and kicking up a flurry of dust and dead grass. He whipped his head around to see Van on the barn roof, steadied in a sitting position with his elbows on his knees to balance the rifle he wielded. "Shit!" He pushed against the ground hard, launching himself toward the homestead. A second round went off, hitting the door to the home. *Thank goodness he's a terrible shot.* Nearing the home, another round went off. This time it came from the upper window of the farm home. The bullet hit several feet from Van on the barn roof. John noticed an opening of a crawl space leading under the home. The crisscrossed paneling appeared to have been broken a long time ago and it stood as a stage of neglect. The three quickly scrambled through the opening.

"Git the one on the barn. Where the hell'd they all come from?" A man yelled out from above them. They rotated to face upward and used the beams of wood to drag their way across the floor to the other side of the house. Using the gunfire to cover the noise, John rammed his axe hard against the subfloor cover, creating a hole just wide enough for them to squeeze in. John poked his head out of the hole and laid eyes on the next house. The door stood wide open. Looking to either side, he determined that the only cover he had was going through the homes until they made it back to the vast, thick forest.

"We have to head to the next house. It's our best bet for cover, John hissed to the others. "We need to move all together or we might be seen. Stay as close to me as you possibly can."

John held his finger up to his mouth motioning to be quiet. He made a countdown from five with his fingers before making his move. One after another they drifted through the property and over a run-down picket fence. Nearing the front door, John pressed against the ground, once again getting the right angle to send him right to the door's threshold. A head peered around the corner and immediately withdrew upon seeing the new visitors. John had no time to react before the wooden club crunched over the top of his head. John's vision blurred as he tried to focus his vision on the new threat. Betty and Kristen lunged at the blond attacker, scratching at his hands and trying to wrestle the wood away. John's senses were screaming at him to help. Willing his arms and legs to move was no simple task at the moment, however. He felt around his head where the man had hit. It was tender and shot pain through his skull, his hair slick with blood. The man freed one of his hands and cocked back to have a go at Betty. A loud pop mixed with the shattering of a board that had been nailed over the front room window. The man's head kicked back as a slug entered the bottom of his chin. The bullet barely had enough momentum to exit the back of the head, accompanied by other pieces of him.

"Thanks… keep moving," John grunted, still somewhat disoriented. As quickly as they could they gravitated through the first floor and out the back door. The next three homes they navigated more warily, electing to move around the outside of each one. He had not heard any gunshots in a while. Fearing the worst was yet to come, they upped their pace going next house. The farm they came to face seemed to be the biggest they had yet seen in the town. John noticed the mailbox had "Fred Studebaker" crudely painted on its side.

"We should be safe here for a minute. I doubt that narcissist has any family." Kristen said softly.

"No willing family, at least," Betty said. Kristen shuddered at the suggestion. Slowly, they entered the home through a side window, moving into the living room area. The room was once furnished with a light green floral couch with dark stains on the cushions. Equally green were the curtains with gold leaves pressed into the fabric that decorated the windows. John could see that the cloth had been nailed into the wall near the bottom to hold it in place. Any passerby from the outside would think that their house still held a gravitational pull. The ever-lingering dust that seemed to inhabit any indoor space these days held the air.

A group of voices began shouting across the road. John pushed against the wall to flatten himself on the floor. Using the old red carpet as a handle, he scaled along the floor toward the window and peeked his head up to see out. Two robed individuals sat above the house directly across from him, holding old, light-brown hunting rifles. A third sat in the doorway, barking orders and pointing a sleek, attachment-heavy, matte-black gun that looked like it was made for an action movie. They backed up several feet, using the porch post as a counterweight.

"Is there anyone else in there?" It was a female voice.

A middle-aged man and a teary-eyed child both shook their heads in response as they moved slowly out of the front door. "I'm coming in," the woman warned. "Anyone who doesn't want to die better speak up now!" The robed lady held, hyper focused on the door and waiting for a response. "So be it!" She raised the firearm to a low-ready position and made her way inside. Two deafening shotgun blasts shattered the silence that followed, each one causing John to flinch. The robed figure re-emerged from the doorway. She yelled something that John's ringing ears did not pick up and pointed inside. The two threw their guns over their shoulders and entered the home.

"John… John! We need to go," Betty cried to him as he watched the two robed men come out of the home, each with a body in tow. John turned to see that Kristen was gone.

"Where did she go?" John whispered as they left the living room. Down a narrow hall and through a small kitchen area they found an opened door containing a staircase that led down. Upon peaking his head around the door frame, John saw Kristen at the bottom of the steps with her hands covering her mouth. A strong smell of copper filled the stiff air.

"What is it?" Betty asked, making her way down the stairway. At the bottom rested a horror that would haunt John's dreams. Betty stopped near the bottom step and instinctively mimicked Kristen's pose. Suspended in the center of the room hung Jack. His limbs were severed in a symmetrical manner and were very carefully placed around his torso, in the correct location physiologically but extended away from the body so as to leave a small gap. His legs were cut at the ankles and upper thighs, arms severed finely at the wrist, elbow, and bicep. His head was dealt with in the same manner, a frozen expression of remorse and exhaustion. The artist of this freak sideshow had taken his time with each cut in order to preserve the meat. The body as a whole resembled a ventriloquist dummy, a man-shaped jigsaw puzzle from hell. Ronney's torso could be seen in the corner of the room. The skin was stretched tightly from the built-up pressure in his untouched organs; expansion of a nightmarish proportion.

"Oh, Jack… Ronney… I'm… so sorry you went through–" Betty broke down, unable to finish her thought.

John felt as if he should be crying, or even comforting the deceased's family. Instead, he kept a steel face with only a stronger resolve welling within him.

"We need to leave," he said coldly. "I think this town has already taken too much from us." He turned and trailed back up the stairs, leaving Betty and Kristen to grieve for a moment and waited in the small kitchen. To keep his mind busy he methodically searched the cupboards and drawers for anything that may help them on their way.

Kristen and Betty reappeared a while later with solemn expressions bringing out the sunkenness of their faces even more. Not a word was spoken – *nothing to say right now that would help* – while they passed through the home to the back and disappeared into the forest. They traveled for what seemed to be hours, headed east judging by the direction of the sun. They kept a steady pace, too slow for John's liking but he was not going to hustle them along after what they had been through. Arriving at a clearing, they stopped on a large birch tree overlooking an old highway. A large sign stood off to the side. "Oregon Welcomes You" it read, decorated with silhouetted trees. The sun setting over the horizon caused the sign to glow a deep orange. A man was posted up on the sign, shadowed by the sunset in such a way that blocked all features from view.

"So, you must be John?"

Lynn watched patiently yet eagerly as the remainder of the townsfolk were rounded up and brought at gunpoint to the center of their small city. One of the robed men indicated to Lynn that the town had been cleared. He had been running over a speech in his head to inspire the heathens that knelt before him. He thought about filling them with hope or telling them how Science can redeem all, but he knew he would just give them false hope about their destinies. They were little more than cattle going to the slaughter now. He pressed off the ground toward the mass and steadied on a wooden porch post. A cough to clear his throat and announce his intent to speak, just as he had done dozens of times.

"Now that the fighting has stopped I would like to take a moment to instill some knowledge in you that will help you along your way. It was by pure coincidence that we ran into your borough, but, as Albert Einstein once said, coincidence is just God's way of staying anonymous. As you can see before you, the state of humanity is at its end. The fall of man some might say. When you are a scientist for as long as I have been you find that there is no such thing as "destroy" or "ruin." Einstein also said that energy cannot be created or destroyed, it can only be changed from one form to another. So, you see, the destruction of society is not upon us. We are simply reshaping the world in the image of our creator, Science."

One of the men on the edge of the group swung his legs underneath him and jumped at the Atomist nearest him. The robed man shifted his weight to one side, causing the man to miss his target and sail off into the sky. The group watched as he drifted over the trees and out of sight, his pleas for help going unanswered.

"Well, now that that is over… Science has given us a truth that we are now going to share with all of you." Lynn lifted his arms up in the air." The atmosphere has completely degraded and blasphemed. If we are to heal our bonds with Science, then we must give back to it."

Lynn indicated to his followers to begin their next assignments. A muscular man stepped forward, grabbed an unsuspecting elderly woman by the hips, and threw her straight upward. A few surprised gasps from the crowd rapidly turned into a mass panic. Frantic crying and pleading as several more cultists stepped in and made quick work of the inhabitants of Briarton. Satisfied, Lynn watched the sacrifices hurtling toward the heavens, taking solace in the fact that he alone had just made a great contribution to the restoration of the old world. To an onlooker, the scene would remind them of party balloons that had been liberated, sailing off into the unknown. Once they, too, were out of sight Lynn raised up his voice.

"Fantastic work, everyone. Now, brace yourselves. Gravity should return any moment and it will be shocking to the body, so get to a safe place." The faithful settled themselves near the ground, anxious to receive their reward. Lynn thought about how this would only strengthen the resolve of his congregation and take him one step closer to earning exaltation. They awaited their recompense in vain.

Chapter 19

"You know I don't like havin' to do that." Sean lit up one of his cheap cigarettes. He always made sure that nobody was snooping in on their business before reminding Jessica of her place. People these days were so sensitive and always blew things out of proportion. It used to be once a year she was talking with the Wyoming state police, explaining that nothing happened and that it was just an argument. Now it seemed like it was every day.

"I'm sorry…" Jessica whimpered, feeling her cheek that would surely be bruised for the next several days. She has to remember to put the right amount of concealment on this time. Jerry, her boss, had pulled her into the office and told her that the bruises were making the customers uncomfortable.

"Dammit… you just don't get it. I don't like bein' angry, but I ain't going to let that disrespect slide. Then you go and start cryin', making me feel like the bad guy." Jessica sat in silence, afraid to even speak. He never liked it when she spoke her mind. The smell of oil and long expired food overwhelmed her senses. Struggling to say those demeaning words out loud she took a short, sharp breath.

"I'm sorry."

"Whatever." Sean pulled the truck into their usual gas station. Something within the engine whined constantly. Metallic and plastic rattling with every bump in the road, the old Chevy was all they could afford on her meager hourly wage. The man who sold them the truck said it was just the result of bad engineering, Sean had told her it was the fan. They stopped in front of pump number seven. A cheery *ding ding* went off as they drove over the black line. The whole vehicle shuddered as the key was turned and the systems powered down. The exhausted engine hadn't received proper maintenance for years. Sean gave Jessica a side glance.

"Stay here. I'm gonna go grab some beer. We're gonna have to stick with ten dollars for gas." He opened the door and ducked out.

"Can't even manage to get decent enough tips for some gas money… You're lucky I'm around," he grumbled as he slammed the door closed, patted his pockets to ensure he had his phone and wallet, and walked around the truck to the passenger side. Sean reopened the door and leaned across the seat. The smell of stale cigarettes and sweat filled her nostrils.

"You know I love you. I just… I just get mad sometimes." Sean leaned in for a kiss that was not reciprocated. He felt like he was kissing a pretty mannequin, lips clenched, unmoving. Sean's face went from pity and sympathy to hurt and anger. He gripped her face, pinching the outsides of her cheeks. The taste of copper emanated from fresh cuts where Sean's fingers dug. He released her, slammed the door shut, and walked towards the gas station store.

Jessica felt like she was suffocating. She was rarely alone with her own thoughts. She hated that she didn't have the strength to just walk out on him – disappointed that she had got to the point in life that she would allow someone so awful to even lay a hand on her – despair at the constant, looming threat of pain each moment of each day. She was losing herself to this man.

Once Sean was out of sight, Jessica allowed the hot flow of tears to fill her eyes and run down her cheeks. She quickly wiped them away with the sleeve of her hoodie. Jessica felt one of her panic attacks starting up. The ability to get a clean draw of air in her lungs made her mind start to panic. Her stomach spun, feeling like a witch was using her insides for a newly-brewed potion.

I need air. I don't care if I pay for it back at home. I can't sit in this damn thing anymore.

Yanking on the rust-tarnished door handle she opened her door and began walking down the sidewalk in the direction in which they had just come. She let fresh air fill her lungs as, for the hundredth time that day, she thought of what more she could be doing with her life. Her parents lived all the way down in Louisiana, and she had no money to pay for a plane ticket. She had no friends here in Wyoming, mostly thanks to Sean. He did not trust her around other people, so she was not allowed anywhere without him.

Maybe just getting down to Boise would be far enough away that he wouldn't come looking for me.

"Jess!"

Even after all of the violence and hurt she still gave credence that one day things will be different. Every independent step and every breath felt freeing and magical. Even knowing the coming argument was inevitable, her heart still sank, and fear twisted in her stomach as Sean yelled at her. She could almost feel the anger in his voice pelting her in the back of the head. She subconsciously hurried her pace, even though she knew it would ultimately do very little to delay the tsunami coming her way. Hearing the squeal of the engine of their truck starting up, Jessica decided to stop where she was and rest her back against the chain link fence beside her. Beyond the fence was a small canal – runoff from a larger river on the north end of the town. As the whining and rattling got closer, frustration built up inside of her – frustration from years of being talked down to and treated like an unwanted pet. The more she thought of it the harder she gripped the chain link, feeling the tension build in suspense. Her chariot rolled up onto the sidewalk blocking her from going any further.

"Jessica!" Sean yelled to her again as he slammed on the brakes in front of where she stood. He punched open his door, the hinges screaming as they swung open. "Where the hell are you going?"

"I just wanted some air." She refused to meet his gaze so as not to challenge him. Sean placed his hands on the fence on either side of her head, trapping her. Tension hovered in the air as she waited for the blow.

"You can roll down the window if you want some air. Get back in." He moved to grab her arm and pulled her toward the running truck. She jerked her arm back from his grip, something she had never done before. She felt an odd twinge of confidence inside as the thoughts of moving on from this chapter in her life had excited her.

"You want me to stick my head out the window. I'm not a damn dog, Sean!" She had barely gotten the last word out of her mouth before the back of his hand connected with it. Her head snapped to the side and she instantly knew that her inner lip had been cut open by one of her teeth. Sean started in on a loud tirade about her ungratefulness and disrespect. Jessica didn't hear a word, though, as something inside of her snapped. Adrenaline was pouring into her veins, her peripheral vision began to blur, and the sounds of the world outside her thoughts became muffled and distant. She turned to look at her lover just as he began to step toward her once again. She lashed out at his face with her untrimmed nails. He reacted swiftly, allowing only a graze of the nails to make contact with his cheek and ear. Still, the strike did enough to bring blood to the surface of his face. He stumbled back. As quickly as her internal frenzy had begun it subsided. She snapped back into her senses upon seeing the blood she had drawn. A fresh, powerful wave of dread paralyzed her, heeding not to her thoughts to make a run for it.

He stepped forward once more, this time tightening his fingers into a fist, and drove it straight into her abdomen. Jessica felt as if her eyes popped out of her head. She pleaded silently for air to enter back into her lungs as her mouth hung open. It took what felt like an eternity of fifteen frightening seconds for the soothing embrace of oxygen to return.

Sean took this time to look around. He saw an older couple had pulled over about half a block behind them and were standing halfway out of their SUV. The woman had her phone up to her ear and appeared to be speaking into it. Sean turned back to Jessica as she was finally beginning to catch her breath. He grabbed the back of her hoodie and began to pull, trying to drag her back into the truck so they could leave before any police showed up. Jessica latched onto the chain link as she fought to push her head upward. She was going to do anything just to buy herself enough time. She started kicking toward him and screaming as fiercely she could manage with the shallow breaths she could draw.

An uneasy, sick feeling suddenly engulfed her insides. She would not realize until much later that this sensation was not a side effect of her getting punched in the gut. Pressing her left foot into the pavement and kicking upward with her right, the toe of her sneaker connected with the underside of Sean's chin. The impact was enough to make him lose his grip on her clothing and fling his head back. Her foot continued upward after the kick, her sense of balance and direction dissolving with the natural balance of the world. Having the sensation of falling, Jessica gripped the fence like a newborn to her mother. Her lower body circled up and over her head, eventually meeting the fence.

What the hell?

She took a moment, waiting for her body to return to the ground. Dread filling her stomach with bile as she did her best not to panic. Sean was no longer in front of her.

"Jess! Jess!"

The shouts came from above. Jessica looked up and laid eyes on Sean, who was about one hundred feet in the air and flailing his arms, trying to steady the continual rotation of his body. She dared not move another muscle. She looked to her left and saw the couple inside of their SUV. They were also drifting upward, though not as quickly as Sean was. She watched as they panicked inside the vehicle, faces contorted with confusion and terror. "Jess!" The more distant-sounding shout made her head snap back toward Sean. His facial features were no longer distinguishable, approaching the size of a fly rapidly. A slight smile danced around her lips as she stared until he was no longer in view; his shouts no longer audible. Then, she began to sob through the smile. Tears clouded her vision as she hung onto the chain link and began to wail, relishing in her newfound freedom.

Chapter 20

Sliding the slender axe from behind his back, John took up position, expecting an ambush from either side of the trees. "Whoa, whoa, sailor. Why so jumpy?" the large man asked with a chuckle.

"How do you know my name?" John answered with his own question. Both Betty and Kristen remained stationary, wishing that they could sink back into the shadows unnoticed. John wasn't sure how much more excitement he could take. Over the last two weeks, he had been sent through the most trying of circumstances. He had never wanted rest so much that it almost brought him to tears. Now at his back was a town full of lunatics, whether it was the Atomists or the people-eating freaks, and in front of him was a new threat.

How long can I keep this up? Sometimes I wonder if it would've been easier to let Van just shoot me. At least I would get some sleep.

"Listen, man. Not only do you look like Tom, but you have his bite as well. Kind of funny who you run into when the whole world falls apart – or floats away." He awkwardly knelt, peeled himself off of the sign, and slowly approached the trio. John was frozen at the mention of his father's name, so much so that he was letting a stranger waltz right up to him. Each footstep caused a puff of dirt to form out from the ground. "I'm Frank." He introduced himself while extending his hand out to John. "I work with your dad sometimes. Every so often I have to travel to the state border, looking for any wanderers that may want to join us in our town."

John remained steadfast and ready to swing. The air started to cool as the day was weaning.

"Stubborn, too. Also a… quality of your father's."

"Prove it," is all John said.

"Well, now, the thing about that is that I can't. No cell coverage, no radios – hell, I'd be happy just to be able to watch the weather report again. I live in a town called Seaside. Just have to follow this highway 'til you reach the coast. You will find a thriving community and all the food you can eat there. It usually takes me about a week and a half give or take to get there, depending on interference.

Oops, actually, I do have this."

Frank pulled a small side bag from around his back and produced a picture-perfect ripe tomato. "I picked this little puppy from the greenhouse just before I set out. Not the prettiest, but I bet someone that hasn't had real produce in a while might enjoy a bite."

He gingerly rolled the steak tomato through the air toward them. Kristen caught it out of the air, giving it a hesitant, unbelieving look over. The tomato was without flaws like it was created in a lab. The aroma of fresh garden permeated the air as she examined it. John's stomach turned and gurgled. *I haven't eaten in a while. We ran out of those fish from the lake.*

"At least humor me. Look over the tree line." Frank pointed out west. "The sun is starting to go down. There's a cave near here that will allow us the privacy we need to talk and rest for the night. I usually rest there if I'm out here more than a day."

John looked at the two women behind him.

"This isn't always JUST my decision. What do you guys think?"

"John, you have spent how long traveling west? We have gone through so many unfortunate events. Now, someone says they know your dad and the first thing you do is pull your axe on him?" Becky said with a calm demeanor.

"Please, just give me a chance to at least tell you about the town. That's the whole reason I'm out here in the first place after all," Frank said.

John apprehensively put his weapon away. "Fine. But I'm searching you first."

"So be it, John. I promise I have nothing to hide."

Frank first handed over the pack he wore. John discovered a cornucopia of produce and dried jerky when he opened it up.

"You never know when you'll get trapped or waylaid out on the road," Frank explained.

At the bottom of the pack were prescription bottles by the fistful. John raised a handful out of the bag with a questionable look on his face.

"Oh, right. I also go through the houses on occasion to see if there is anything of value to me. I'm bringing those antibiotics back to the town."

Where was this guy when my hand was cut and Jack was covered in burnt boils?

Seeing that John was finished, Frank pushed closer as he continued inspecting each pocket with careful precision. "Whoa, buddy," he chuckled. "I haven't had someone get this fresh since my wife and I got married."

John, unamused by the joke, looked up at him in silence, trying to read the man for any deception.

A sharp pinch immediately drew his attention away. Looking down, he saw a small ant hill next to where he was standing. He smacked at his leg to brush off the colony of large black ants who had decided to try and make him their next meal. Some were resistant to his swats and clung on to his skin and leg hair. Multiple little stings started pulsating on his calf. Taking an annoyed, sharp breath he raised his legs one at a time and picked the ants off. He couldn't help but feel irritated that most of the bugs surviving in the world liked to bite and bite hard.

"Alright. Lead the way. But if I even get the feeling that someone's eyes are on me I won't hesitate to plant this blade in the back of your skull," John threatened.

"Well, let's hope we don't have any prying eyes for my sake then, eh?" Frank turned and led them deeper into the forest. He pointed out a set of descending stairs that curved in and out of sight. Using the handrails built next to the steps they pulled themselves deeper and deeper into the lush green forest.

The forest in which they traveled varied from gorgeous vibrant evergreens to starch white birch trees with a periodic dried-up, brown meadow in between. Weaving left and right, the pathway opened up to a large, rectangular clearing and a little guard station on the other side.

"It's just across the way there," Frank said, pointing at the runty rundown building. "I ran into this cave a couple of months ago on one of my trips down this way. If we're lucky there is a surprise waiting." John stopped with a defensive look. "Alright, Mr. Paranoid, I found a couple little pockets of water," Frank said with a touch of annoyance in his voice. "Not much of a people person, are ya? Another trait you probably inherited from your old man."

The guard station stood weathered and resolute besides a large opening that dug further into the mountain. A one-room workstation meant for checking tickets. The glass windows were shattered, leaving behind sharp, jagged geometric shapes along the edges. One window had simply been opened as if someone had finally had the thought to check if they were locked. Peering inside, John had a hard time making out the contents with the low light of early dusk.

"Do me a favor, John, and reach in under the desk. There is an obvious switch that will kick on the lights if we're lucky," Frank instructed. John reached in and ran the tips of his fingers across the coarse wood. He felt a pinch and pulled his hand toward him, expecting another ant, only to see a small sliver as the culprit. *Great... Imagine that headline, "Man dies from infection after surviving the apocalypse.*" Locating the switch was like playing a game of battleship. This time he patted around the desk until he located the switch and hit it. A series of string lights trailing down the walls of the cave flickered on.

Staring into the cave gave John a nervous feeling that things were only going to get worse. Frank gathered several large sticks in one arm and passed through the entrance of the cave. Betty, Kristen, and John followed. Cold air blanketed them upon entering. They stood in the large opening of the cave as Frank worked on starting a fire with a metallic lighter. The outer walls of the stone held a sleek appearance with grooved lines, formed over thousands of years.

"You asked me to humor you and I did. Now, are you going to answer some questions?" John asked sternly.

Frank stood up, turning his back to John as he looked deeper into the cavern. "I'm going to go see what water I can find. After that, we have the whole night to play twenty questions." And with that, he dipped down a narrower side tunnel and out of sight. John furrowed his brow and stared after him for a moment before deciding that he might as well stick around and wait.

Bulbous stalactites spattered the walls and roof around them. An odd sparkle caught John's eye, drawn to one substantial pillar of rock that rose from the ground several feet. Directly above it was a large cone-shaped formation pointing downward, as if trying to reach its other half just below. John leaped forward slowly and witnessed something he had never seen before. A thin string of water had attached itself to both tips of the opposing rocks, giving it the appearance of a tightly strung harp chord. For several minutes they sat in silence, worry and paranoia trickling in. John began swiveling his head constantly, waiting for Frank to appear from the shadows and take them out one by one. John looked over to the sisters and noticed Kristen gently crying. She stopped and looked up at John.

"We never ran into any problems until you came along. They would still be alive if it weren't for you." John was taken aback at the sudden accusatory tone. "You brought that psycho right to us and forced us to leave. We could have been happy at that cabin! I can still see his face… I can't stop seeing his face."

"Are you really blaming me? I haven't forced a single thing onto anyone," John replied, fighting back the urge to raise his voice and match Kristen's anger. In truth, his heart ached at the hostility from someone he was beginning to consider a friend.

"Blame? My family is dead... DEAD! You really don't feel any kind of responsibility, do you? You knew he was crazy and you said nothing. That's like seeing a bus heading for a kid in the street and not even calling out to the mother before the bus hits it. How long did you know? How long were you going to wait before saying a damn thing?" Kristen was screaming through painful tears. John looked desperately at Betty. She let out a sigh.

"I knew, Kristen. John told me about Van and we agreed to keep an eye on him. I'm to blame as well." Betty said as she watched Kristen's heart break even further, holding back the urge to now scream at her sister.

"Ronney and Jack's blood is on both of your hands," she said through clenched teeth. A look of embarrassment washed over her face and she backed herself into a corner of the cave, tucked her knees in, and sobbed.

A soft light began to light up the scene as Frank came around a corner on the opposite side of the cave from which he had left. "You guys sure are a dramatic bunch... I have something that might cheer you up." Frank held up his arm and showed off two small fish. The fish had a peculiar soft-pink color with white fins. The place where their eyes would be was an extra thick padding of scales. "I've heard of cavefish in the past, but I always thought they were fake. These two guys were hanging out in a big ol' water bubble resting against a wall." He settled up to the fire and warmed his hardened, cracked hands over the still flame.

"I suppose I should start at the beginning. Like I said before, I live in Seaside, a small town twenty or so miles north of Portland. The town was started by a couple of young engineers with a vision: the vision that we don't have to allow this gravity business to destroy everything that we have built as humanity. They decided that someone had to pick up the pieces of the world and rebuild. Starting out, they tackled the basic necessities like food and water. Once they had a steady stream of both the town started to thrive. We have saltwater filters, greenhouses, and an overabundance of fish. A designated council was voted in later on. Their job is to work with the engineers on deciding which tasks or issues to focus on. When I left for this trip they were preparing for the town's yearly festival. That's where the tomatoes came from. They were also building several tunnel systems for safer means of travel."

"That's kind of hard to believe..." John grumbled. "I've been traveling for a long time and have never seen any kind of positive outlook. Only death and disappointment."

John decided to change topics. “How do you know my father?”

“Questions for later, John,” Frank waved his hand as if dismissing the words from the air. “I’m getting to that part. So, in Seaside we have a government and organizations. Idle hands are the devil's playground after all. When we all started we were given daily tasks to build up the community. As the population grew and there was more help to go around we usually only received jobs once a week or so. About a year into it all the people stopped flowing in and the community, in general, thought that could be an issue. Hence this outreach initiative was created, designed to snag any stragglers that are still struggling on their own and give them a place to go and a purpose.”

“Don’t you ever worry that you are bringing in bad people?” Becky asked. Frank looked annoyed from yet another interruption.

“I mean, I am far from perfect. Once The Lifting went down – or up, heh – we all had to do things to survive. I don’t think anyone’s hands are blood-free these days. Any who, we are at least a week and a half from Seaside. I have ample time to determine anyone’s true intentions. Every couple of months it’s my turn to come out here in hopes that we can reach everyone with the success we have had."

"That doesn't explain how you supposedly know my father," John piped back in. "Just last week we discovered a family living in a town that invited us to dinner. Want to know how that ended? We were shackled in a barn waiting to become a meal. All this sounds like a big coincidence and I don't have much belief in those."

"Right… I do see that trust is in short supply with your bunch. I had the luxury of joining this colony soon after its establishment. Albert Einstein said that coincidence is God's way of staying anonymous. I met your father when the town started assigning living areas. I moved into a small little RV next to a boat named the "SAINT JOHN." Your father and I became fast friends and if it weren't for the festival he would have been out here with me. He has pictures of you all over his home."

John had a million questions rolling through his head, but one stuck out among the rest. *Can I trust what he is saying?* The resentment of treating his father like a monster all those years racked John's heart and soul. As he grew into a man he realized he wasn't losing one loved one, but two. Here was a man who was trying to stay strong for his sick wife and surviving son, trying to be the steady foundation that any father needed to be. *All I did was put the final nails in the coffin.*

"Alright, Frank, I'll bite. But–"

"Right, right, death threats and axe to the head." Frank made quick work of the odd-looking fish. It wasn't much meat to go around, but it was enough to halt the stomach pains. John wondered as he ate light-colored flesh what kind of worms or diseases it probably held.

John finished his meal and drifted into the further recesses of the cave. Sleep wouldn't come easy tonight – the cave held an unsettling stillness. Ultimately, any sleeping position felt the same on the body. And yet, he tossed and turned, trying to free himself from the anxiety of what tomorrow held. The walls of stone started to play tricks on his mind. John wondered if the woman way back in Fernwood ever made it out alive. The vivid image of her awkwardly rotating in the air… he could almost smell the piss, hear the pain in her voice as she pleaded through cracked lips for saving.

What have I become? I devoted my life to saving people from the brink of death. How did I become so indifferent?

He wondered how he would feel finally seeing his

father again. A touch of fear pierced the veil of his thoughts.

What if this is just another play to trick us?

John's arm skimmed the side of the cave wall, causing him to jump, half expecting Frank to be there in the dark, waiting. As the paranoia subsided, sleep finally took hold of him.

John found himself in a meadow surrounded by lush green pine trees. He was ten feet off the ground in a stillness, frozen in the air. A man approached from a distance, but something odd about the man caught his attention. He was walking on the ground, and the blades of wheatgrass reacted to him as he pushed them to the side. He had a red flannel shirt on and some roughed-up blue jeans. A straw-brimmed hat protected his head from the sun. The ground walker stopped in front of John and called up to him.

"Why do you insist on floating there? Why don't you come down and join the rest of the world?"

As much as John tried he could not move, trapped by nothing. The man looked up – a familiar face with graying hair. It was his father, or, at least, what he thought his father would look like now. His face held deep sadness, accentuated by the deep wrinkles around his eyes.

"Dad, I can't do this... It's too much. I feel like I'm losing my humanity," John said as tears welled in his eyes. "I don't think I will be able to forget the faces... I've caused so much pain."

"You have held onto your pain, and mine, for too long, John," Tommy replied.

John looked around him, sudden screaming erupting throughout the trees. Several figures shot out of the thicket like spears. The wailing grew louder and louder as they flew closer. He began to make out the faces, flooding his whole being with dread – all of the people who had died at his hand. John did the only thing he could and curled into a ball, forcing his eyelids together, and waiting for the clash. A different voice rang out above the rest. Opening his eyes, he saw them tearing his father apart piece by piece.

He jumped toward him and began tearing the lost souls away from him. The more he tore away the deeper he seemed to be sinking into the pile of bodies. When only a shoulder remained visible, John shoved his hands down and around his torso.

If they're taking you, they'll have to take me, too.

All at once, John felt the pushing and ripping stop as

a deafening silence replaced the screams. He looked up to see fire engines on either side of him with their emergency lights flashing. The massive hoses were unraveled from the sides of the trucks with teams of firefighters manning each one. He could feel the heat from the apartment building, charred from the fire that was seeking to consume it entirely. His team members turned their head to look at John, still clutching the body, making him jump. All facial features had been erased; eyes, nose, mouth… nothing remained. Each one a frozen manikin with no expression.

John looked down to the man he was holding. Staring back at him was no longer his father's face, but his brother, Colby. John had carried him out of the building, a beam had fallen on him on the second floor. His eyes were lifeless. John moved his hands to cradle the back of his little brother's head. What should have been solid skull was now replaced with a sinking hole. His fingers pressed further then was natural. The contents of Colby's head enveloped John's fingers. John felt the need to vomit, but as he opened his mouth he could only force out a harrowing wail.

John woke up howling. The echo of the cave made

a resonating chorus of his fear. A faint, orange light caught his attention, the glow growing steadily.

It must be morning. I wonder where the others are.

He stretched and followed the string of light bulbs out of the cave.

"Ha, and the dead finally rise. If we plan on getting there anytime soon we best get on our way." Frank said.

"I have something to say," Becky said as she clung to the side of the guard tower. "We won't be going with you." The words pierced John's heart. "Kristen and I decided that it would be best if we head north, back to our homes, and hope to ride out whatever time we have left living."

In the back of his head, John has assumed that these were his new friends, his new family, for life. He felt almost betrayed. The words that would beg them to stay nearly erupted from his throat, but he swallowed them back, choosing his sense of pride.

"Well, if you ever change your mind, head west till you hit the coast. Follow it south and you'll eventually run into Seaside. One other thing before you go…" Frank pulled his pack around and fished around inside. He pulled out several cans of various foods and handed them to Becky and

Kristen.

Becky pushed off of the guard tower, stopping just inches from John, and embraced him like a friend who was off to war.

"I know this wasn't what you expected but we have to do this for ourselves."

Half of John felt urged to follow them as they turned to leave. What life could he start with Becky if he gave up this quest to find a man who may not be alive? He still was not sure if he could put full trust in Frank yet. The other half of him screamed that he needed to find his father and mend their shattered relationship – apologize for the heartache he had caused. Becky let go of John with tears in her eyes.

"Goodbye, John."

Chapter 21

Mr. Ridmore,

We wish to receive your feedback and assistance with ongoing community issues. We invite you to join us today in lieu of your regularly scheduled work details. We look forward to meeting you.

The Engineers.

Tommy stood dumbstruck as he read the scribble written on the paper he was given. His vision drew across the coast as the sun crested over the ice caps of Velum that extended to the top reaches of the atmosphere. The massive pillars, blocking entire sections of the sky, reminded him of the time he worked in New York City. High noon was the busiest time of day in the city, as it was the only time you could feel the warmth of direct sunlight on your face. Tommy stood within the threshold of St. John as the growing heat grazed his cheeks.

Velum stood as a screaming reminder that things were different and they weren't changing back. Having a beachfront property is supposed to be accompanied by rolling waves and the sounds of seagulls calling. He would always joke with Frank and Maureen that Velum looked like blue-dyed dreadlocks with white tips.

A sick joke... ironic, really, how close I am to the ocean with a boat and I can't use it. He looked back to the note and wondered what it was that the Engineers wanted with him. *What could I have possibly done to even catch their attention? I am one man that does just the basics in this community. I don't even know anything about engineering.*

He studied the looming wall of water that was the newly-formed ocean and noticed one of the fishing aerial tramways. In Seaside the trams were designed by the Engineers to harvest fish on the icy peaks at the top. The fish were all frozen in place; all the people had to do was break them out. One side of the tram was secured to the largest piece of ice at the top of Velum, providing secure passage from the ground level. Tommy recalled the first couple of months he was in town and was put on fishing duty. Mesmerized, he would always take a moment at the top of the ice to look out at the world – gazing upon the majestic horizons, mixed with the calm, quiet stillness of the air, gave him a sense of peace that he craved.

Pulling himself inside the cabin, he rummaged through his cabinets to find something to nibble on his way down to the Engineers' council room. The oak cabinet door let out a whine as Tommy opened it. He pushed several old dishes to the side to where he kept his stash of treats and retrieved a bag of chips that Frank had brought back from one of his runs to the state's border. As stale as they usually were, junk food always gave him a feeling that someday things would be made right again.

He stuffed the potato chips in the side pocket of his pants and left through the door, locking the sliding door behind him. Tommy's boat and RV sat on a lot on the upper side of town. Each was tethered to multiple large stakes he had hammered deep into the earth and one longer rope to a small, freestanding bundle of trees nearby. Tommy preferred the distance from the city – he did not trust people. He spent his working life dedicated to shielding the public from the evils of the world, only to realize that there was no divide. Besides, it took much less time and effort to cover the distance to town, being able to simply float his way down.

Springing from one redwood tree to the next, Tommy made his way down the hill to the clip-in area, pulling on his harness straps as he coasted. The one thing you didn't want to do is put all your faith in one piece of your equipment. You maintained your gear or you could quickly find yourself flying away. He clipped in and gingerly made his way down the street, heading for the meeting hall. Occasionally, someone would stop him for light conversation, but Tommy would politely cut it off quickly. He didn't want to be caught ignoring a summons from the Engineers.

One thing that always amazed him when he traveled through town was how Velum affected the lighting. The sun rays fighting through the water tendrils would often create a rainbow effect on the streets and building walls. Most shadows, rather than simply dark spots, had copious amounts of color – a thin border of reds and blues at the very least. The city sat, in one of the most dreary and hopeless times, illuminated in beautiful, joy-inducing hues.

Steadying himself, Tommy had arrived at the building doors. The Engineers used the old city courthouse. The walls were built with a sad, tan granite that gave the whole building a feel of bureaucracy. The three-story structure had windows evenly spaced with a light brown pillar in between each of them. The front door was the most daunting: two large, dark-stained wood doors. He pulled himself up the chilled stone railings and found the front door was left ajar. As he entered he was greeted by a middle-aged black man who looked overjoyed to be there in a meeting hall.

"We were wondering if you were going to show up! We are all gathered in the courtroom hall. Thank you for joining us." Tommy apathetically nodded at the man and followed him through another pair of sturdy wooden doors to the main courtroom.

Coming through the main door, Tommy saw several groups of people congregating in different corners of the room. Three men could be heard arguing about the state of the roadways. Another group laughing among each other. Upon seeing him they all quieted down, gazing at him without a word. Tommy could feel a tension rise in the air as rapidly as if someone had opened every window to let it in.

A fleshy, bald man slapped a gavel against the railing, calling order to the group. Each of them readily scuffled to a different podium facing the speaker's podium at the front of the room. Tommy felt awkward, not knowing where to position himself. The speaker started passing around sheets of paper to the others. Tommy was surprised when he received a paper himself. It had been printed from a computer on a real printer. *We barely have the means to produce food and water and they're using up our limited electricity on an agenda?* Making his way back to the front, the man who seemed to be conducting the meeting confirmed as much.

"Welcome, and nice to see that everyone made it. For those who don't know me, my name is Brett Halverson, interim head of the Committee," he said, looking in Tommy's direction. Tommy finally spotted an open podium and moved to it as inconspicuous as he could.

"Does anyone want to add to the agenda for the day?" he asked. Tommy raised his hand. "Right, Tommy, you will just have to wait your turn. If you look at the agenda you are number seven on the list."

Annoyed, he skimmed down the typed-out lines and bullet points until his finger trailed down to see written in bold lettering, "Invitation to New Member." Tommy's name was listed below, along with two other names he did not recognize. Looking up, he quietly watched as two members of the Engineers argued over the food supply usage. Tommy had always wondered if he would take on a real role in the community someday, but nothing like this. He wanted to speak up and say something to make a good first impression – show that he had good ideas like they were after. Maybe a new tunnel system or a way to naturally process medicine.

"Alright, Tommy, you have been more than patient. We now move on to item seven, which we are all very excited about." Brett pulled a large cardboard display with several hand-drawn illustrations and a map of the coastal area. "We have been pouring over this particular problem for a few weeks now, though I would dare say it isn't the most urgent. In the town of Seaside, we have not only survived this desolation of a world but are thriving. We have greenhouses, fresh water, and security. The problem with that is we now have become so successful in growing our community that we are at the point of overpopulation." He shot a glare at one of the women across the room as he continued. "Some of us thought it reasonable to consider kicking people out. Others think we need to secure the border of the wall and stop anyone else from entering. However, the reality of it all is that we need to tackle this problem before we have to explain to people why their food rations have been halved. That's where you come in." He pointed at the poster. "If you don't mind, Tommy, Wendy, and Karen give a wave." Tommy scanned the room. A middle-aged black woman on the opposite side perked her head up and waved her hand wildly. Karen, who was just a few spots to his left, raised her hand high while adding a kink to her wrist, giving the impression that she was not exactly thrilled to be there.

"We believe that we have the answer to the problem and it can only be solved through you. You, with a few others from this group, are being tasked with recreating – no, expanding upon – the dream that started this place. About twenty-five miles north of here, on the other side of the canal, is a large town full of what should be abandoned homes that we can put to use for our growing population."

Karen raised her hand, "This doesn't sound like it's my problem. It sounds like we should just stop giving food out. I mean who says we are responsible for saving the world? Why can't that be someone else's problem?" Brett ignored her whining.

"I don't understand... Are you saying you need us to start a new city?" Wendy asked.

"That is exactly right," Brett beamed. "Well, almost. Starting a new city is more than overwhelming for just a few people. What we need is a responsible group to go out to the town of Ocean View to assess the area. We need to verify there are no current residents and the condition that the homes are in. We thought it appropriate for a member of the Engineers to go and figured this was a good way to introduce new minds to the group."

"So, what do I get? I get that I have to do jobs to get my food ration but this seems way out of the realm of normal labor. I mean, you are asking us to go into an unknown location where we could likely be killed." Karen accused.

"For one, being a member of the Engineers means no more weekly work details. Your job will be this. Secondly, being the first to assess the new area means you get the first pick of the homes over there. Lastly, a new area comes with many different challenges and we will need reasonable leadership to step in and run things. We have established a couple of basic points that we will need to tackle first, but we are excited to continue to rebuild humanity."

Tommy eyed Karen and Brett arguing back and forth for a moment before coming to a realization. They don't need grunt work from him. They need him to head off bringing another city into the fold from scratch. He had the opportunity to insert a huge amount of influence into how things operated in every aspect.

"How big is the town?" Tommy asked, cutting Karen off mid-sentence.

"Good question. At least one of you isn't into arguing," Brett said in a low voice. "The town is just as big as Seaside. It would allow us to avoid overcrowding. Once we get settled in we would have to set up a safe trade route for the first little while to make sure everyone is fed properly and could build their self-sustaining systems."

"I would like to help with this project, but on one condition," Tommy said with affirmation in his voice. "I want Frank and Maureen to join me. Not these lost nobodies."

Karen went from a look of contempt to one that had the potential to shoot a dagger into him. Her lips contorted while spewing almost random words in a defensive rebuttal.

"Let's give it up to a vote from the council. By a show of hands, who votes to allow Tommy and his two acquaintances to go in Wendy and Karen's stead?" The vote was unanimous, Tommy was chosen to traverse the unknown to continue picking up the pieces of the world.

Frank and John traveled slowly and methodically, being careful to not attract the attention of anyone along the way. Each small town they came to was accompanied by a large list of strange facts from Frank.

He's had to have been doing this for years...

While passing through the most recent town, Frank told John about how he had found several interesting trinkets, one of them being a short journal that had belonged to a young boy. Frank took them to a spot on a hill to rest after clearing the municipality. He went to a small knot in a tree and pulled out the book.

"You know, two years ago the only thing people would want was gold and diamonds to fill the empty spaces. I have been traveling for a long time with plenty of time to reflect. You know John, I think we lost the most important piece of us that is hard to get back – the true human experience." Frank pushed his way to John who was resting under the shade of a large redwood pine. He handed him the journal. "This isn't just a meaningless journal. We were meant to grow. We were meant to settle down and have a family. Feel the anxiety and nerves of holding our firstborn child in our arms. That," Frank placing the book in John's hands, "is a record of someone that has been robbed of those joys… Robbed from his human experience."

John rolled his eyes but decided to indulge Frank by reading while they rested. While taking his time with each page, John started to feel a connection to the young boy in the book. The hunger and the need to find warmth tugged at his heartstrings. He remembered being that age and all the sleepless nights waiting for the monsters to get him. He could not imagine having to deal with the world as it was now at that age. About midway through, John stopped on a passage that he could not get past. He read it over and over in his mind.

"When will my mom and dad find me?"

John remembered the day he left home. He fought with his father for hours about who even remembers what. Storming out of their small shack of a home, he vowed to never return. However, that soft voice would crawl into his thoughts on dark, lonely nights. John had asked himself the same question the boy had in the journal. *When will my father come for me?* He perused the small, battered pages, now unable to put it down. The regret of unresolved hope poured through each line. As much as he tried to focus on the rest of the words, that simple line bothered him. The child longed for the safety and comfort of his family – the one thing that John so readily threw away. Nudging John, Frank indicated that it was time to move on. John stretched out his hand, offering the book back without looking up.

Frank waved his hands and said, "The only way we can understand each other is to put ourselves in the shoes of others." Cheesy as they were, the words hit home. John tucked the book into a side cargo pocket and followed Frank onward.

From tree to tree, rock to rock, John could feel the weight of the journal. He wondered why the boy never gave up looking.

I'll bet he saw more horrors while looking for his family than he would have by staying put.

Was that what John had done? Had he given up too easily? Was it so bad to swallow his pride and return home? Minutes turned into hours and they slowly made their way across a more barren part of the landscape. The sun inched closer to the ground, ready to call it a day. Frank stopped them on the edge of a ridgeline sparsely decorated with long-dead foliage. The cliff edge must have had a large amount of activity over the last two years. Dotted along the ridge were fist-sized rocks and clumps that held inches from the cliff line like a ring of Saturn. Frank motioned him to stay quiet, scanning the treetops for any movement.

"This is a well-traveled area for water," he whispered to John. "We need to stop here to fill up or we will have a hard time on the last leg of the journey." John felt a familiar sting as his stomach growled and whined. Frank fished around his bag and retrieved a small glass jar of green beans and handed it over to John. As the two men ate, John found himself drawn back to the journal. He downed the can, even drinking the salty green bean juice, and turned his focus on the next journal entry.

"Day 37

I went through Aunt Carol's house today thinking maybe mom and dad were there. They were not. I heard a noise coming from one of the pantry closets which turned out to be a rat. I think it was hungry and scared. After leaving her home I went to my hiding place. There are lots of people who come out at night with flashlights, I think they are looking for me. Tomorrow I will go into town. I have no more food and my stomach hurts. I find old neighbors dead in their houses some days and I'm afraid they will come looking

for me when I'm sleeping. I miss my mom and dad, I wish they were here to protect me."

Frank pulled in close to John and told him it was time to move and he tucked the book back in his pocket. They began scaling down the cliffside head first. As they slowly moved downward John noticed that there was something peculiar about the forest below. A thin haze blanketed the ground, eerily similar to an eldritch cemetery.

"Is that what I think it is?" John asked. Frank stopped and looked in the direction that John was pointing then nodded.

"That's the reason why we're here, John. I haven't the faintest idea as to why it happens, but the water never left this basin. When the night falls the fog draws together into tiny balls of water throughout the forest. I have a favorite spot where I wait for the night. It lies on the other side of the tree line just over there." Frank pointed to the other side of the basin cliff line. "The problem is there are a handful of people that reside here that like to give me trouble any chance they get." They continued to the bottom of the jagged cliff. Frank wasted no time in pulling himself to the nearest pine trunk and began cutting a dead branch off.

"What are you doing?" John asked in a whisper.

"In order to make our way across safely I'm going to make a distraction." The sun had set down low enough that it just kissed the edge of the horizon. The light faded as John watched him tie several large, dry sticks together in a bundle. "Alright, John, once I light these we need to move as fast as we can to the other side while staying hidden. Use the fog as cover, it's thicker than it looks."

Frank removed a small rod and struck it with the back of his knife over and over until the dead branch took flame. Frank then pushed the ball of flame in the opposite direction.

"Wait until you see the movement," Frank whispered in his ear. The noise of several branches breaking echoed off the stone walls of the cliff. John could faintly see the shadows of several people moving following the glowing cluster of sticks. He waited in anticipation, his heart rate rapid. Without a sound, the light from the fire splintered in different directions as the twine that had been holding the wood together finally gave.

"Go!"

Frank shot forward like an arrow through the gray

mist.

No way he can see where he's going!

Trying to keep up, John noticed that with each push to the next tree, a swirl in the fog trailed behind him. The air was colder in the dense mist – the thickness of it almost gave him a claustrophobic sensation.

Frank paused for a moment to catch his breath. They had been moving hard for several minutes. "Hopefully they were dumb enough to chase after it to the other side of the basin. That should give us enough time," he said through slow gasps of air. There was no sun remaining above the horizon and the yellow-orange glow of the sunset had nearly left the skyline. "We are nearly there."

John could see the fog quickly thinning out and forming large bubbles of water. He reached out and touched one. It was chilled. "The mist pulls together at night into what you see before you. When the sun comes out it evaporates, causing it to turn back into the fog." Frank said.

Several creaks and moans of tree branches approached their position. John searched the air to discover that they weren't alone anymore. Frank's ruse had run its course. A sharp break overhead caused John to look up. By instinct, he crouched down but before he could press forward Frank stopped him.

"They don't know where we are so don't be so hasty," Frank whispered so quietly it was almost inaudible. The longer he sat there the antsier he became. *I refuse to be someone's prisoner yet again*. Right as he was about to make a break for it, the noise of rustling trees faded off in the direction of the far side of the basin.

"Damn idiots," Frank muttered under his breath, joining John in drawing a breath finally.

"Who are they?" John asked.

"On one of my trips through this area, they got lucky enough to catch me off guard and had me locked up. From what I can tell they stay in the valley and live off maggots, pine cones, and who knows what else, which would rot anyone's mind. They cornered me with sharpened sticks and tied me, or at least they thought they did. I was able to escape faster than it took them to fumble around with the straps of cloth they were attempting to use."

Frank started again and John followed. It was hard to see the trees in front of them now. With each press forward John caught several large globs of water to the face. John half-expected his head to meet a tree. The temperature had been getting noticeably colder as they traveled. The further they moved through the forest the more moisture his skin and clothes held onto. The combination of the cooling air and moisture caused him to shiver.

A few minutes later, the pair found themselves in a small alcove between several large rocks that shielded them from all sides. A chill ran through his body, reminding him he was wearing wet clothing. The worst part about being sopping wet is the fact that John couldn't remember the last time he bathed. The smell was so thick he was repulsed by himself.

"Can't risk a fire tonight, at least while they're looking for us. Do you think you will be okay?" Frank asked. John, devastated, briskly nodded as he wrapped his arms around his chest and began rubbing his arms, seeking any warmth that friction could bring.

In his fleeting dreams between episodes of violent shivering John could see the boy from the journal. He pictured him to be no more than ten years old, standing in front of him with dirt-stained cheeks and ragged clothes.

"When will my mom and dad find me?" the boy said softly as tears poured from his eyes. John reached out to comfort him as the boy faded from existence. He decided he had had enough of this broken sleep and rubbed the sleep out of his eyes, noticing a multitude of colors peeking through a crack in the rocks, creating a band of color throughout the alcove. Exiting the cave, he was struck by the scene. The whole western side of the mountainous bowl was aglow in a rainbow of colors. The valley that he now found himself in was filled with the glow of the morning's first rays. Before him were millions of small balls of water spaced only inches from each other, hovering on an unseen barrier from the ground. The sheet of drops held suspended chest-high to John. The reflection of colors from the Western sky danced with the spheres of moisture, causing the water to give the appearance of a quilted blanket fit for a god. *How could something so beautiful exist in this forsaken land*?

Frank was already moving up the western rock face to the top of the precipice. John did not want to be left behind and quickly caught up to him.

"I think we just might arrive in time for the festival," Frank said as they reached the top. John could see across the tops of the towering redwood trees to the edges of the horizon. Catching his breath, John saw a large, dense wall of water that extended from the base of the ground to the top of the sky. At the top of the anomaly, a prism of colors spewed forth, coating the whole landscape with colorful life.

“What is that?” John asked Frank breathlessly.

“That, John, is what we call *Velum*.”

Chapter 22

In the passing hours, Lynn had been eager to share his findings with the Doctrinate, sending everyone to scour the town for a radio. In Van's impression Lynn didn't care for the cause, he only wanted power and recognition. Lynn had seemed hell-bent on crawling over anyone to get what he wanted and the town of Briarton was proof of it. He had no care for the well-being of Science or humanity, his motivations were selfish. As the sun was setting and the thrill of executing such an intricate rite had died down, Van had taken to searching for the town with the others. Each small farmhouse looked like it had been through the holocaust, bullet holes and broken glass scattered the landscape before him. His gaze stopped when he saw Weston moving in and out of the group of people, his body restrained by the gravity they all strove to restore. *This can't be good,* he thought as Weston stopped in front of Fred's home and pointed at the upper windows.

A cry came out from the upper floor where Weston had been pointing, someone had located Fred's radio.

After locating Fred's radio setup, contact was made with Doctrinate's office in Boulder, Colorado. Occupying the living room floor of Fred's dusty, manure-stained house, Van waited with the others as Lynn privately made a report.

A soft click warned him of their completion of the conversation. Both Lynn and Melody descended the stairs like a ghostly apparition would pale and scared. Melody had been in the room with Lynn at the time. Her typical professional demeanor had also fractured into an aura of nervousness, a wisp of dust swirled around her feet as she followed down the stairs. She repeatedly wiped her sweaty palms on her pants and tucked them behind her back.

A quiet hush fell over the room as they waited for him to speak. "This ought to be good," Professor Weston said out loud as he fazed through each person moving to the front of the group.

"Since Boulder is about 800 miles from where we currently stand, the Doctrinate has agreed to travel and meet with us in Fernwood. It seems I must give an in-person report of our findings," Lynn relayed to the rest of the group. His nervous tick coming out Lynn picked at his beard, methodically pulling out hairs.

"We must now return home. We have much to do to prepare for our visitors." An allure of excitement washed over the Atomists like a child going to meet Santa Claus for the first time. Van turned to see Weston standing at his side inches from his face. He winced, seeing his carnage so close before, Van could almost smell the copper from the blood dried on Weston's face.

"Like a lamb to the slaughter," Weston said. "They don't even know the horror that will meet them when they return, all but him." Weston pointed to Lynn. "He knows that an example will be made." In saying that Weston sighed and walked to the couch and sat down.

He spent the night kicking himself for missing his one shot on John. *Maybe if I had set up in a better position... more stable, I might not have flinched on the trigger pull...* He refused to allow the thought to cross his mind that some piece of him did not want to go through with killing John. That would open the door for more doubt and stupid choices, much like the ones that landed him in this situation, in this dusty, repugnant town. He had to remain convicted. He could not take any more self-doubt.

"Van." Lynn singled him out as he sat front and

center of the audience.

"Yes, sir?"

"I am sorry that we were not able to find your man. They must have slipped through as we were clearing the homes. There was a report that they were last seen heading due east out of the town."

"That adds up. Yes. I am familiar with their intended destination. "

Lynn looked him over as if sizing him up to judge if he was ready for what he was about to tell him. "If you wish to pursue your endeavor I will not stop you. As far as I am concerned you are a man who can make his own decisions – one who no longer needs to live under the constant supervision and protection of the herd." Van blinked dumbly at him, trying to comprehend what Lynn was getting at. Van felt a political motive behind his decision. Nonetheless, luck was looking in his favor.

"I volunteer to go with him." Van's confusion grew as Jessica's voice piped up from behind him. She moved through the sea of robes to join Van in front. Her expression was calm and resigned; not a common look for her. Van felt a twinge of hate and resentment as he caught the shape of her atom symbol resting on her forehead. He fought the urge to touch his head with his hand.

"You wish to accompany Van?" Lynn asked somewhat incredulously.

"I do. Not as a supervising companion as I have been since he joined us. But as backup, since this John guy has companions as well."

Van was astounded, speechless. He could not think of someone more torturous to go with him on his chase. *Yesterday she ran her thumb in my eye. Is this just an opportunity for her to off me?* "Professor," he piped up. "I appreciate the offer by Sister Jessica, but I would kindly refuse. I feel strongly that this is something I need to do alone." As he spoke, he could hear a deep, frustrated breath leave Jessica's nostrils. Melody was staring her down hard enough that Van thought she was going to punch holes through her head with her gaze.

Lynn took a moment to consider the two young adults, trying to figure out for himself just what Jessica's intentions were. It would, however, give him a break from her incessant critiquing and hostility. He agreed to allow it as long as Van allowed it.

As if reading his mind, Jessica whispered out of the corner of her mouth, "This isn't about revenge. I need to get him just as much as you do." Van almost scoffed at the last bit, only seeing her through his good eye.

Trust the girl who beat the absolute dog piss out of me after I'd already nearly been killed... right.

He reiterated his desire to take on his mission alone. A curious peek out of the corner of his eye showed her clenching her jaw so hard he thought her teeth might start to crack under the pressure. Lynn concluded the meeting and began to gather his pack and the rest moved to do the same. He noticed Jessica hesitating to follow the group home.

"Young lady," he called to her. She noticeably tensed up her shoulders. "You are to return home with us. He has made his decision and we must respect it." She kept her back to him as she begrudgingly grabbed her belongings and joined the back of the group. She shot one last scorching look toward Van as they moved off. Van watched them as they moved back toward the ridge and into the trees until they faded from his sight. He was alone, and strangely at peace, for the first time in a long while. Mostly alone, that is.

"How about it? What say we get going after those heathens and get you on your way to glory?" Weston walked up behind him and laid a hand firmly on his shoulder. A tide of weariness washed over his body and mind.

"No." Van waited a moment to see if this would anger Weston, who did not reply. "I know John's plan. I know his direction of travel. His group probably wants to rest, too. I'm going to rest up. But not in this town. It's giving me the creeps."

"Fair enough. But if you expect Science to give you prophetic inspiration then you must fulfill your proof to him." The pair of them meandered their way out of town in the same direction John had. Van felt more at ease in the thick of the trees, opting for a thick branch to tie himself to for his slumber. He could not have gone far by himself in the blackness of night that now enveloped him.

After getting situated, he decided to get some food in him while he had the chance. The group had been thoughtful enough to bring him a small pack of supplies and give it to him before they moved out for their assault. He took out a can of miniature sausages with a pull tab and popped it open. His brain was too exhausted to go through any process to remove the meat from the juice that held its form, refusing to spill out of the can. He shook the can until the entire cylindrical blob plopped into his hand and ate it like a smelly, watery cookie, washing it all down with a couple of gulps of water. Somewhat satisfied, he shifted to a horizontal position and drifted to sleep. It was the first time in a while his thoughts did not keep him tossing and turning for the first time in a long time. Even Weston had chosen to leave him alone.

Van awoke with a despicable, salty aftertaste in his mouth. From the frontmost zipper of his pack, he produced a travel-size half-empty toothpaste. He scoured the insides of the bag and all the pockets but did not find a toothbrush. *Lovely. Guess it's still better than nothing.* Putting his lips to the opening of the tube he squeezed some of the minty paste into his mouth and used the forefinger of his good hand to wipe it around his teeth. He chose not to rinse, wanting to preserve his precious water and keep the clean sensation, the chill air adding with each inhale. He swiveled himself into a sitting position on his branch and removed his shirt. A small red spot had appeared on the gauze that bandaged his side.

I should be good. I think there'd be more blood if it were still actively bleeding... I wish I knew more about this stuff.

He twisted his leg up onto his opposite knee and inspected his calf wound, similar in appearance to his side. The wound on his hand had a slightly larger red spot that he chalked up to having to use his injured palm more than he would have preferred during the raid.

The rattling of leaves from behind and above him, followed by a sharp, familiar "Hey!" made him nearly jump out of his skin. He shot his head around to see Jess, bright blonde hair and all, squatting down on a branch like a monkey and smirking sinisterly at him. "Miss me?" Van scrambled to his feet, nearly causing himself to spin upside down in the process. As he was finally able to correct his positioning she had already made it to him with a fleeting jump, landing almost soundlessly even among the dried foliage. She pressed a hand against his mouth and held his good hand against his chest with the other, squeezing his wrist to the point of cutting off blood circulation. "Like I said before, I'm not here to kill you. I would've done it by now. Plus it's not like you are that inconspicuous, I bet even if you tried to ditch me I'd still find you."

I guess that's probably true…

He released some of the tension in his muscles. Jessica, feeling him do so, let go of his wrist and mouth. "Then why are you following me? The Professor is going to be pretty pissed off that you're defying his orders."

Jessica's eyebrows turned down into a scowl. "The Professor can shove it." Van raised his eyebrows in surprise at the sudden hostility.

"I mean… I know you two don't really agree on much but he is still in charge."

"He's only in charge because Weston is dead." Her voice became louder and Van could feel the hostility turning toward him. Her expression then turned sorrowful. "Lynn just likes the title. He'll do whatever he wants and drag everyone else along if he thinks it will make him look good. Weston actually gave a damn about me. Us. You. That day you weren't the only one to lose a mentor." She gazed down and away from Van, willing back her tears. "Does he really talk to you?" If Van thought he could not be surprised by her anymore he was proven wrong. He regarded her with suspicion as he slowly nodded his head. Out of the corner of her eye, she noted his response. "I would give anything to talk with him one more time… does he look the same as before he died? Or is he, like, younger? Or thinner?"

Van's eyes flashed to the apparition, who had been watching silently as he sat leaning back against a trunk. The cleft forehead worsened in appearance still, albeit slowly. "He looks just like he did when we last saw him," Van replied, avoiding the detail of carnage. A solemn silence hung between them until Van became uncomfortable, eager to break the awkwardness.

"They're making their way to the coast. I assume they're following the freeway or whatever main road takes them in that direction. That's how John and I traveled." He slung his bag onto his shoulders, then his rifle, watching her as he did. He expected the usual hate to take over once she heard John's name.

"Okay," she said moodily and waited for Van to lead the way.

She's being weird... Is it because of Lynn?

Van decided to ignore her mood for now and turn his attention to tracking, and dealing with, his old posse. They kept the sun between their three and six o'clock position. Tracking people, Van had found, was more difficult than it had probably been back when gravity existed. Instead of being able to find a trampled path through tall grass or footsteps in the mud, you have to scan above and below you – inspect the trees for broken branches or chunks of bark missing or floating nearby. Maybe you would get lucky and someone would leave behind a piece of garbage, or forget to take a rope with them they had used to tie them down for the night.

Unfortunately, John's smart enough not to leave

behind any easy signs to follow him by.

They had been hopping trees for what he estimated to be over an hour without saying anything to each other. The uneasy feeling of having Jessica behind him out of sight had subsided, mostly convinced that she was going to be true to her word. He was about to break the silence when the trees abruptly gave way to open space and a wide road. Van had to reach for a group of twigs with his hurt hand to prevent himself from going airborne over the highway. He grunted at the sharp pinching feeling in his palm.

"Are you alright?" Jessica asked. She had sped up and stopped on the same tree as him. Genuine concern in her voice and on her face freaked him out even more.

"Yeah. Peachy." She seemed annoyed by his slight sarcasm. She glanced right then left down the road.

"Over there. Looks like a sign about a mile down the road," she observed, pointing west. The two stuck to the tree line as they worked toward the sign. Van was able to read the wording before Jessica as they approached.

"Oregon Welcomes You," he read aloud.

It had a pretty background painted behind the wording. Two figures emerged from the thick tree line and shrubbery on the opposite side of the sign. Van locked eyes with Betty. His hands began to reach for his gun, then he stopped himself. He looked at Kristen, eyes puffy as if she'd been crying just moments before. She scowled at him. The two stood no more than twenty feet from each other.

"Are you going to do anything?" Jess asked rather calmly. Van looked at her. Normally, he would have expected her to be itching to take these two out herself. Instead, she looked at him almost indifferently.

"Are you saying I should shoot them?" he asked in a soft tone.

"I'm not saying anything. I'm along for the ride, remember? I'm asking what your plan is so I know how to back you up," she said defensively.

Van looked back toward the pair of women as his brain scrambled to think of what he should do. He ripped the gun sling over his shoulder and half-heartedly raised it toward them.

"Really? You're going to shoot us?" Betty called out, placing her arms out to her sides to show that she presented no threat. "We were good to you… Shared our stories over dinner. Then you tried to have us killed." Van's forehead began to sweat. Betty's words only scrambled his thoughts even more. His stomach began to churn and hurt. "You were the one who betrayed us. If anything, your issue lies with John. Who, by the way, we parted ways with. We want nothing more to do with your conflict. Our brothers are dead because of you two. If it were up to us, we'd see you dead with them… But we know that won't bring them back to us." Still no response from Van, whose hands were now shaky despite the weightlessness of the rifle in his hands. Jessica continued to watch him with interest. "Just let us be. Please. You don't need to worry about us trying to track you down for retaliation. We just want to go on living out the rest of our lives in as much peace as possible."

Van finally lowered the gun. His heart was in his throat and he was breathing heavily through his nostrils. He slung the firearm back around his shoulders. "You're not going back to that town, are you?" he asked them.

"Of course not. There's an exit back down the road a ways that starts toward Montana. We figured we'd head there to find a nice community, perhaps."

Without waiting for a response from Van or Jessica, or offering further explanation as to their plans, Betty dipped back down the slight hill between the side of the road and the tree line to continue on her way. Kristen looked after her for a moment, then turned back toward the others.

"There's a cave not too far that way," she told Van, tense in her jaw, jabbing her thumb in the direction from which they had just come. He could tell she did not feel quite the same as Betty about letting everything go. "That's where we separated from John. Go crazy on each other, you lunatics." She turned away and floated away to catch up with her sister. Neither Jessica nor Van moved, following the women with their eyes until they were out of sight. Jessica turned her head back to Van.

"So… should we get after it?" she suggested. Van took a moment to process what had happened.

I feel… angry. Why do I feel angry? Why did I freak out just now over nothing?

He looked down at his bandaged hand and waited for it to stop quivering. He flexed it into a fist a few times. The sting of it seemed to help him gather himself. "No. We know where he is, or at least where he was. Let's have some lunch."

Chapter 23

Squeezing the last of the sweet, pine-flavored water from a bag, John looked out at the wall of buildings that made up the city of Portland. The dull-colored buildings grew in density the further you looked into the massive city. Velum stood as a canvas against the foreground of weary skyscrapers. To the rear, John could see the peaks of Mt. Hull – a resolute giant for all of the locals to see. He wished he could have seen this view in the winter, snow covering the landscape and capping the mountain. As it stood now, it resembled a pile of uneventful rocks ending at a fine point. While moving towards the city, John had told Frank that he wanted to see the area from the top, but Frank insisted there was no time. John tried to do the calculations of how long it would take him to float there from his spot. He guessed it to be between twenty and thirty miles.

Three hours, give or take. That's quite a long time

to be floating... The view would be incredible, though.

Pulling his attention back to the city, John wondered how much food they had left. Frank drifted beside him and handed him a pair of binoculars.

"For the first year, the survivors felt like they had to protect the town from intruders, so they built that." John's eyes followed Frank's finger while looking through the binoculars. There was a wall of rusted, broken cars that wrapped around the lower half of the city's edge. They had been stacked together three to four cars thick, extending edge to edge.

"Don't they know that anyone could just crawl over the top of it? All they did was box themselves in," he said, handing the green binoculars back to Frank.

"My hope is that we can pass through without any trouble from the locals. Once we get outside the city we'll only be about a day's travel to Seaside." Frank handed him a piece of jerky. His lip turned up in instinctive disgust as he remembered Artemis, the man selling human jerky. He held up his hand in denial. Frank shrugged and readily scarfed it down. "You see that large building over there? That is going to be our directional bearing. It's the Wells Fargo building, and roughly halfway to the other side."

The men became more cautious and alert as they

started toward the metropolis. Closing in on the wall of cars, John could make out small gaps in the wall of metal, allowing glimpses inside. It appeared that whoever had worked so diligently to move these in place wasn't worried about the big holes of broken windows and removed doors. At the edge of the man-made wall, he noticed that the construct was wrapped together with an assortment of items, ranging from loose wiring to braided clothes. One van presented a sizable opening that appeared to be able to fit at least a family of eight. He pulled himself to the outer threshold of the car window.

"John, don't go through, it's a wired trap," Frank warned. Taking a second look ahead of him, John saw a sawed-off shotgun that had been duct taped to the headrest of the chair. A thin wire wrapped strategically around the interior of the car was rigged to pull the trigger if anyone crossed through it.

"As you said, the wall from the outside perspective doesn't make sense. They set up the whole wall as a massive booby trap to keep any unwanted people out." Frank said in a hushed voice.

"Are there any traps at the top of this thing? Wouldn't people be able to just go over it?"

"Originally, they were going to set up traps at the

top. Once they began running out of supplies, along with realizing they would just have to keep setting more and more traps elsewhere as people found ways around the wall, they simply left it as is. Their new way of thinking was that they could lure people into simply going over the barricade where they could easily see them. Funnel them in, essentially."

"Not the worst idea I suppose… So, aren't we going to be walking into a trap by going over it?"

"Nah. They gave up on keeping people posted a while ago. Doesn't mean someone won't see us, though, so be wary."

They started the climb up the barrier. John had found two other rigged traps awaiting an unsuspecting victim. Pieces of sun-worn plastic snapped under the force of their hands and feet as they scaled. He peered in the window of a rust-red sedan near the top of the wall. A yell nearly escaped his lips as he came face to face with a corpse in the driver's seat. The poor soul had been snagged by what looked like a crude bear trap. The body had also expanded to extreme proportions. Its abdomen had bulged outward with a great build-up of unreleased gasses. John hastily continued his ascent, forcing the image from his mind.

I have seen a lot of death, but that was brutal.

Lurching, his stomach desperately wanted to physically expel what he had seen. When John blinked he saw the face of the man in his exhaustive despair. Frank pointed out a small coffee shop with several broken-out windows.

"Make your way down to the shop. I have some supplies stashed in there we can take to get us to Seaside. Unless someone else managed to find my goodies," Frank said. John could see loose barricades meant to block off side streets with graffiti written on them: Autonomous Zone. Spray paint decorated the majority of the building walls with anti-police rhetoric and violent slurs. From what he could see not a single edifice had every window still intact.

John pushed away from the wall, thankful to put space between him and the carnage. Landing on a sturdy light pole, John steadied himself for the next jump. He began sailing out toward a bench no more than fifty feet away when motion from across the street caught his eye – a man who had been lying in wait, slinking from around an alleyway corner. John threw his feet down onto the hot asphalt, stopping himself in the middle of the street.

The man held a rusted pair of scissors in one hand.

His shirt and pants alike were covered in holes, stains, and patches. John shot a glance behind him, noticing that Frank was not behind him.

This better not have been some dirty trick, old man.

"Stay where you are," the man called to him. "No need for anyone to get hurt here." The man seemed like he could barely consider himself a man. John guessed him to be only nineteen or twenty, although his skin was loose, clinging to his hungry body. One by one, more strangers looking just as ragged came out from their respective hiding places, a total of five people in all. John, bracing himself for an impossible fight, waited for them to make the first move. A woman wearing torn tie-dye produced an old .45 Colt handgun that gleamed in the sunlight.

"If you got something of worth we'll let you pass," the woman said as she shakily pointed the pistol in his direction. Her eyes held a scared, unwilling gaze.

I don't have anything other than my axe. I doubt that pistol even has bullets.

Frank stepped into view, causing them all to shift their attention toward him.

"I'm guessing you guys remember me." Frank took out a small baggy containing a small green ball from his back pocket. A couple of them shifted at the sight.

"You're going to tell me where you keep the rest, old man, or I'm going to blast you away," the woman said, her gun now directed at Frank's head.

"Hey, hey now. You said to give you something of value to pass, right? I'm just giving you something to look forward to when I come around again. If you shot me, how would you get any next time?" Frank said as he pushed the closed baggy toward the woman with the gun.

Quickly tucking the gun away, she raced for the bag, snagging it like it was going to try running away at any moment. The remaining four young adults gathered around the woman, eager to get a piece of the good stuff. Frank gave John a nod and they both quietly moved by. As relatively smooth as the encounter went, it only packed on the paranoia John had inside.

"Why would they want to smoke that crap? Wouldn't that just make you hungrier?" John asked. Frank stopped himself on a park bench with a half-faded picture of a woman selling insurance and the letters "ACAB" sloppily painted over the face.

"I think most people just want to feel normal. They want to go back to the past and not stress every day about where their next meal is coming from. Plus, the stuff we grow is as strong as they come." John looked confused. "Still stuck on the preconceived notion that drugs are a gateway, huh? The city grows it because it is one of the only consistent things we can grow to use as medicine. It's the same concept of drinking water from a sink pipe. When times are tough, and you're desperate, societal norms tend to change." Frank nodded as if to punctuate his stance and began moving in the direction of the Wells Fargo building. Feeling a bit more at ease, John pressed off from street level, gravitating toward the middle of the tall spire, and landed gently on an unusually clean and intact window. Oddly enough, this was one of the only buildings he had seen thus far with mostly intact windows. Frank joined him and pointed upward, indicating that they were aiming for the top of the building.

Once at the top, John surveyed the roof. A series of large metal boxes spread across the small, pebbled walkways — air conditioning units, coated in rust. A large antenna grew from the roof extended to the sky and was held steady by several thick, metal cables. Frank drifted over to one of the intake pipes and opened a side panel. He produced a dull red duffle bag from within and unzipped the top to inspect the contents.

"I told you, I have stashes left all over town. Looks

like this one, however, is a little light on the supplies we'll need." He discarded loose cans and other garbage, shaking each one to check their fullness. He tossed one can over to John; a can of old pineapples with an odd bulge from pressure in the side of it. John pulled on the quick tab and a hiss of air escaped the can, sickeningly reminded of the bloated man sitting at the edge of town.

"Do you honestly think this is still edible?" John asked skeptically.

"See, there you go again. You think it's bad simply because it has a bit of pressure to it. You need to shake off the societal norms," Frank told him. John looked at him incredulously as he peered at the pale-colored food inside the tin can. He had come across plenty of canned food in the last two years but none had shared the bulgy appearance. Using his pointer finger John scooped the food into his mouth, ignoring the tingle it gave his tongue as he chewed. *I would feel better eating bugs, I think.*

"Are you nervous to see your father again?" Frank asked suddenly.

"No. I have a lot to say to him. Things I should have said a long time ago."

"I got to warn you, John, if you plan on sticking around in Seaside they have some expectations. Each member of the public is tasked to do something every day, even if it is something menial. Everyone pitches in for the greater good of the community."

John shrugged as he finished off the last of the fermented pineapple juice in the can.

"All this talk of changing the society culture, yet I still have to hold up a job that gets me nowhere in life."

"Before The Lifting, my wife and I would go out to eat at a buffet once a week. If it just so happened to land on a Saturday, we would be surrounded by crowds of people. The only thing worth eating in the whole restaurant was the subpar steak cooked in the middle of the buffet area. On the weekends the line of customers stretched from the grill to the front door. At the time, societal norms said that I had to go to the back of the line and wait my turn. As I watched from an outside perspective, I saw that some people remained in the line for salad and others for the taco bar. I didn't want any of that so I walked up to the steak counter and asked for a piece. Once I got my steak, I looked down the line and saw everyone giving me the stink-eye. They thought that because I jumped in line I had wronged them, even though most of them didn't even want the steak." John remained silent, waiting patiently for Frank to make his point. "Now, if you look at the big picture, everyone wants to be needed and everyone wants to feel safe. That, in my opinion, is a good social norm. Everyone wants the fulfillment of putting in a good day's work, even if the job is small. But, enough of that. We need to make our way out of town before we run into another group."

Hopefully, we get there soon. Frank's lessons are getting a bit old... Damn, is this how Van felt when I would lecture him?

John shook the thought from his head. He had no desire to relive any of those days. He and Frank pushed off after surveying the area a while longer. They would periodically stop as they heard voices draw near, waiting for them to go by before proceeding. At one point they dove into a small shop as a group of men and women flew through the streets in the direction they had come from. As they waited in the backroom, John took a moment to check the cabinets for food, just in case. Nothing.

The city is definitely picked clean at this point.

John opened the cabinets under the sink to expose the plumbing. He proceeded to make small knocks on each one, waiting for the dull thud that would indicate water. Rapping on the final pipe, connected to the p-trap, he found the resonance he was after. Carefully, John unscrewed the pipe fittings to find just a gulp-worth fixed to the inside of the pipe wall. It tasted of mildew, but he had had worse in the past.

Frank indicated it was safe to move and they pressed on. The noonday sun blazed overhead as they flowed from one building to the next. After several blocks, Frank halted in front of a large plate in the ground that looked like it led to a sewer system. Cracking it open, they both slipped along the ladder to the bottom. Frank clicked on a dull flashlight and led them further down a man-sized corridor.

"A couple years and it still smells awful down here," John complained.

They arrived at a barred door. Frank pulled out a key, unlocked it, and pushed it wide open. As John crossed the threshold he noticed a sharp change in temperature from chill to cozy.

"What is this room?" John inquired. "This is what I call my bachelor pad," Frank chuckled. "I like to have a place on the road where I can relax. Let my guard down just a little without worrying about someone stumbling onto me." John could see floating piles of cans among other odds and ends. "We have the night to rest. Tomorrow, we should be coming into Seaside near the end of the second sunrise," Frank said as he ruffled through some items. He flipped a switch on the wall and several bulbs flickered to life.

"Second sunrise?" John asked.

"Have I not told you about that yet? Apologies. It's a nickname we use to refer to noon. The ocean wall typically blocks most of the sunlight until it crests over the Velum, at least in Seaside. We call it the "second sunrise." Frank pulled himself into a fluffy sleeping bag. "I'm going to catch some sleep, you should probably do the same," Frank said as he closed his eyes.

John suddenly remembered the journal in his pocket and figured this was an opportune time to finish reading the entries. He positioned himself directly underneath one of the dim bulbs to best see the boy's words. He poured through the remaining pages until finally coming to the last one.

Day 92

I made it across town to check grandma's house. It was the last place I could think of. I had to push my way through grandma's screen on her back patio to get in because the front door was locked. I found dad in the back bedroom and mom in the downstairs basement. I didn't stay long. I have been on my own for a long time and I'm having a hard time finding food and water. I cry

most nights because of how hungry my belly is. I found some spare toilet paper that no one had taken yet. I have been going without it.

I'm not sure what to do now. The town is all gone except for the man at the end of the street who always yelled at me. Before the world got scary I saw him go down a tunnel in the ground. Maybe he will look after me.

Closing the small book, John found that he had tears of his own clouding his vision.

Damn it... I hope you're okay.

He wondered if he would have the will to go on if he had seen what the boy saw. He rotated his body to be parallel to the wall, pulled himself to the door, and secured the lock. Calmness warmed his inside knowing that, at least for tonight, he would not have to worry about something going bump in the night.

Chapter 24

A low light shade stretched across the quaint town as the townsfolk prepared for the festival set to begin later that afternoon. Tommy wondered if Maureen had been right — was it wrong of them to bid a celebration for a cataclysm. Based on last year's dismal event, Tommy was worried about what this year had in store. As much as it was interesting to pontificate on today's reveals, Tommy couldn't help but ponder on his newly appointed assignment. How was he going to convince Maureen and Frank to join him? Maureen was already a worrier and Frank was off on his usual trips to the border, so he had some time to think about how to sell it to them. Looking up at the crisp sun as it was shielded by the Velum, Tommy figured it was no later than eleven o'clock. That gave him an hour to make his way to the city square.

Securing his clip to the tether wire, Tommy pushed off and drifted lazily through the air. The aroma of fresh-baked bread caught his nose. To his left were several large, netted bags stuffed with beautifully bronzed rolls, ready for the mid-day feast. The sight in the street as he passed the bakery puzzled him. Along the whole street, people were hauling large mirrors from within their business buildings and homes. Each mirror seemed to be angled upward to some degree. Tommy steadied himself near a woman who was struggling to keep her mirror from twisting to the wrong angle.

"Why are you doing that?" Tommy asked bluntly, startling the woman.

"Oh! We're preparing for the Color Festival like we ought to. We were told to place mirrors on the ground and hang any kind of crystals we had for the celebration. The Engineers say that the rainbow prisms would not only shine down but would create a whole tapestry of colors."

Upon closer inspection, Tommy could see that crystals had been set adrift, floating in the air, each one secured with a string. He gave the annoyed woman a nod and continued floating past more people eagerly preparing for the day.

He rounded a corner and the center square came into view. It looked exactly as one would expect such an area to with its spacious, grassy area and willow trees bordering the edges of the walkways within. The willows were long dried up but the long branches remained stretched out and tangled like a witch's hair. Along the outside of the park area, various produce and baked goods stands had been constructed. The table tops were not firmly secured to the ground but were floating about waist height with a rope at each corner securing it to the ground. Each of them kept their goods from floating away using either one large net stretched across the table or keeping the product in bags.

Tommy loitered and watched as the crowd in the square grew in size as noon drew closer. The empty willows filled with onlookers. Several families with children congregated toward the northern end of the field where an awkward platform had been erected. Mirrors had been attached to the podium, all of them angled toward the spot where the speaker would stand. Tommy found himself a small space at the top of a corner shop. It looked out over the square and provided him some distance away from the masses.

Wouldn't take much panic to send someone flying in a group this size...

Three portly men wearing sharply pressed business suits approached the stage and unpacked a trumpet each. Hovering shoulder to shoulder, the trio remained ten to fifteen feet higher than the crowd. They brought the mouthpieces to their lips and blew three resonant, drawn-out trumpets. As if by magic, Brett and several of the other Engineers appeared on stage and waited for the trumpeting to seize. Brett drifted forward and poised himself at the edge of the stand.

"Welcome, welcome, to the second annual Color Festival. With how dreary last year's occasion was, we wanted to bring a brighter touch to this day. I want to start by saying that this isn't a place to remember the horror or the depression. Today is a celebration of remembrance for those we've lost. Today is about looking inward at ourselves and our community and how far we have come." Brett motioned with an open hand toward the pillars of water and ice out past the coast. "At the peak of the Velum, we have a bounty of food to choose from. Stationed all along the streets are delectably prepared food and desserts to eat. Also, a unique carnival has been set up on the far left side of the field where your kids can play all assortments of games. This evening we will convene for the lighting of the lanterns. For that, we would ask that you all bring an item that holds some remembrance to be sent to the heavens." He clapped his hands and grinned at the crowd. "Having said all that, it looks like we are ready to begin!"

Brett shielded his eyes as he looked up at the sun – it had just started to crest the ocean wall. An indescribable array of colors split the air. The sun reflected off of the water and ice caps of Velum, which in turn hit the dozens of mirrors that surrounded the speaker's station causing the whole square to become a kaleidoscope of dancing colors.

Tommy squinted at the sight. *Wish they would have told us to bring sunglasses.* Looking downward while shielding his eyes, Tommy could see a magnificent swirl of colors as if they were mixing in water. A tingle began crawling up his exposed arms to the tips of his fingers. The heat of the reflection started to itch and burn his skin uncomfortably. Fading as fast as it started, the colors dulled out to a soft hue of reds and blues then disappeared altogether. Tommy looked down at his arms to find they were badly sunburned from the intense pressure of the sun. Different shades of red wriggled across his skin just as the colors had done, his burns varying in degree of intensity. The deepest reds imagined that of crimson marbling. The radiating skin intensified at the parts that the sun still beat down on him.

Bewildered, and annoyed, Tommy aimed to get his fill of tasty foods and made for the stands. Especially the baked goods. It wasn't every day you got fresh cooked rolls from the oven. Sure, they weren't the same as before due to the cooking process, but they still hit the spot. He touched down on the concrete sidewalk and spotted a table three booths down from him filled to the brim with sweet-smelling cakes. Eagerly he made his way over and graciously thanked the baker as he grabbed two fat rolls with a sweet-tasting icing smeared over top, one for each hand.

"You, sir! Hmm, come, and let me tell you what your future has in store," a plump man said from inside a dark purple canvas. Tommy was surprised to see one of these guys in today's world. Why would anyone waste their time on this nonsense when there were tasks to be done? Nevertheless, he thought it would be a good excuse to get out of the sun's rays beating down on his cooked skin.

He pushed forward and drifted into the makeshift carnival tent as he finished off the remainder of his treats. Wondering how the tent stayed up as it did, Tommy was underwhelmed to find it simply was a common tent. One pole raised the center upward and the sides were carefully hammered down with stakes. Tommy pulled the flaps closed, causing the tent to become pitch black as his eyes worked to adjust. The plump man readily lit several candles, carefully holding them still in the air and then letting them float in place. The ambiance of the tent made Tommy's nerves grow. When his eyes adjusted he saw the big man beckoning him over to the center of the space where a large ball hung in the air in a slow, disciplined spin. A single light was flipped on, causing the crystal globe to explode with many needle-thin light beams that slowly rotated. He watched in fascination as the lights danced across the canvas walls.

"Now, let's see, hmmm. I see you are set to start a new adventure. Hmmm. There are many dangers ahead, yet one image stands out from the rest. A grand reunion before an agonizing loss – a sorrowful catastrophe."

Tommy rolled his eyes at the man.

"What could make our lives any worse?" he asked skeptically.

"Mother nature can always choose to rain down destruction as she sees fit, as is the karma of the world. With each prize comes a bully ready to snatch it away from you. Beware the giants, for they will be your demise if you are not careful." The man grasped the ball and spun it faster, which caused all of the lines of light to fuse as one. The ball shone as bright as a search spotlight then disappeared once again sinking them into disorienting darkness. The flap flew open, and children and teenagers came pouring in demanding their fortunes be told. Tommy slipped out into the fray of chattering kids. He was reminded of his burns as he entered daylight. A willow tree welcomed him with its patch of shade where he sat to think for several minutes.

After eating a hearty meal of fresh vegetables and other treats he decided it was time to track down Maureen and give her the news, still unsure of how he was going to ask her to do something so unpredictable and dangerous. She had not made an appearance in the square as far as he had seen.

Maybe I'll catch her at the next event.

Linking once more to the steel, woven cable, Tommy drifted to the outskirts of Seaside to what had been coined "The Tossing of Flowers." He found it a bit archaic himself but if it helped people grieve then that's where he needed to be. Tommy remembered the tense conversation that he and Maureen had just a few days earlier. She hated this holiday more than anyone he had met. He carefully paced along as the beach-goers gently tossed flower petals into the water of Velum, seeking its approval until next year. He was told that tossing the pedals one by one was a prayer to the water and all its majesty. He didn't care to join them; there was no point in praying to a natural phenomenon. He just needed to find Maureen. As he drifted back toward the town he wondered if she had even left her home.

Maureen lived alone, as she was the last surviving member of her family. She resided in a white rambler house that once overlooked a cliff and over the ocean. Before the lifting, it would have been an enchanting residence with the waves crashing against the rocks. Most of the residents of Seaside avoided living in the houses nearest the ocean since they were now the last to receive direct sunlight.

How depressing it must be to wake up in the dark alone and be there 'til midday.

Once he had gone by her house and did not find her, Tommy scoured the town, inquiring any person if they knew her whereabouts. No one had seen her. Why was he so drawn to her? Not in a romantic sense – she and he held the same pain, only he was able to mask it better. Each had suffered the same loss. Tommy paused near a street lamp. The bond he felt was molded out of subtle pains and built strong through perseverance. He needed to be with Maureen, and even Frank, to fill the voids in each other's cracked souls.

Tommy continued searching as the sun started to wane. The festivities were coming to a close, leading up to the new event this year, a solemn occasion for those who may be hurting. Following a crowd of men, women, and children up the main hill, Tommy pushed forward. He chose not to use the safety of the wire to pace himself and launched himself up the street, passing by the multitude of onlookers, a metaphorical lamb to the slaughter. Even in this time of disorder people craved to walk in lines and wait their turns. Civility was ingrained in their very character. The street opened to a large meadow clearing, more willows bordering what probably once was a beautiful sanctuary.

Tommy crested the hill and finally laid eyes on his friend. All but her head was covered by the overgrown grass. She sat cross-legged just above the ground with her hands resting on her thighs, still as a boulder.

"Maureen!" Tommy cried out. Slowly opening her eyes, she saw him flying to her and could not help but crack a smile. He looked like an old, overweight hero awkwardly flying over to save her. Tommy's body had been rotating counterclockwise so that by the time he sailed past her his back was facing her. Tommy reached the edge of the grass, bringing his hands up to stop his motion on a medium-sized rock. Slowly this time, he made his way back over to Maureen, who had resumed her apparent meditation.

"I have something important to ask you," Tommy

said as he approached her, giving caution that there wasn't much to hold onto for safety.

"No, Tommy, not today." She drew out a small box from behind her. The edges were made from a thin, brown material.

"Where have you been? You missed the feast." Tommy tried his best to steady himself beside her. Maureen pulled a small photo from her shirt's breast pocket. A picture of a young girl holding a baseball bat and dark blue hat.

"I went to a place that I knew would hurt me. Last month I went to see the Engineers and asked them to include an event for this year. I need to move on, but I have to do it my way. This last event is meant for that reason. The Chinese called it "Yuan Xiao" or, in English, the "lantern festival." Throughout history, it has been used for all kinds of sentimental things. For the color festival, it's to lift the burdens from our hearts and send our loved ones to a better place." Tears welled in her eyes as she gazed beyond everything in front of her. Tommy wanted to do anything to take her pain away. Maureen lifted the picture so Tommy could see it better.

"I went home. I haven't been back there since..." Maureen's voice drifted off as she tried to stifle memory. "I needed to get something that represented my loss to lift to the sky." The color of the sky had shifted from a light blue to a dark gray. She tucked the photo into her makeshift lantern, leaving it for the right time. "I don't mind if you join me, I just… I need you to let me say my peace." She told him in a low defeated voice.

Looking around, Tommy could see that many families and individuals alike had found their own spot in the field, spaced apart enough to allow for some privacy. Many of them hugged or told stories around their handmade lanterns. Eventually, the dark gray sky turned black and the first stars speckled the sky.

Raising the small shrine, Maureen spoke softly. "I remember the day you came into my life. You came out scared and crying. I told you that everything was going to be alright. Do you know what you did? You stopped crying and stared at me like you already knew who I was – like you were there before you were even born. The hardest thing I had to go through wasn't the destruction of the world… It was losing you. This isn't goodbye… This doesn't mean I am forgetting you. I need to be free of the hurt. I want to only remember the smiling, happy person you were. Please, look over me like I was meant to do for you."

Maureen lit the end of a skinny stick that stood in the middle of the lantern and lifted it into the air. In silence, they watched as dozens of lanterns were cast up, lighting the sky with the memories of so many lost. Tommy wondered why he didn't feel the same way at this moment. Why didn't he feel for the loss of his family? Perhaps it was because his wife had died many years ago. His son had made it clear he was not interested in including him in his adult life not long after. Maybe there was no loss for him to feel after all.

Chapter 25

The remainder of John and Frank's journey was refreshingly uneventful. They had passed a pair of Seasiders, a man and a woman, who were out collecting some firewood to take back to their home. Frank introduced John, exchanged pleasantries and they continued on their way.

John could not stop staring at the monstrosities that made up Velum. The gargantuan pedestals of ocean water made him feel vulnerable and insignificant. As he drew closer he could see the specks that were the carts transporting workers miles upward to the icy lids. The knot in his stomach tightened as the distance between him and his father closed. He had made up his mind that he would start the conversation with an apology, leading to a real Hallmark-like reunion, hug and all. John always thought it was weird that as a kid a hug meant nothing so it was frivolously tossed around, it held much more weight as an adult.

"You know your father isn't exactly the hugging type, right?" Frank had reminded him.

"Well, neither am I. I figure after the end of the world we can move past that sort of thing. Besides, you didn't exactly provide any great alternatives to an opening line..."

"What? Your dad loves that joke about the three nuns arriving at the pearly gates!
No? We'll work up to it."

Now, here they stood, at the main security checkpoint at the entrance of Seaside. The pine trees followed on each side of the road meeting two tall towers. From inside the gates, John could hear the hustle and bustle of the population within. He had not been around so many people since before The Lifting.

Man, I forgot how much I dislike crowds.

He found it ironic that he had chosen to enter a career of service – one that required him to constantly interact with strangers. There was something different about tending to a few folks' injuries versus feeling swarmed by hundreds of people, though.

The towers were constructed differently than he would have expected. A large tree trunk was set flat against the ground and extended upward to a platform above. Four braided ropes were fastened to various objects so the sentry could clamber up the pole without fear of tipping it off angle. John could see that one sentry at the top was tied to a rope. He held a serious demeanor, ready to leap at any moment for a wayward citizen.

Frank, friendly as ever, approached the couple of guards that had been placed at the gate for the day. They required no identification from him as they recognized him immediately.

“We’ve got another one joining us here at Seaside, fellas,” Frank grinned at the young men. “Tommy’s boy, as a matter of fact.”

“I didn’t know Tommy had a son,” one of them replied. “Doesn’t seem like the family type, honestly.”

Frank chuckled.

“Yes, well, that’s what we’re hoping to change today.” Something about Frank’s words made John even more anxious. He could feel his breathing speeding up ever so slightly. “Come on, John.” Frank waved him forward to follow. “We’ll go straight to Tommy’s place. If he’s not there right now I’m sure he’ll return shortly.”

Frank handed him a carabiner that had been rigged to a thick leather belt and explained their method for moving around the city. John put the belt on and clipped the carabiner onto the line. The two of them made their way through the streets of mingling people. John was fascinated by how many kids he saw — some of them not even toddlers. On top of that, there was no fear in their faces. Everyone appeared healthy and well-fed, much different from the elastic-drawn eye sockets worn from lack of water and food that he was used to seeing. A feeling of contentment emanated from each one. It almost made him mad to know they had been living like this while he was fighting tooth and nail for his survival.

This is weird... they're just going about their day as if the outside world isn't in complete ruin, filled with masses of psychopaths. John almost laughed at his own thoughts. *Hell, as if I'm not as crazy as the rest of them out there at this point.*

They did not speak as they made their way to the outskirts of the city where St. John rested. Frank allowed John to have the time to mull over what he was going to say to his father when they arrived. When the old fishing boat came into sight John looked at Frank with a questioning look, to which Frank nodded, affirming that he had finally reached his destination. Once they were about fifty yards away Frank called out for Tommy, but there was no response. Frank shrugged.

"Must've gone out for a treat. That man loves his baked goods. We'll let ourselves inside. He showed me where he keeps a spare key." He maneuvered his way to the stern. From within a knot of rope secured around a cleat, he slid out a simple, silver key.

Unlocking the door, both men went down into the cabin. It looked as John had expected. Everything was tidied up and in its place. On the left side was a short, square table with single, cushioned seats on either end with storage underneath. A couple of cupboards for a pantry. On the right was a tiny sink sitting on more cabinets and an uncomfortable-looking sofa. At the end of the space, through a small entryway where a curtain had been hung, was a bed big enough for one.

John moved into the seat on the far end of the table, resting his head in his hands. The position was not as comfortable with no gravity, but it felt familiar and he stuck with it. On the limited amount of wall space hung a couple of photos. One was of Tommy and his former beat partner receiving their Lifesaving Award from their Chief of Police. Frank followed his gaze and smirked.

"I love giving him crap for that mustache."

The other photo, hanging right above the sink, was

a photo of Tommy, John, and Colby, his little brother, Colby. The three had gone on a fishing trip for one of Tommy's birthdays. They stood with an arm around each other's shoulders as Colby held up the hefty largemouth bass he had caught.

Ah, so now he cares.

The fact that the photo was hung up as if it were some treasured memory of his father's, irked John. His thoughts began to race. His sentimental feelings waned as he sat and stewed over how his father had handled everything back then. The loss. The heartache. The abandonment. He was beginning to think that he had some other words he would like to say to his father.

Frank decided to go back up to the deck to watch for Tommy and give John some alone time. They had been practically joined at the hip the last few days while heading to Seaside, he was sure that John would appreciate some space.

A glint of color caught John's eye from the skylight affixed to the center of the ceiling. Large white square crystals with pictures attached to them. Pushing from the seat cushion he drifted closer. Nearing he recognized many of the pictures, they were of him and his brother. The largest held a picture of his mom. The glare from the sun combined with the size of the cube caused his mother to glow like an angel. John sat and thought for another fifteen minutes or so, wandering the space and finding artifacts from his past, before Frank spoke up.

"Hey! You ornery old bastard. Happy to see me?" John could tell Frank was smiling as he spoke. A second man's voice, familiar, yet a stranger's still, called back from further away.

"Not even close, buddy." The man's voice also contained a smile. "I do have something important that I've been waiting to discuss. It involves you, me, and Maureen."

A few seconds passed and John heard the two above him embrace and exchange small talk. He felt awkward, unsure if he should make his way topside. Just as he was about to leave his seat and go for the stairs Frank's voice came through clear again.

"We'll go over the details of all that later. Listen, I've got a surprise down here for ya."

"Ah jeez, Frank, it better not be another–" Tommy stopped mid-sentence as he ducked into the cabin, laying eyes on John. His mouth gaped, but no sound came out. John froze, he could not remember a single thing he wanted to say to the man who now stood in front of him for the first time in multiple years. He thought his father looked more tired and aged than he had expected him to as if he had been in constant worry since they last saw each other. Frank, noticing the hesitancy from the other two, broke the silence first.

"Can you believe it? Your boy just wandered on up to where I was posted one day. Nearly hacked me to pieces, too," he chuckled.

John finally found his voice.

"Hey, Dad." John felt his throat tighten as he forced out the words. John had at least known he was coming to meet his dad – Tommy was getting blindsided.

"John…" Tommy was at a loss for words.

"Pretty nice bachelor pad you got here." John motioned around him with his hands. Tommy blinked rapidly a few times. John shot a glance at Frank. He was beginning to think that he had actually sent his father into shock.

"Nice place, but a little cramped for all of us. How about we get outside into some fresh air?" Frank offered. Tommy and John nodded and silently followed him out. John found himself becoming irritated – upset, even.

I get that he didn't expect to see me, but does he really have nothing to say after everything that happened and after all this time?

Once they got up to the deck Tommy turned to face John. John felt like giving him a shove but stopped himself, reminding himself that it would likely send him flying and cause harm. Tommy finally recovered his ability to speak.

"John... I can't believe you're–"

Tommy's words were cut off by a warm, dark red splash on his face and shirt. John's vision flickered then returned as he began to feel a searing hot sensation under his right collarbone. His ears had not even registered the boom of the round being fired from the rifle while the bullet seared through the back of his shoulder and out his upper chest. His stupefied gaze locked onto the piece of lead and copper for just a moment before Tommy was dragging him by his collar over the side of the boat. Frank followed.

Immediately, Frank brought his pack around to the front of him and dug out his makeshift first aid kit. He ripped John's shirt at the shoulder to expose the wound. He began applying bandages and pressure to the holes on either side of John while Tommy moved to the far end of the boat, peaking around his cover to get eyes on the shooter. Further down the tree line, about two hundred yards or so, he caught a glimpse of a young blonde man moving back into the trees flanking the trio.

"I only see one, but I don't recognize him from town. A blonde guy with a hunting rifle. What the hell is that about?" He directed the last sentence John's way, looking for some explanation as to why this stranger would randomly open fire in city limits. John did his best to answer through his gasps of anguish.

"Van… I can't believe… he followed us…"

"Van? Well, who is he?"

The whistle of another bullet flew by Tommy's ear. He instinctively ducked and moved to another position behind the boat.

"Dumb guy I met… insists on killing me for some… ritual."

Tommy looked even more confused than before but decided not to push the issues of who and why right now.

"Is there anyone else with him?" John asked as Frank put the finishing touches on his patch job.

"Not that I've seen. Should there be more?"

"Possibly. There were plenty in Briarton."

"Frank," Tommy turned to look at him. "You okay running into town to get help if I draw his fire?"

Frank nodded. The two older men held such a level-headed demeanor that it made John feel the need to do likewise. He tried not to think about the gaping holes in his shoulder and moved to a crouched position, ready to spring in any direction needed. He drew his axe with his non-injured arm and kept it at the ready. Tommy hesitated.

"John, I have my pistol down in the cabin. Just stay behind the hull until I get back out."

It's weird not being the one with the plan but I can't think of a better one. Seems like Van might've had some target practice since he last shot at me, the bastard... I'm going to make sure there's no chance he lives this time.

With a nod, Tommy sprung upward and grabbed hold of the side of the deck, throwing his legs over the edge and planting his feet onto the floorboards. Using the bend in his knees from the landing he sprung for the opening to the cabin and sunk into the hole without slowing down. John was astounded at the agility the old man still possessed.

Frank took his only chance and used Tommy's athletic performance as a diversion for his exit. He anticipated the snap of another shot from Van's rifle. Except the round did not go for Tommy, it nearly took Frank's ear off.

Damn kid... he knows Frank's going to get backup. It's me he wants, though.

Before Van had another chance to take a shot at

Frank, John stood up from behind his cover, waving his axe overhead. A glint off of the rifle scope flashed from within the trees. John knew his distraction worked and that he only had a split second to move before he was taken out. Three smaller, closer cracks of a gunshot made John jump. Tommy had reappeared with his Glock 17 handgun and fired back at Van.

"Follow me!" Tommy shouted to John.

John clawed his way around the other side of the boat. As Tommy dropped himself down to meet him, yet another bang sounded from the wooded area, followed by a sharp ping of metal on metal. Tommy let out a yell. Fearing the worst, John tried to help catch Tommy on his descent while keeping his axe tucked under his arm.

"Where'd he get you?" John asked in a panic. His father lifted the back of his shirt for John to see. A hole, rapidly filling with gel-like blood, welled on his abdomen. "From what I can tell, you must've caught a ricochet. Luckily it wasn't a direct hit. It looks like one of your ribs stopped the bullet in its tracks."

"Then it can wait. We got to move," Tommy grunted. The pair bounded away in the opposite direction of the tree line that concealed their attacker.

"We need to stay and fight, Dad," John growled.

"He isn't going to stop until he finally gets to me."

"Not when he's got the drop on us. We fall back, gather ourselves, and maybe get an ambush in place if he wants to follow."

John wanted to disagree. He was seeing red. How could Van be so determined to come after him all this way? Why could he not just let it go – find a new victim for his insane ritual?

They moved along the outskirts of the city within the abundance of trees and shrubbery, providing enough concealment to prevent Van from lining up a good shot on them. The distance between them and the main streets was too far and too open for them to risk crossing.

"If this guy insists on pushing us, and he may have helpers, then I think our best bet is to go for the tunnel system Seaside has started digging out," Tommy said. "It'll force them into a smaller space where they can't flank us. If he's as hell-bent on coming for you as you say, he'll be easy to draw in."

"Glad you care enough to help out now, Dad," John murmured, taking a moment to duck behind a mound of dirt and boulders to adjust the sling for the axe. His father was a proud man – and got defensive easily. John was worked up now, thanks to the surprise attack, and was itching for a fight, even if it was with Tommy. He needed to get this off his chest.

"Meaning what, exactly?" Tommy retorted. He joined John to catch his breath, wincing from the wound on his back.

"Meaning you left things like you did without a care in the world to fix it. You never called or checked in during my divorce, to see if I was doing okay after Mom and Colby…" John had to stop talking to keep himself from showing tears.

"You know, you're an adult, John. I don't remember you putting in any effort either."

"But you're… Dad! It's your job to take on stuff like that!"

"I'm not a perfect father. I don't need you to explain that to me, son. Look, I—"

Tree bark and slivers of wood erupted from the nearest tree to them, followed by the sound of the gunshot. Without a word Tommy and John abandoned their hiding spot, staying as low to the ground as possible while they continued clambering their way through the woods. For several strenuous minutes, they followed the curve of the tree line as it wrapped around the outskirts of the city to the eastern side.

"How much further is this tunnel?" John panted through deep breaths.

"There!" Tommy called as he pointed just to their left.

Across a short opening in the tree line was one of the holes in the ground leading to the transport tunnels. There was an orange awning-type covering what appeared to be a simple, yet massive hole in the short hillside. Such a short distance felt further with the impending doom that one good shot is all Van needed. Looking around in quick desperation, he focused on a section of thick bark hanging from a nearby tree.

"John, give me your axe!" Tommy urged.

Taking the axe, Tommy hacked away at the trunk. He had to readjust several times to be able to slice at the right angles while John helped keep him steady on the ground. Finally, the large piece broke off cleanly from the base and he pried it from its owner. In one hand, gripped firmly, was John's axe, and in the other a piece of bark nearly as tall as he was. He placed the axe back in John's sling and then laid the bark horizontally in front of them.

"Alright, John. When I say go we are going to jump straight for the tunnel. Hopefully, this thing can shield us until we get there." John drifted in and clamped to his father's body. It felt awkward to be in physical contact with his father. Tommy gave an indication and they both pressed off of a boulder. Tommy held the bark like a shield as they drifted across no man's land.

A sharp crack whipped through the air and a hole appeared through the bark. John prayed that Van would waste his ammo and that the shield would hold. Two more rounds sounded off and sizable sections of their makeshift cover exploded around their faces, causing dried bark to vaporize in a puff of dust. Tommy felt a warm itching on his cheek from where a sliver had punched its way into his skin.

Finally, they collided with the protruding side of the cave wall, crashing away from their tattered wooden armor. They had made it just inside the hole's opening.

John let a breath he had not realized he was holding in. Now that his adrenaline had a chance to slow down, the pain in his shoulder was starting to become overbearing. Tommy noticed John's face contorting in the on setting agony. He brought around his pack and pulled out a sun-worn pill bottle and a vial of a yellow, oily substance. From the bottle, Tommy shook out four painkillers and handed them over, which John gladly swallowed.

"Here's some clove oil." John peeled back the bandaging and allowed his father to lightly rub drops of the oil around his wounds. "It ain't morphine, but it should take the edge off." John stayed silent.

Opening before them was a tunnel, not quite a box-shaped rectangle, yet not as round as a semicircle, about twenty-five feet wide and fifteen feet tall. Just within the opening, there was wooden scaffolding lining the tunnel like you would often find in an old mining tunnel. What surprised him was that he could not see the earthy walls of the tunnel. Sheets of all different sorts of materials – netting, blankets, tarps, and more. Lights had been strung along the ceiling.

"They were going to pretty it up a bit," explained Tommy, "but they decided to focus on other sections of the tunnel first after they realized how much manpower this takes. Turns out mixing concrete to line the entire tunnel takes a lot more effort than it used to with gravity." He approached one of the walls and flipped a lever on a power box, bringing light to their surroundings. "Lucky for us, they left the power connected. We'll move further in and hope it draws in your friend out there. It runs about a quarter mile deep."

Still panting, John and Tommy descended into the passage in silent tension.

Chapter 26

Weston grinned at Van as he stood between him and Jessica.

"Marvelous sight isn't it, boy?" Weston beamed.

The three of them rested in the trees that topped a hillside overlooking Seaside in the distance. In the background of the town stood pillars of seawater that extended miles up.

"Is that a tram system going to the top of the water?" Jessica wondered aloud. "Why would they need to do that… how would they even do that?"

In response, Van only offered a grunt. He was not focused on the wall of water that extended miles up, nor did he care about the methods of the people who lived here. He only cared about catching John, and they had followed him all the way here. Rather than work themselves to death to catch up to John and his new friend in the wilderness, Van and Jessica followed at a distance, watching through binoculars to keep the men in their sights and ensure they could see where they were going. Once John ended up in whatever town he was looking for, it would be easier to get close to him without being noticed.

Jessica had not brought up the idea of abandoning this personal crusade of Van's again during their travels. She had, however, made it a point to show her disapproval and lack of enthusiasm.

"I'm doing this because I want to believe that it's what Weston thinks is right," she had said one night while they quietly discussed their plans for when they got to John.

"It is," Van reassured.

She noticed that his attitude had been changing as well. He had become more irritable, quick to anger over seemingly small things. He had begun mumbling to himself before falling asleep at night. When she would try talking to him or asking a question it was as if he had a hard time focusing on her words, prompting her to have to repeat herself multiple times.

Now, as they approached the city of Seaside, Van's obsession no longer brought him excitement or fear. Although he knew his goal, and he was set on achieving it, he was calm – almost unbothered by the thought of it all. Weston had remained with them for nearly the entire time since they left Briarton.

Why is he always here? He would wonder. *Trying to control what I think and do... still treating me like a kid.*

He was beginning to tire of Jessica's company as well. Avoiding conversation was preferable – even just having some distance between them while they traveled helped soothe his mind for some reason.

They followed the faint outlines of John and his friend to the southern outskirts of the city.

What are they doing out here? I need him in the busy part of town.

"We'll figure out a way," Weston assured him. Van shrugged him off.

They watched from afar until the two men reached a fishing boat of some sort and made their way down into the cabin. Van decided to work with it. He and Jessica moved swiftly through the wooded boundary of Seaside to get closer. They decided to wrap around to the other side of the boat where the tree line offered more positional advantages. As they got close enough to see the boat again they slowed down, focusing now on stealth instead of speed. Several trees back from the edge of the tree line they found a patch of dense, prickly, dried-up bushes to duck behind.

Another man, who Van estimated to be in his late

fifties or so, appeared on the opposite side of the boat from where they sat. He waved at the man they had seen John traveling with, who had not been visible on the deck until he moved to greet the newcomer. They spoke for a moment then ducked below deck. Van itched the bridge of his nose. Anticipation filled his gut as he brought his rifle from his shoulder into his hands, which were beginning to moisten with sweat. His peripheral vision had already begun to tighten. The dulling of his outside senses made him completely forget about Jessica. His moment was coming – he could feel it.

His instincts were rewarded by the sight of John joining the others as they all re-emerged out of the belly of the vessel.

"We probably ought to wait it out, see if he wanders off alone," Jessica recommended.

The words did not reach Van's ears. His mind no longer controlled his muscles as he raised the rifle to his shoulder and filled the circle of his sight with the white of John's shirt.

"Van!" Jessica whispered loudly at him.

"Aim at the top of his shoulder at this range... Squeeze the trigger slowly... breathe out steadily..."

Weston coached.

Though the sensation had become familiar, he was always astounded at the punch the butt of the gun gave his shoulder whenever he fired it. Unable to watch the bullet make impact due to the recoil, he knew it had found its mark as he brought his scope back down and watched as the three men scrambled away from the red mist and bubbles where John once hovered.

"Damn you, Van!" Jessica was fuming. "You're going to bring the whole city down on us."

Van ignored her, staring intently through the glass for any flicker of movement.

Then I'll take them all with me. The more sacrifices the better.

One of the men suddenly appeared over the side of the boat and leaped for the entrance to the cabin. Van had the trigger pulled halfway before the other stranger dashed out to the left toward the town. Without releasing an ounce of pressure from the trigger he flung his crosshair to the side and fired. The bullet ripped a hole through a tree just behind the man's head.

"Tsk tsk. You'll need to be better than that, boy," Weston warned.

"Shut up!" Van snarled. He glimpsed at Jessica who

was staring at him as if he had grown a second head. "Loop around and cut that guy off! Don't let him get back to town." Jessica scowled.

"Or, we just go get John and his buddy right now. We're even numbers now and you already put one hole in John."

"NO! Go get him!"

Jessica flinched as Van got close enough to nearly touch his nose to hers. They stared each other down for a brief, intense moment.

"Screw you, Van." Her voice was quiet and shaky. She jumped away and through the trees toward Seaside. Van was not sure if she was going for the man or if she was leaving for good.

Whatever. Either is fine with me.

He had to move forward as if she had abandoned him, that much he knew. He could no longer rely on Jessica or anyone else to achieve his goal – not even Weston. Turning his attention back to his targets, a surprising sight made him hesitate a second. John was standing in the open, looking right toward him and waving his axe in the air. Was this a challenge? Was he trying to die? He had barely raised his scope to aim when three snaps, followed by the whiz of a ricochet, made him duck down behind the bushes. He scampered behind a thick tree trunk. He had never been shot at before. Even having suffered as he had these last few weeks, the thought of someone shooting back at him filled him with fear. He started feeling dizzy.

"Get back up and take them out!" Weston demanded. Van sat a minute longer, forcing himself to take deep breaths to force calmness into his body. By the time he peeked out from behind the tree, gun at the ready, a flash of color in the trees far behind the boat told him that they had already retreated and were on the run.

"Dammit!"

"After them, boy!" called Weston maniacally.

Without taking the time to sling his rifle onto his back he dashed after them, relying on using one hand to help navigate the woods while carrying his gun in the other. The wounds that had been healing well now groaned in agony. The gash in his side, he was sure, had reopened. No time to care. Rest could wait until this was over. And it would all be over very soon.

Van was almost to tears while listening to Weston

berating him; not because he was sad or guilty or any of that but out of anger.

"– waste of space! Science itself does not have the words to express the disappointment you have caused! For once–"

They had chased John and the other man for some time until they had covered themselves with a large piece of tree and dove into what appeared to be an abandoned mine. He had been debating whether it was smart to follow them in. He knew nothing of the tunnel system down there or where it ended. He had his flashlight from his pack, but would he be walking right into a trap? His fatigue, both physical and mental, was beginning to take its toll on his ability to reason. It was at this point that Weston started on his tirade.

Van tried everything in his power to drown out the voice. When he was unsuccessful in mentally pushing Weston out, he resorted to getting physical. He lunged for the dead preacher time and time again, only to have him reappear behind him whenever he got close enough. In his desperation, Van even threw a few punches to his own head.

"– think for one second you can silence me, you imbecile! You'd be better off–"

"Jacob." A familiar, feminine voice cut off Weston,

silencing the relentless stream of insults and threats. Van's eyes widened. He swung his head side to side, looking for the new voice that rang with clarity. There, in the middle of the clearing, he watched as his mother, blond hair flowing to the middle of her back, contrasted against her loose black dress, walked away from him in the direction of the tunnel.

"Mom," Van called out. She continued her strides as if she had not heard him. "Mom!" He scrambled to the edge of the trees and out into the opening, throwing away all caution. She reached the entrance and disappeared down into the earth as Van had just about caught up with her.

"Mom, please!"

Why is she walking away?

As he soared over the opening in the ground, digging his hands into the dirt to stop his momentum, she had already disappeared into the depths. He felt like crying.

No... She must be leading me to them. I must be on the right path, she wants to see me succeed.

His mind began to race again. Intrusive thoughts became overbearing once more and his emotions began fighting for his undivided attention. Nonetheless, with newfound determination, he dove into the tunnel.

In an instant, Van knew the darkness a cave brought. The air felt cold and had a stifling smell that he struggled to remember. Confused, he took in the acrid odor of oil with a deep breath. He could have believed himself to be covered in it with how strong the smell was. Drawing himself across the wall, Van blinked his eyes rapidly, trying to adjust his eyes to the deep blackness in front of him.

A faint crack produced a dull glow that grew several feet in front of him. A newly snapped glow stick. A shadowed face drew near the light; the scarred, sun-worn face of John.

"You want me? Now you have me," John said as he held the stick next to his face. Van looked around, trying to see the trap that he knew was waiting for him. Nothing moved.

"What are you waiting for? He is right there! Just put the old boy down like the rabid dog he is." Weston said in a whisper in his ear. Van could swear Weston's mouth was devoid of saliva with how each word smacked with his tongue.

One shot and I can be free to move on...

Van pulled his rifle up and pointed it at John, knowing the scope would be useless at this distance and in this darkness.

"DO IT!" Weston's scream echoed across the walls of the tunnel. Van's cheek rested against the hunting rifle.

As his eyes adjusted to look past the barrel's edge, his breath caught in his throat. His mother stood in front of John, blocking his shot.

"Move, Mom. Please, I have to do this for you. I am so tired of being alone," Van cried in desperation. John tilted his head slightly in confusion.

Weston appeared to his side, rage in his eyes, and punched Van in the stomach. Van knew that he wasn't real but he felt the air escape from his mouth all the same.

"If you aren't strong enough to see through that disguise, I will take things into my own hands," Weston said with disgust. Weston's person vanished, but his voice rang out in Van's head.

"You kill me and you think you can just walk away?" A two-toned voice came out of Van's mouth. Van felt frozen – paralyzed in his own body. Even the words he spoke were alien. "I can still feel the blade you planted in me, you heretic."

Van felt like he was losing time with each passing moment. All he wanted to do was leave here, unable to tell what was real anymore. He felt a tightening around his throat.

Is Weston trying to kill me?

He could have sworn that something was cutting off

his air. His vision blurred and his mother was gone; in her place was a single floating glow-stick. Van touched the back of his neck and immediately knew he was in trouble. His senses began to become his again as panic filled him. While he fought for control of his body the rope was tightening on his neck. Pawing at the scratchy thick rope, trying to remove it, only seemed to be making it tighter. He heard a voice that made it freeze.

"If you're so obsessed with sending people to Science why don't you give it a try?" John said, his ominous sentence echoing off of the walls. At the entrance of the tunnel, a wall of fire erupted, blocking the exit. The cave became illuminated, hurting their eyes with the heat and brightness. John and Tommy were a distance away with their backs against a wall, holding a large boulder in their hands. Van's eyes followed the rope that was around his neck. It weaved loosely side-to-side close to the ground and was firmly tied around a massive rock.

With the remainder of their collective strength, John and Tommy launched the boulder toward the entrance, yelling through the searing of their wounds. Van quickly aimed the rifle in desperation and fired, missing them entirely. The boulder sailed past Van, taking the rope with it.

A violent jerk ripped at his neck. Deafening cracking filled his ears. A sharp pain, unlike any he had ever known, shot through his upper body, followed by numbness in all his extremities. His limp body hurtled toward the wall of fire. No matter how much he willed his arms to move they heeded him not. He whipped through the fire, setting his body ablaze. Propelling upwards out of the tunnel's opening he squinted from the even brighter light of day. As he soared over the tree line, his arms and legs flailing on their own, he closed his eyes and let the tears come as they may. A squeezing sensation enveloped his body. When he opened his eyes his mother was holding onto him, hugging his body as they flew. A soft expression of love shone from her face; her beautiful eyes, the excitement in her smile, it all smothered out the retching feeling of dismay. At this moment Van did not feel alone. He drifted off to join the stars.

Chapter 27

Maureen held onto the railing inside the tram as it traveled up to the icy peaks of Velum. She and the small team were set to mine and harvest the fish for the day. It would be one of her last shifts before she would venture out with Tommy and Frank on their task of setting up the new city. As the tram meandered along she thought to herself how proud she was to contribute to the success of the whole city. Adjusting the hood of her parka to fit over her head, she did a final check of their gear for the day including a simple, rusted hammer in her satchel. The hammer would feel quite heavy under normal circumstances but it was nearly effortless to swing it around now.

The tram traveled several miles at a steady pace, pulled along by a thick, metal-woven cable. One thing that most of them never got used to was the absurdly steep angle at which the tram traveled. When entering through the cabin's doors each person had to rotate their body ninety degrees so they were facing the correct direction.

She pulled out a foot-long chisel, meant for breaking away the ice, and a metal ring with colorful pitons. The tram leader pulled himself to the center of the train, steadying himself on the cabin's ceiling cross beams.

“Hope you all had your morning nap on the way up. Yesterday’s shift passed on to us that they had stumbled upon a pretty large tuna. They had been working in the southern section, about a mile across the Velum. The majority of the prep work has been done to pry it out but we need to finish the job today.”

The tram hit the end of the cable line, causing the group to sway wildly. Anyone not paying attention would be spun and slammed against the cabin wall. The air felt still as the cold cut through her layers like a razor blade. Rotating the nozzle gauge, she checked her oxygen tank pressure level to make sure she had enough to make it through the day. Normally, they would have spent all day trying to locate a fish but she knew it would be a shorter day. All they needed to do was finish pulling the one-ton fish from the ice and transport it safely down. In her opinion, these were the easiest days.

The scratched, blue cabin door screeched open and then locked into place. Stepping out, Maureen took in the most magnificent sight. Far below was the bustling town of Seaside. Further back stood the point of Mt. Hull, barely poking above the horizon line. This was her favorite part of the ride. She paid for it in sweat, anxiety, and time, though she felt it was well worth it. She strapped the oxygen mask to her face and pulled her hood back over her head.

The team of misfit excavators kept a steady pace as they traveled south across Velum. The front man's job was to slam a metal piton down and secure the line, while the last man was to retrieve it from the ice. West of the shore the Velum extended as far as the eye could see. Some parts of the ice extended well out of the atmosphere. She always wondered, provided she had the food and water to last the trip if she could traverse to the next continent. For some reason she did not understand, her mind always went to Hawaii, and if anyone had managed to stay alive out there. Had it been swallowed up by the sea? She pictured the large island cocooned in a bauble of water like a snow globe but with more sinister consequences.

In the distance, a flash had caught her eye. When they found a fish that required more work than a day would allow, they used a bundle of spinning reflectors about as big as a grown man's leg that helped the next group find their work sites.

The otherworldly noise of deep, thick ice cracking made Maureen's heart nearly jump out of her chest. The team members gave each other looks of uncertainty. She looked back toward the reflector. Was it moving upward? She was sure it had been level with them just moments ago. She then noticed the small ridge that had formed between her and the mark, extending the entire width of the ice from what she could see– the source of the cracking noise. Hand-sized shards of ice began kicking outward as the two sides slid across each other.

"Look!" another woman on the team called to the rest.

Maureen followed her pointed finger. The cable on which the tram had transported them up here was beginning to slack, while very slightly, steadily, and consistently.

We're... sinking? Falling?

In her new state of panic, her mind fixated on what the appropriate term would be in this scenario. She did not allow her mind to accept the truth that they were all coming to realize: Velum was descending.

Tommy felt tired – more tired than he had been for many weeks. With every part of his soul, he wanted his son to be alive. He did not want to go back to feeling the pain that Maureen or any of the other grieving parents knew from losing a child. The memory of those lanterns as they drifted into the sky filled his heart with sorrow. He felt that he now had the chance to meet the man that his son had become; this was his chance to be there for John. Tommy pictured John waiting in his living room, both of them without words. Always finding it freeing, Tommy had no reason to hold back or place himself in dangerous situations until now. Now he only lived for John and he would make sure that he never let him go again.

As much as it pained him to leave John's side, Tommy had to give his account to the Engineers. This town was built on honesty and bureaucracy. He felt it necessary to relay the details of the event that had occurred so that the town could learn from it. Sitting outside the office building, he was hit with a sense of déjà vu. It was only a couple of days earlier that he was offered the chance to build up their little corner of the world. Now, all he wanted and needed was to focus on being John's father – take advantage of being given a second chance. The sun came down on his shoulders, his shadow casting out in front of him like a slumbering giant.

A distant, thunderous snap echoed through the air, pulling him out of his thoughts. Looking up, he witnessed large chunks of ice slowly drifting through the sky. He was surprised by the sensation of his feet touching down on the concrete and a strange pressure weighing down on his neck, back, and legs. The air stood still as the implications began dawning on him.

Awestruck, Tommy struggled like a toddler to stand as he watched the solid ice peaks of Velum cascading down through the tendrils of water. Like molasses it unfolded before him, so slow that he had to look away and back to make sure he was seeing it all correctly. Water surged like syrup as ice pressed into the water, forcing it outward, overcoming the first line of homes and buildings nearest the coastline. The smell of saltwater grew strong. Velum, which comprised thousands of thin water tendrils reaching up into the sky, was once again merging into one destructive body. Tommy's mind went to John resting in the boat on the hill.

I need to get there. Now.

As quickly as he could manage, Tommy bolted for home. Townsfolk bolted out of windows and doors to flee the incoming tsunami, the returning gravity making the whole scene move in eerie slow motion. He glanced at the safety cord, knowing that he could easily push in the wrong direction if he wasn't careful. A man landed on the ground in the street in front of him and rolled onto his back. It reminded Tommy of the old clips of Neil Armstrong walking on the moon for the first time. No time to think. Time was against him and dwindling rapidly. He hunched down, pulling his knees into his chest, and sprung for the nearest building's roof.

Tommy’s aim was true. His body launched head-first toward a second-story red-brick building. He never made it to the roof. Instead, he drifted forward and his body descended back to the ground. Head first he met the asphalt as he stretched his hands forward bracing for impact. His palms pressed down and Tommy somersaulted with an awkward rotation. He caught a glimpse of the wall of water that rolled closer.

Velum rolled over the building, swallowing them whole and trapping their inhabitants. A distressed old man was seen crawling out of a window just as the salt water melted over the top of him, forcing him to the ground where he was further engulfed in ocean water. Velum rolled with a downward spiral, catching any drifting objects in its wake. The dense wall ripped through each home and shop. No one, and nothing, was spared.

Tommy caught hold of a secured bike rack with one goal in mind. How would they escape even if he did reach John in time? Tommy pushed off the rack with all of his strength, pointing his body well above the horizon. If his intuition was right, he would finally touch the ground again near his home. If he was wrong, then it would not matter how much planning he did or how fast he moved. As he sailed out above the rooftops, other citizens, some friends and others strangers, joined him in leaping away from Velum. He finally drifted down after passing nearly four different side streets.

Fearing he wouldn't make it, Tommy glanced back to see the edge of the water only a couple hundred feet from his feet and was closing in fast. He threw a hand out and caught the edge of the rooftop, pressing off once more. St. John's mast could just be spotted over the treetops.

I'm not going to make it… Am I?

He jumped once more after landing on top of a hill. The roar of the wave grew louder still. Luckily, he had gauged his final bound well enough that he was set to land just shy of the deck. Chancing another look behind him, his heart sank further somehow. He would only have mere moments to get John out.

"John!" Tommy screamed, his voice cracking with how hard he pushed the words out. Hopefully, John had not wandered from the boat.

John appeared rather quickly from inside, moving with a purpose at the intensity of Tommy's tone. His face dropped as he saw the water surging forward. Tommy landed near a skinny tree. Gripping the abrasive bark, he made his final push for the vessel. Coldness enveloped his feet. He looked back and gasped. The wall of water had finally caught up, and it was attempting to absorb him. His speed nearly matched that of the water, but he was not putting any space between it and himself.

Tommy reared his head forward again. His mouth dropped open. He had overshot the boat. Sailing past the deck of the boat, he locked eyes with his son as John braced himself for what was upon them. Netting greeted his fingertips as he strained to reach anything he could. Though exhausted, he sucked in a mouthful of air as the water consumed him.

Thirty-five million years ago, a combination of ash and pumice mixed with a flow of water. The ash then oxidized on the surface, forming layer over layer. This mixture combined with great compacting force, creating a form of cementation. Through this process, the desert landscape, built upon thousands of layers, shaped what is now known as the Painted Hills. The Painted Hills' alternating tan and red rock, curving up and around the hillsides, were home to many natives for approximately eight thousand years. The area was good for collecting many different types of plants and roots for medicinal needs.

John stood reading these facts off of a sun-worn bronze sign that was affixed to a rock overlooking the vast desert land. At his back was his father's boat, tilted on its side atop a sloped mound. Rattled was a bit of an understatement for John's current state of being. He wasn't sure how far the waves had swept him away but he did not recall Oregon having a desolate wasteland.

The mounds of orange and red sandstone sloped up and down with vast dipped areas in between hills. John gazed at all of the pools of salt water that had settled in the rocks.

Too bad that water isn't suitable to drink.

Tommy opened the hatch on St. John's deck. In an awkward leap, Tommy jumped twenty feet off the ground and slowly returned to the sandstone. Finding it easier to walk now that he had had some practice, Tommy put his arm around John's shoulder.

The rules have changed again, John thought as he tried to wrap his head around the, once again, new world.

Epilogue

A slender old man dressed in a newly-pressed pinstripe suit sat on the edge of a leather reading chair. Smoke drifted up from an unattended cigarette held in his right hand. Ash dropped from the cigarette into a slender dish affixed to the floor next to where he lazily sat. The wasted smoke filled the large room, adding to its musty, dank smell. The walls were lined with humming computer screens that displayed several settings throughout the world. Drawing on the cigarette, his eyes focused on a small panel built into the chair's arm. He pressed and held a small blue button.

“Haley, come in here,” he said through his cracked lips in a low strained voice. The echo of heels could be heard drawing closer in the hall outside. The door screeched as it opened into the room. A thin, young woman approached from around the chair. She wore a long, tight, black dress that extended past her knees, matching her square glasses and heels.

"What can I do for you, Mister Colorado?" she asked as she anxiously drew a small notepad from her side. With some effort, he pulled himself upright in the chair and dabbed his almost diminished cigarette off to the side.

"Get the states online. We are about to come out of the convergence."

The assistant curtly nodded and briskly walked out of the room. On the far wall stood a large map of the country. Each state had an affixed iridescent light. All states were shown red except for Colorado, which remained green. A sharp chime sounded off and the map lit up in a flickering frenzy like a Christmas-time display. Mister Colorado sat waiting for the distinct alert tone notifying him that everyone was present.

"Mister Colorado, we were able to get everyone online except Mister New Mexico and Mister Illinois. Both of them failed to take the call," The woman said from a council speaker. "Mister Illinois did report several months back that he was having mechanical issues and that the locals had found his pod."

"So be it." Mister Colorado pressed several more buttons on the armchair panel. "Gentlemen, ladies. We are at the edge of the convergence. According to the reports given to me, we seem to only be a couple of weeks away from the end of this annoyance. Missus Maine, can you give us an update on the East Coast?"

A young, melodious voice buzzed in.

"We have seen only a handful of colonies that have been able to self-govern but the remainder of the state is in utter disarray. I have the Geo-report as well. It appears that our planet has lost about fifty percent of its ocean water and wildlife. Coming out of the convergence, we will have some serious issues with desert spreading and decaying deforestation. It has yet to be determined where the majority of the lake and river water has gone but we suspect we cannot count on its return."

Mister Colorado sighed as if this was just one more annoyance to him – a mosquito biting his hand.

"Mister Kansas, how soon after the convergence will you have the farming up and going?"

"It's Miss Kansas now. My father passed away several months ago and I have assumed control of the state."

"My condolences."

Miss Kansas cleared her throat. "Our recent inspection tells me that we are at seventy-five percent ready. With some minor fixes, we will be ready to move forward."

"Thank you. I believe our final necessary report is

population count. Let's start with West territories."

The map on the wall flickered and the Oregon light flickered and turned yellow. "We were able to amass the majority of the region's people into a small town by the ocean, we suspect we will have casualties with the re-convergence but not enough to worry. We estimate that approximately one percent remain."

A red light on the wall started to rotate and an alarm sounded off.

"Sir… Sir, we have a problem," Haley called in.

Mister Colorado flipped a switch and the screens that surrounded him came to life. The alarm screeched so loud that he could barely hear his thoughts.

"Haley! Turn this damned thing off. Can you hear me?"

The light map of the country displayed the state of Colorado flashing red. All at once the sound stopped and an uncomfortable stillness held the air. He could hear the mumbling voices of the other states in the distance but couldn't make out what they were saying.

"Haley!" he screamed.

The stress of the silence grew like cancer, starting as a small seed in his stomach and growing out of control. He called for his assistant several more times in vain. Only the echoes of his cries reverberating off of the walls could be heard. Anxiously, he scanned the screens that displayed the area surrounding his pod. The red light turned yellow and an automated voice came over the speaker system.

"WARNING. WARNING. SPHERE SPEED SLOWING."

Why would that be happening? He thought as he began to panic. His eyes turned to his now burned-out cigarette, the smoke appeared trapped in a mushroom-shaped cloud at the end of the filter.

"SYNTHETIC GRAVITY OFFLINE."

Mister Colorado was now inches off of his seat. The sensation of being weightless was not foreign to him – he sent people out all the time to gather information. He could hear popping sounds echoing through the walls. From the screen, he could see his military force being decimated. One by one they fell. What he could not see is from where they were being taken. The camera that pointed at the front doors showed people wearing tan robes accented with green actively hitting the doors. Mister Colorado carefully pulled himself around the armchair and pushed to the door.

I need to get my pistol.

The door in front of him was secured with a hand-crank metal wheel that pulled the piston locks out of their sockets. Bracing his old legs on the door, he managed to pry it open and peered down the darkened hallway. Fifty feet from him was a lit wrap-around receptionist desk where Haley spent most of her day.

If they haven't made it in the pod why would the gravity come off?

The handrail that traced the wall acted as his guide down the hallway. High ceilings were decorated with tasteful silver and gold-trimmed lights. The walls were made of polished concrete, making the whole complex feel like a cultured tomb constructed just for him. He inched down the hall hand over hand until he reached the granite counters of the desk. Haley was nowhere to be found. Several of her effects gravitated around the countertop.

"WARNING. FRONT DOORS OPEN."

His heart jumped to his throat. A cold sweat made him shiver. He felt like a cornered raccoon in a cage – a fancily-dressed, tired, old raccoon. He remembered what he had come this way for and threw his legs around to the inside of the circular desk. Haley kept his small revolver in the bottom drawer of a cabinet. Mister Colorado desperately dug around the drawer creating a cloud of floating office supplies as he did so. It was not there. She had abandoned him and taken his only form of defense with her. Voices started to echo down the corridors, growing closer to him.

I must hide.

Pulling a pretty, leather-wrapped high chair up from under the desk, he tucked himself beneath the counter. Mister Colorado drew any item within reach to cover himself, like a floating camouflage. The voices grew ever louder as he waited. He knew deep down that he would be found eventually. He could only hope the intruders would not care to look too closely for him. Before he could offer a prayer in his mind, a shadow grew over him, blocking the overhead lights.

Outside, the sun cut brightly overhead. The exterior of the pod was surrounded by a thick grove of overgrown blue spruce pine trees and quaking aspens. The pod complex had been intentionally designed to be naturally hidden from unwanted eyes and distant from any nearby towns.

Mister Colorado waited in a flat outcropping of the grounds tied with braided ropes which appeared to be from ripped clothing. His hands and legs were bound and he knew his old muscles stood no chance against his restraints. Turning his head, he saw that over a dozen individuals were donning those tan robes, resting in the trees around him, waiting, staring. Without his glasses, it was hard to tell but it looked as if they each had something crudely carved into their forehead.

A bulky man pushed his way through the pine needles and out to the exterior of the grounds, garbed with a dark green robe with gold laced throughout the chest and arms. His head held a rounded hood that came up to a point just above his forehead, accenting the scar on his head. As he drew closer to Mister Colorado, he could tell now that it appeared to be an atom. Gold lines stretched outward from the atom symbol, giving it a more sacred appearance. More surprising was that he recognized the man.

"Oh goodness, Dr. Houston, you gave me a scare. I thought that I was being overrun by transient serfs. Why am I tied up?" Mister Colorado asked as Houston approached through the air. He had soft leather moccasins covering his feet. They rested on a pile of dried pine needles piled on the ground in front of Mister Colorado.

"I do not go by that name anymore. You may address me as the Doctrinate and accept my standing with the one and only Science."

Mister Colorado hesitantly looked around at all of the other people watching with flat expressions.

"I don't understand what's happening here. I have been supplying you with food and clean water for years. I single-handedly insure your life and success. Why am I tied up?" He tried to mask his nervousness with a demanding tone.

"I have been thinking, Mister Colorado. Science has given me insight that we are not meant to play by your rules anymore," the Doctrinate spoke forcefully. "The rich and the pompous have had their chance to build a better world, yet all you did was create death and despair to build up your coffers. It is now our turn to take control, and that won't happen with a bunch of old men pulling the strings from the shadows. You are unbelievers, and for that, you are granted a one-way ticket to meet Science himself."

The crowd of robed figures individually moved from the trees, drifting in on Mister Colorado. He felt hands gripping all around his clothes, pinching his skin and bunching him uncomfortably.

"Please, don't do this. I believe! I believe in

Science! You can't kill a believer!" he groveled.

"Your lies sicken me, and make you look weak."

The Doctrinate reached down and gripped a small handful of dirt. He brought it up to his mouth and spit into the dirt. Rolling his fingers in his palm, the mixture had a reddish coloring. Once it was mud, he carefully drew a large atom symbol on the old man's forehead. He nodded to the others and Mister Colorado, writhing like a trapped bug in a web, was hoisted above their heads. They brought him lower once more then briskly drug his body upward and let go simultaneously. Mister Colorado rapidly glided upward. He continued to plead like the Atomists could reverse his impending death. The group stood and watched for a long time, ensuring he made it out of sight and into the stratosphere.

An odd sensation, small enough to almost go unnoticed, welled in the stomachs of the robed men and women. As they looked to each other for confirmation they fell, landing hard on the ground. A few laughed incredulously, others began to sob. After several minutes of trying to remember how to stand, one pointed up to the sky, calling to the rest. The Doctrinate raised his head and watched as Mister Colorado descended from the sky. By the time he had reached ground level again, he was traveling fast enough to shatter most of his bones. His screams ended with one loud thud and an odd grunt as the remainder of the air from his lungs was forced past his vocal cords. The Doctrinate turned to his followers.

"Science has finally ended our trial. Now, we must pick up the pieces in his name and move forward with Its plan.

Afterword

As funny as it began, we looked at each other from across the work desks and concluded that we both had wanted to write a book for the fun of it. Both of us have enjoyed successful careers so far as Deputies at our local county jail. In this profession, some find that a nice sci-fi fantasy escape is nice to break up the monotony of the day. After three or so weeks of arguing about the general logistics of the book we had a strong vigor to accomplish something hard. It seemed like the hardest part of starting this book was just that: starting. For a year we poured hours of time and energy into what we consider a novel we can take pride in.

A lot of what was put into this book stems from researching old wilderness survival books and speaking with other first responders. We tried so hard to find ways for John to simply stay alive without "giving the cow away," so to speak. Along the way, we discovered that many of the basic elements react vastly differently in a gravity-free zone, causing us to lean heavily on watching videos of astronauts doing demonstrations and living within a space station. We hope in the future to return to this story and continue diving into the complexity of a new, growing society and the lives of those who were lucky enough to survive The Lifting.

Arguments

We were encouraged to add this by the people who listened to the many ideas put into writing this book. From the start, we had to overcome many logistical obstacles when simply stating that gravity had disappeared. We wanted to put down some of the interesting things that change when dealing with an environment devoid of gravity. The Earth rotates at such a fast speed that if gravity abruptly turned off the contents of the whole planet would launch into space, ending life as we know it. But, overlooking that for the sake of this story, here are a couple of topics we found to be exceptionally interesting.

Water

We found that water disbursement would be a tricky one. In the novel, John runs into many different types of water situations. Water without gravity means that the water itself doesn't rely on gravity's weight to dictate how it moves. If you were to empty a cup of water into a gravity less state it would remain a sphere. Not relying on gravity the sphere then has a strong reaction to the tension of the water molecules and how they interact with other objects. Placing your hand in water without gravity causes the water tension to react to the oils in your hands and it tries to maintain that tension on your hand.

When you place a heating element to it the sphere does something even more curious. A video from the International Space Station displays a test done on what water does when it boils without gravity. In the video, a metal pin was inserted into the sphere of water and then heated to try to get the water to boil. When it hit the boiling point a small pocket of oxygen formed on the top of the pin. Normally when you boil water the air boils up and disperses in the air. With a lack of gravity to tell the air which way to go the pocket of extremely hot air remained on the pin because of the water tension holding it in. In the book one of the characters enters a lake and almost drowns because when faced with the water the tension held the sphere of water to his face because gravity didn't tell it to move otherwise.

Fire

Fire was another interesting occurrence we found when researching the book's details. On a regular day when the wind isn't blowing striking a match causes the flame to reach upward because of the dispersal of the gasses burning out. The gas burning rises, making the flame look like a typical flame. When you remove the gravity aspect of lighting a match it causes the flame itself to do something peculiar. The flame without gravity rounds off without constraints and even burns outward not upward. You can find a small clip of astronauts lighting a match in space and see the effects of it. We had fun trying to think of different ways someone would utilize fire in the novel from campfires to drifting lanterns.

Bugs and Animal Life

This portion was a struggle and a half to overcome. All but a few animal types run off of primal instinct to simply stay fed and be alive. Peter spent hours arguing with AI technology on what kinds of bugs and animals would be able to temporarily remain alive or borderline thrive in this kind of environment. Unless by freak design all of the animals that jump or move quickly as a necessity were gone. AI stated that some Primates and very slow-moving animals, like sloths, would likely be the only survivors. Speaking of bugs, we know that a great deal of them use crawling as a main mode of travel, and for that reason, they would somewhat be able to manage a normal bug life with a slight variation in their eating habits.

Human Anatomy

Your body has so many things that change, for example, how your body heals. In zero gravity your blood coagulation gets slower. Having this in mind all minor cuts will bleed longer and harder. Most wounds without artificial intervention will bleed for twice as long before scabbing. The body relies heavily on gravity's downward pressure. Without that pressure, the intestines would move and regulate slowly causing additional methane build up.

Jordan found an interesting event that happens with a long-term living in an environment with no gravity called SANS or spaceflight-associated neuro-ocular syndrome. Lack of gravity caused astronauts' brains to swell more, altering both the shape of the eyeball and pupil. In more extreme cases this can ultimately lead to blindness. We gave this condition to one of our characters to really give weight to living in such a survivalist-like world with no sight.

Plant life

Now this topic caused some arguments on how long a tree would survive before really dying. Without gravity, the plants and trees would have to use what was left of the groundwater. From what we found trees would survive no more than a couple of years on the minimal water intake. What is also interesting is most plants don't like constant saturation of water. It causes a sickness on the plant from mold that grows on always wet roots. The mold responds to the plant like it's living in drought conditions and usually kills the plant. On the International Space Station, the astronauts use hydroponics. The system allows water to pass by the roots without the fear of mold by using a drawing method. By no means in the environment setting had we created would plants come close to producing fruit because they would just attempt to remain alive.

Food

The CDC recommends that people stay indoors in their homes for 2 weeks after a large catastrophe event. Some of the reasons that were given were that most deaths from looting and mayhem would happen at this time. CDC states that if our country faced a huge problem we have a storage of about 2 years of being fed before running out of canned foods. One of the reasons Peter wanted to start the story where we did was simply from this fact. We wanted to have the reader see the survival through the idea that there was no loose food lying around and that people couldn't easily get hold of it.

Co-authored by:

Peter Anderson

Jordan Nuffer

Made in United States
Troutdale, OR
01/14/2025

27968294R00257